ALL IS CLAM

A Shores Mystery

ACORNPRESS

P.O. Box 22024
Charlottetown, Prince Edward Island
C1A 9J2
acornpresscanada.com

Printed and Bound in Canada
Cover illustration and interior design by Matt Reid
Editing by Sherie Hodds

Library and Archives Canada Cataloguing in Publication

MacLeod, Hilary
 All is Clam / Hilary MacLeod.

ISBN 978-1-894838-77-1
 I. Title.

ebook ISBN 978-1-894838-81-8

Canada Council for the Arts   **Conseil des Arts du Canada**

The publisher acknowledges the support of the Government of Canada through the Canada Book Fund of the Department of Canadian Heritage and the Canada Council for the Arts Block Grant Program.

ALL IS CLAM

A Shores Mystery

Hilary MacLeod

The Acorn Press
Charlottetown
2012

To all the students, in 22 years at Loyalist College,
who challenged me, laughed with me and kept me young.
Chase your dreams.

"Si-i-len' nigh'...ho-ho-l-e-ee nigh'
All is clam...all is brigh'"

—"Silent Night," as sung by Millie Fraser,
The Shores Hall, Christmas 2012

Prologue

A sparkle of light glimmered beside a deep blue coastline, like a diamond set in a sapphire sea. It was a still photo, but the light appeared to move, to radiate.

The tiny jewel was The Shores in a satellite photo taken of the island from space on a late December night. The newspapers had dubbed the shot "Star in the East."

It was that time of year again, and, in The Shores, everything that didn't have the legs or sense to get away was strung with lights. Thousands and thousands of Christmas lights. More every year. The Shores was just catching up. Electricity hadn't arrived until the 1960s. When it came, the villagers lost all their traditional restraint.

One year The Shores was strung with so many lights, it caused a province-wide power failure, plunging the whole island into darkness on Christmas Eve. Except The Shores. The villagers were used to power failures. Those who had generators fired them up and plugged in the lights again. An official limit had since been set on how many they could hang, but they ignored it.

There were Santas and reindeers and elves. Christmas angels

and stars. The holy family – complete with crèche and wise men – on roofs, on front lawns, on mailboxes and well houses, in empty lots and on boats parked on land for the off-season. The Hall, at the centre of the village, blazed with lights on a massive spruce at the front of the building, and Santa and his sleigh and reindeers rode the green steel roof. Some houses dripped lights like falling snow; others had clumps tossed up on their roofs – shining drifts of lights. There was hardly a tree or plant of any kind – lilac, maple, dogwood, anything that had branches, that was without decoration. The Shores glistened in the night, from everywhere within plugging distance of an electrical cord. Extensions snaked around the village, straining every household's fuse box. Breakers hadn't reached The Shores yet.

The villagers' Christmas spirit had created the twinkling diamond seen from space. From the first of December until the New Year, The Shores lit up the Red Island sky at night – announcing the existence of this tiny village to the universe.

Apart from Ian Simmons' place, and he was from away, there was only one house in the village that wasn't lit up. It had been dark for years. That was about to change. Wild Rose Cottage was about to be lived in – and died in – again.

Until then, the villagers wished for snow to complete the Christmas portrait.

They would regret it.

Chapter One

The house appeared to be weeping. The tears fell from its eyebrows, the high gables with teardrop gingerbread trim, and dripped onto its eyes – windows clouded and streaked with grime running like mascara over the sills.

Wild Rose Cottage was massive and ancient, nothing like a cottage, and in the summer, rose bushes grew around it out of control. They had become an eyesore, like the house itself, windows broken, shingles rotting, deserted.

Except for the rats.

Rats skittered across the wood floorboards stained with their excrement, competing with mice and ants for crumbs still to be found in the floor cracks.

And, today, one two-legged rodent.

Jared MacPherson was tearing away at the walls and floorboards, finding plastic bags of rodent treats that someone had buried there years ago. Whenever he found one, he flung it across the room and the rats scrambled for it, tearing at the plastic, wolfing down the poison.

Dead or alive, the rats didn't bother Jared. He had them at home. If one got in his way, he just kicked it aside. It would squeal, run off, and start a stampede of scurrying rodents, melting into a stream, flowing like liquid across the room.

Jared was looking for something. His job was made easier by the plaster peeling off the walls in big chunks, baring lath made of fish crates. The first owner, a young architect, had constructed his house on the cheap, with leftovers from his wealthy clients and whatever building materials he could scrounge in the village. Even so, when finished, it had been magnificent. That had been more than a hundred years ago.

Now the floors were littered with the remains of lives lived – broken furniture, clothing, old books, toys, hockey equipment, all chewed and peed on by rats.

Frustrated at finding nothing, Jared stood up and planted a dirty boot on a plastic place mat. It was the one with the satellite photo of The Shores, lying with the garbage on the floor.

Hy McAllister was the last in the village to string her Christmas lights. Even Jared had already put his up. That was still causing a stir. He'd never done it before. Maybe because he was usually in Sleepy Hollow, the provincial jail, at Christmastime. Not this year. Busted for dealing cocaine, he'd served almost no extra time for the grow-op he'd been operating from inside.

The wire had become tangled. Hy hadn't bothered to straighten the twisted cord before she'd climbed the ladder. She struggled with it, and the ladder jumped off the wall and slammed back onto it again, nearly making her fall. As she steadied herself, she saw a strange entourage coming down the road.

The circus has come to town, she thought. Leading the parade, at a snail's pace, was a half-ton pick-up. A young boy or girl with blond hair, head stuck out of the passenger window, was keeping an eye on the uncertain load, covered with a tarp. Hy could see it was filled with household goods – a microwave and a couple of chairs sticking out the back. A dog ran slow circles around the truck. The driver paid no attention, not bothering to alter his speed when the animal darted past the front wheels. Its paws were bloody.

Behind the truck was a donkey, tied to the bumper. Behind the donkey was a woman, her brown hair streaked with grey and tangled in a scarf wound several times around her neck. She had one hand on the donkey's rump, guiding it and steadying herself. Her shoulders were slumped, feet dragging, her head down.

They descended into the "holler," a dip in the road where there was a sad collection of abandoned or rarely used houses, and Hy turned her attention back to the lights. She reached up and they cascaded down. The ladder rocked and she gripped the gutter. It creaked, and she felt it give. She brought her hand back onto the rocking ladder, shimmied down, and ripped her jeans and gashed her leg. Wincing, she raised her pant leg for a look. A big lump was swelling up, a bruise forming along the scraped and bloody shin.

The ladder fell and hit her on the head.

Trembling with shock, she hopped inside, stumbling and teeth clenched, to clean and bandage the wound, and make herself a cup of tea.

There was a message on her phone. That would be Ian. No one else in the village left messages. They felt embarrassed talking to a machine. She'd call back later, because right now she might be tempted to ask him for help, and she didn't want to do that.

After she'd finished her tea, she fastened her jacket and clipped on her earmuffs. They disappeared into her thick red curls. The cold air pierced her skin through the ripped jeans when she opened the door.

There was a man on her ladder, a child holding the lights up to him, the dog now dancing around them. The overstuffed truck was parked in her driveway. The woman and the donkey, no longer attached to the truck, were still walking up the road.

The man grinned down at her. One front tooth was missing and he was unshaven. An unwashed smell wafted off him. But he had a peculiar attractiveness. Rakish, Hy decided. The child looked like a fairy tale prince, with chin-length golden-blond hair. Great big eyes in a face with the flawless complexion of youth. An open, honest face. Smiling. Hy smiled back, then cast a look at the woman labouring up the road.

The man caught her expression.

"Her…don't worry about her. She could of got on the donkey if she wanted."

Hy winced at his grammar, and looked at the animal. The donkey's ribs were sticking out, its breathing laboured. It didn't look able to carry itself.

"Give me that, boy."

The man grabbed the lights, secured them, and dropped down off the ladder with the agility of an acrobat. Up, down. Up, down. He kept going until they were all in place.

Hy was relieved. She wouldn't have to ask Ian after all.

She held out a hand to the man.

"Hy McAllister," she said.

He dusted off his hands on the seat of his pants and shook hers.

"Patrick Fitzpatrick. Fitz."

A small hand thrust at hers.

"James Fitzpatrick. Jamie."

"Like father, like son." The man swiped his son across the back of the head.

"And this is Freddy." Jamie grabbed the dog's collar. It was a black lab. Skinny.

"Freddy?" Odd name for a dog. "Where'd he get that name?"

Jamie grinned a wide grin. Toothless, too. His eyeteeth gone, and one just growing in.

"He's a she. Frederica. After Dad's mom."

"Both bitches," Fitz snarled like a dog himself.

The woman coming up the road with the donkey had passed Jared's place.

"Would you like some tea?"

The man flashed a smile. The missing front tooth, oddly, had a certain charm.

"Wouldn't say no." He and Jamie followed her into the house.

She poured the tea, filling the boy's with lots of sugar. Fitz pulled a flask from his jacket pocket, and poured a slug into the tea. It was then that she noticed the chain around his neck, a bicycle chain. He saw her looking at it.

"Last bike I ever rode." He plucked it with a finger. "Used to do stunts. Gave that up when I was eighteen for bigger and better things. Had the chain made into a necklace." He stuck a finger under the chain and yanked it. "I'll die with it on. They'll bury me in it."

He looked around.

"Cozy place." It's what everybody said. It was tiny and as overstuffed as the truck outside in the driveway. Fitz was standing right in front of the woodstove. Hy sat with Jamie at the harvest table she used for eating and working.

Fitz pointed at the computer.

"You a writer?"

"Yes," she said. "I edit and write for websites. *Content*, that's my company." Which syllable of the name she stressed depended on how she felt. Today it was the first.

"Do you now? Maybe you could write a website about us."

"That's not really how it works."

"We've got quite a story." He held out his cup for more tea, but didn't budge from the woodstove, hogging the heat. Hy got up and poured. He splashed more rum into the cup.

He reminded Hy of Jared. *Two of a kind.*

As Hy had guessed, the two would find they had more than a few things in common.

Causing trouble was just one of them.

Chapter Two

Wild Rose Cottage had been the pride of The Shores. It still was, in a way. The villagers basked in its former glory. It was what was called a Victorian cottage, a simple house in a rural setting, simpler than the grand mansions in town, used in the summer to escape the heat. The cottage had eighteen rooms, almost twice as many as any other house in the village. It had six peaked gables, front and back, and a wraparound verandah.

The main body of the house had never been painted, and the grey cedar shingles that looked charming on smaller buildings looked grim. The trim and gingerbread hadn't been touched since the turn of the last century. The paint was almost peeled off. The house looked as if it hadn't been lived in for years, but it had. Just a few rooms on the first floor. The rest had been empty for decades. The foundation was caving in at the back.

It was through the rotting foundation that Jared MacPherson had entered the house. A tarp had been stretched across the crumbling island sandstone. It would have been easier if he had brought a knife. There was one in his truck, concealed in the woods behind the house, but he had been too lazy to get it. So he had ripped away at the tarp with bare hands, hands red and cracked, stained with nicotine. He held a cigarette in his mouth as he worked. When it came close enough to burn his lips, he spat it on the ground next to several others, and crushed it under his boot.

Finally, he had been able to rip off a big strip of the tarp, only to find another layer underneath. *Probably the best insulated part of the whole dump.* He had yanked the new layer free.

He'd been in there an hour and had found nothing. He stood where he was, big dirty boot on the placemat, thinking, and smoking another cigarette.

"What is your story?"

"We've just come all the way from Dawson Creek, British Columbia."

The kettle was boiling. Hy took it off the stove.

"Did your wife walk all the way?" She was grateful that he'd put her lights up, but she didn't like him. Little Jamie was different. He grinned at her, and she smiled back. She was nearly forty. She'd never had kids. She couldn't imagine it. Except she thought about it sometimes at this time of year.

Jamie jumped up from the table. "We took a train." It sounded like "twain," which made him seem even younger than he appeared – eight, no more than ten.

"All the way across the country?" Hy popped several bags of tea in the pot and poured the water. Jamie's head bobbed up and down.

"Did you have a sleeper?"

"We had a whole car." Fists to mouth, giggling at her look of surprise.

"A boxcar," said Fitz. "I rented a boxcar. We put everything in it and came across the country."

"Including the donkey?"

"Including the donkey."

"And the dog!" Jamie jumped up, his eyes laughing. He liked how people reacted when they heard the story.

Hy loved animals, but crossing the country in a stuffy, closed boxcar with a donkey and a dog? It must have reeked. It must have been cold. For the man and the boy, an adventure, maybe. For that poor woman struggling up the road...

"Why the donkey? Why The Shores?"

"That's not just any donkey. That's a guard donkey."

"A guard donkey?"

"For guarding sheep...from wolves."

"But there are no wolves on Red Island."

"Give it time," said Fitz, breaking out a pouch of tobacco and rolling a cigarette.

"In the meantime, there are coyotes." He didn't light the cigarette, just played with it.

"But you've no sheep."

"Give it time," he said again. "I'll get some, or maybe I'll just raise guard donkeys."

Hy smiled. "You'll need another one to do that."

"Give it – "

"...time," she finished for him.

"Exactly." He stuck the rollie in his mouth and chewed on the end. "You're like the wife – finishing sentences for me."

Hy looked out the window at the woman just cresting the long, low hill before the house. Please God, not like his wife.

He spat bits of tobacco out of his mouth.

"Not on my floor..."

"Like I said, just like the wife. S'pose that means I can't smoke in here neither."

She shook her head, lips pursed. Now she wished she'd asked Ian to help her with the lights. Except this was going to be a great story to tell Gus. Hy liked to be the first one with the information on what was going on in the village, and Gus, who couldn't get around as well as she used to, liked to be the first to receive it.

Fitz strolled outside, pulling a lighter out of his back pocket and lighting the cigarette when he was just barely through the door. He took a puff and then yelled down the road, "Hell, woman, haul your ass up here."

The smoke from his cigarette drifted into the house, chased by the cold air through the open door.

She was a faded beauty, two or three years older than Hy, and he must be about fifty, like Ian. She was as tall as Hy, long-legged, but where Hy was willowy, the woman's waist and hips were thick, and the camel coat a bit tight. Her hair colour was as dull as the coat, her complexion grey, her large eyes ringed with red and suffused with sadness. Still, Hy could see she must have been pretty once.

The woman had tapped on the door, her ungloved hand shaking with the cold, the other barely able to grasp the rope that held the donkey.

Jamie flew past Hy and launched himself at his mother. She almost fell backwards as he landed against her, arms unable to squeeze her all the way around.

For a moment, the woman's eyes came alive, but a shadow fell across them when Fitz came to the door.

"Get your fat ass in here, woman, this lady has offered us some tea."

The woman looked up at Hy. Hy nodded. Jamie took the rope from his mother, and scuttled off to tie the donkey to the truck.

"Please," Hy said, extending her hand to help the woman up the stoop.

"I'm Rose." Her voice was barely more than a whisper.

"Hy."

"Hi."

It happened all the time.

"No. Hy. H-Y. That's my name. Short for Hyacinth."

"An old-fashioned name."

"Like Rose."

"Yes." A small smile. "Botanical."

"Mine, too – but chemical as well. Drug-induced. My parents were back-to-the-landers in the sixties. Water hyacinths are tall, strong, and free floating…"

"It suits."

It was a compliment. A tentative offer of friendship.

Hyacinth. Also very fertile. Hy didn't say it. But her time to have a family was passing. Would she regret not having a child? Did she want one? Hy liked children well enough – but enough to have one of her own? And with whom? Ian? The thought made her smile. *Nuts.*

"Is it much farther to Wild Rose Cottage?" Fitz was again planted right in front of the woodstove.

Rose looked at Hy hopefully. She hadn't drunk any tea, just warmed her hands on the cup. "Do you know where it is?"

"Wild Rose Cottage. Of course I know where it is. Everyone does." Hy was so surprised that she had to sit down.

These were the new owners? Just wait until she told Gus, as soon as they were on their way. She wouldn't mind seeing the back of Fitz, but she felt sorry for Rose and Jamie.

"Is it still lovely?" Rose took a sip of tea, felt its warmth penetrate her eternally cold body. "Is it?"

Still? Does she know the house? Old photographs maybe.

"Well…yes…and no…You haven't seen a recent photograph?"

"We got it sight unseen," said Fitz, standing upright and pushing his chest out. "But the price was right." He grinned, winked, and Hy wondered what he meant.

"He means it didn't cost us anything. Not when Fitz found out it was for sale."

"Tried to pull a fast one, that real estate agent. It belonged to Rose. Her inheritance. Found that out soon enough. Free," he grinned. "A free house."

"We did have to pay back taxes."

The villagers had wondered about the "for sale" sign that went up and came down almost as quickly, but hadn't been able to find out anything. Sold? Not sold? The realtor was in and out of The Shores only long enough to put up the sign and take it down again. He wasn't related to anyone in the village, so no one knew anything.

Now Hy did. It was a small pre-Christmas gift – a prime piece of local gossip she would tell Gus, and then Gus would tell everyone else and give her full credit.

"I hope you didn't pay too much in taxes. I'm not sure it's worth anything."

Rose's mouth drooped. The rest of her face followed.

"I had a bit aside. That covered it."

Fitz sneered. "A bit she wasn't telling me about. Until it suited her."

"And you." She threw it back at him with what seemed like hate. The tension gripped them all, and Hy tried to lighten the mood.

"Oh, I forgot. Ginger snaps." She opened a kitchen cupboard and pulled out a jar. "Gus's ginger snaps."

Jamie's eyes opened wide.

"Ginger snaps?"

Hy opened the jar and offered it to him. He snatched a couple of cookies and crammed them into his mouth, right into the gap in his teeth.

"Who's Gus?" His cheeks were chipmunk fat. "He makes good cookies." Crumbs sputtered onto his lips.

"Gus is not a he. She's a she."

"Oh." Jamie stopped chewing. "A girl with a boy's name." He chewed on the idea along with the cookies. "Like Freddy."

"Yes. Her real name is Augusta."

Jamie screwed up his face. "That's a name?"

Hy smiled, and Jamie smiled back, a mouthful of ginger crumbs visible when he spoke.

"Well, she makes good cookies."

"Jamie, close your mouth when you're eating." Rose touched Jamie lightly on the shoulder and he responded immediately, stuffing another cookie into his mouth, closing it, his cheeks bulging.

"You'll turn him into a sissy," Fitz growled.

Hy smiled and gave Jamie the cookie jar. His small hand fit right in and he pulled out several more cookies.

"What will you do with the place – besides farming sheep and donkeys? There are eighteen rooms…"

"An inn. We'll open an inn. The wife's a great cook and very artistic. No matter what shape the place is in, we'll do it up right. Maybe this Gus will cook for us."

Hy shook her head. "She's over eighty."

Hy wasn't sure the place even had functioning electricity any more, but she wasn't going to say. Let them find out for themselves.

Fitz burped and farted.

"We gotta get on the move, get up there before dark. Jamie, you're on donkey duty. Rose rides shotgun." Hy could see the relief that swept over Rose's face, mixed with concern for her young son.

Hy gave them directions, which weren't complicated. Down the road, hang a left at the village centre, and up Shipwreck Hill. "You can't miss it," she ended, thinking, *I've begun to give directions like an Islander.*

Except in this case, you really couldn't miss it.

Jared had plenty of warning of the Fitzpatricks' arrival. He was still in the house, on the second floor, from where he could see well down the road and up the hill. He happened to be looking at the hill when they crested it. He couldn't know they were coming here, but something told him that they were – a ragtag bunch, just the types to fall for this old place. Damn. He'd only searched a handful of rooms, and not all that well. It might be found under the floorboards, in the walls. And he didn't even know what he was looking for. The Sullivan legacy. *What the hell was that supposed to mean?*

"You'll know it when you find it," he'd been told.

Jared didn't think he'd find it here. It was an old library, cradled in the large middle gable of the house. It had built-in shelves and benches, and rotting books – eaten away and pissed on by rats, mildewed by the damp air, black spots, and a fuzzy white mold growing on them. Jared kicked a few books around and began to sneeze. He was tempted to torch the place. Bit of fun. He shivered. Bit of warmth.

He finished his cursory search of the room and then scurried down the stairs, out the back, and through the ripped tarpaulin. There was no snow, and the red clay was frozen solid, so he left no tracks.

Perfect conditions for thieving. But what was there to steal?

Chapter Three

Hy's phone rang shortly after her visitors left. Ian again. She'd better answer, or he'd think she was in a sulk, which she was not. Especially now she had her lights up. She knew it would be his first question, and answered it as soon as she picked up the phone. No hello.

"Yes, they're up."

"Good, I thought you might need help."

"No," she lied. "I was fine."

"Look, Hy, I'm sorry I can't go along with it…"

"Forget it, Ian. We've been through it all before. You know, I think you could relax your environmental standards for Christmas, for this one thing. You burn enough electricity on that computer."

"Which is why I try to be rigorous in other ways. Besides, you know I'm not a believer."

"You don't have to be a believer. It's a village tradition. The lights are heathen, not Christian."

It was nothing they hadn't already said the day before. Ian had tried to soften the argument by offering to help put up her lights, but she'd refused, saying curtly, "I'll do it myself." He wasn't likely to find out she hadn't.

"Anyway, that's not why I called. I saw an odd group coming up the road...a truck, a donkey, a dog, and a young boy trailing behind..."

Hy had wanted to tell Gus first. She sighed and told Ian what she knew.

"Wild Rose Cottage? Interesting history, that house..." Ian detailed names and dates, the fame of the original owner-architect, the sad demise of the family and the house, the various efforts to revive and transform it. Hy felt time and patience grinding away in her stomach. She hardly paid attention to Ian, thinking about how she'd tell Gus her news.

Until she heard the words "Sullivan legacy." Ian had been googling while he was talking.

Now he had her attention.

"Sullivan legacy? What's that?"

"I'm not sure."

"I'll ask Gus."

All of Hy's feline curiosity was aroused. Now she was even more anxious to get to Gus.

Jared was getting cold sitting in his truck in the woods behind the house. He wasn't sure what to do. He'd dashed out of the house when he saw the truck coming down the road, sure it was the new tenants, and he'd been right. Now, how was he supposed to drive out of here, with that truck of theirs in the way? He'd have to ask them to move it, but that meant he'd have to explain what he was doing here. He took a long haul on his cigarette and thought hard. Hard. Thinking wasn't easy for Jared.

Hy cycled to the village centre, which consisted of the Hall and two empty lots where the school and General Store used to be. She was stopped by Wally Fraser, husband of Gladys, President of the Women's Institute at The Shores. He rolled down his passenger window.

"See you got your lights up. See some fella helped you. Not from around here." He was fishing for information. Hy said nothing.

"Got a donkey. And a truckload. Wouldn't be the Wild Rose Cottage people, you think?"

"No idea," Hy lied. She took the turn down to Gus and Abel Mack's house.

"And what have you and Wally Fraser got to say to each other?" Gus greeted her. She was putting on the teakettle, her back to Hy.

"They've come."

Gus turned.

"Who's come?"

"Fitz, Rose, and Jamie Fitzpatrick." Hy slumped down on the chair opposite the big purple recliner, from where Gus held court and had a view of the crossroads and the village centre. Over the years, she'd watched it disappear. The church, turned into a smart summer home. The school, burned down by the villagers when it had graduated from fixer-upper to complete ruin. And Abel Mack's General Store, blown up by an exploding propane tank, which had sent Gus's husband flying out the window. He'd landed on his feet, unharmed, if a bit surprised. People said that's when he'd begun to lose his hair. They joked he could use some of his wife's, a healthy white shock that Gus tried to tame by keeping it short and permed.

Gus sat down in her chair, shaking her head. "Fitz, Rose, and Jamie. Don't know any Fitzes. Now Rose...?

Hy smiled at Gus's typical genealogical response.

"The Wild Rose Cottage people."

"The Wild Rose Cottage people? They never came today?"

"They came today."

Gus was sure she hadn't taken her eye off that window all day. Not long enough for anybody to go by without her seeing. It must have been when she'd been kneading the bread. "Would they be Sullivans then?"

"They're Fitzpatricks."

"P'raps on the mother's side?"

The teakettle was boiling over. Hy jumped up, pulled it off the burner, and poured the water into the Pyrex pot that held three bags of tea. Gus liked to boil her tea, rather than steep it. *Joy of Cooking*, North Shore style. Thick as pudding. Dark as chocolate. Life-sustaining.

"I don't know, Gus. They didn't buy it. She inherited it somehow. They plan to live there."

"I thought they was summer people."

"So did we all." The truth was that nobody knew anything. They'd assumed summer people, since the house was such a wreck. "It would be better for them if they were."

"Do they have lights there?" Gus meant electricity, but Hy replied, "No Christmas lights yet. They've only just got here. Probably cracking open the door right now."

"It's not as I remembered it," said Rose. She'd been small. Everything seemed bigger then. But it wasn't that. The house was big. Too big. Able to contain too much gloom. A sad house. Well, that would suit them. How could she have hoped for better? She sighed, turned to see Jamie reaching for the light switch. He flicked it. No lights. No power. As expected.

A scurrying sound from upstairs. Mice? Please, God, not rats.

One came leaping down the staircase and ran right across her boot. She screamed. Jamie laughed. The dog barked. Fitz cursed.

"We'll soon settle that." Fitz marched out. When he came back he stalked toward the stairs. Rose reached out and grabbed his sleeve.

"Not that, Fitz. Not in the house."

He shook her off.

He was carrying a rifle, fully loaded and cocked. He whipped around, and it was aimed at her. He moved closer. He poked her belly with the gun. Something moved in her. Her heart? Rising and turning over, and then still. She shrank back. The dog whimpered, not knowing what to think. Little Jamie didn't either. He slid between his parents.

Fitz uncocked the rifle and leaned it against the wall.

"Jeez, I was just kidding. Soon as the truck's unloaded, I'll go to town for some Warfarin."

When he finally got to town, that's not what he brought back.

"Rose...Rose..." Gus's brow wrinkled. Her memory wasn't what it had been. People depended on her to remember the history of the village a hundred years back. The fifty years before that, too, at least in a hazy way. None of it was written down. Not yet. There was a fat folder bulging with papers and photographs in a dresser drawer in a corner of the room. Gus was putting together a history of The Shores for the bicentennial coming up in a few years. It wasn't much past the idea stage, and no matter how much Hy tried to get her to organize it, Gus wouldn't be budged. She had to assemble it all first, she would insist. Just like a quilt, she'd say. When Hy pointed out that was not the way Gus approached her quilts, Gus got stubborn. "Well, let's say it's a crazy quilt, then." Gus had never made a crazy quilt. She was so organized, so meticulous in her quilt-making, that she couldn't figure it out. It didn't make sense like a nine-patch did.

Gus took another sip of hot tea, and her face smoothed out, her expression cleared.

"Of course. Rose Sullivan, that was."

"You can't know that from a first name."

"P'raps not. But what would bring them here, else it was that? And her gettin' the house 'n' all."

"You'd think that might keep them away."

"Happen it might." Gus gave one of her meaningful looks. Hy could feel a story coming on, no doubt a tangled tale of relationships and convoluted associations. Before Gus could get in gear, Hy fired off the question that had been on her mind since she arrived.

"The Sullivan legacy. What does it mean?"

They might have been brothers, so alike were they to look at, except that Fitz had years on Jared and more brain cells.

That hat, for example. Fitz couldn't stop staring at it. A baseball cap with a bottle opener built into the brim.

"Like it?" Jared grinned, took it off, and held it out.

What fool would wear that, thought Fitz, taking it and examining it closely. Yes, a real bottle opener.

"Comes in handy," said Jared, securing the hat back on, giving it a tug down, so that the lip of the brim jutted up, revealing the beer bottle opener. It had been well-used. "Know what I mean?" He winked.

"What are you doing here, anyway?" Fitz asked gruffly, annoyed by the conspiratorial wink, as if they had something in common.

"Well, I've been takin' a bit of wood from the back there, keeping the woods clean, you know, not lettin' it go to waste, like."

Jared had braved it, and come walking out of the back woods when he saw Fitz taking a leak behind the house. That gave him a slight advantage.

"That ends now." Fitz shook and zipped up. "I need it myself."

"Understood." Jared shoved a filthy hand, with its long, dirty fingernails, into his shirt pocket, and pulled out a crushed pack of cigarettes. He waved it at Fitz, keeping it close, in his own personal space – an offer, but not an offer.

Fitz interpreted it immediately, and though he had a few of his own smokes rolled up, grabbed one of Jared's.

"Don't mind if I do." He shoved it between his lips, and waited for Jared to light it for him. After a small hesitation, he did.

Fitz had won the first foray. He took a long haul on the cigarette, and blew the smoke out in Jared's direction. Jared didn't mind. He breathed it in. He hadn't lit his own cigarette yet. It was a trick he used in bars to make his smokes last longer. It didn't work so well in the fresh air.

Fitz understood that, too, and tossed the remainder of his cigarette on the ground – almost a whole cigarette. He crushed it with his boot and won the second round. He was twice Jared's age, after all. Give it time.

"Now tell me what you're really here for." The few branches loaded in Jared's truck didn't fool Fitz. He didn't believe Jared was here just for wood.

Jared grinned, baring his stained teeth.

"I'm lookin' for something."

"What?" A sly smile.

"Never mind what." Jared was poker-faced.

"You'll have to tell me, if I'm gonna let you in." Fitz jerked his head towards the house. "It's in there, right?"

"I don't know."

"Jeez," said Fitz. "A fuckin' Einstein."

Hy's questions about the Sullivans tickled at Gus's brain, until she hauled herself out of her chair to fetch the fat bicentennial folder.

There was an article by someone from away. A brief history of the Sullivans and their house, a national heritage property in spite of its state of disrepair. But there was more, somewhere. She shuffled back to her chair, pages drifting onto the floor behind her. Hy darted down to pick them up, handed them to her, and Gus shoved them back in the file.

She glanced at the article, then gave it to Hy.

"Nothing much in there we din't already know, including them bits that are wrong."

"Which bits?"

"About the fire bein' a accident. It was set apurpose. I was just a kid then, din't even live at The Shores but everyone knew about it. The one brother started it out of spite. Jealousy, because the house wasn't left to him. He kilt his brother, but went scot-free. It's the last bit there."

That's not what it said in the article. The fire had burned the back of the house and had killed the brother who owned it, but there was no suggestion of murder. The article's interest was not in the death, but in the damage to the home.

"Is the house the Sullivan legacy?"

"Lord no. I don't think there ever was a legacy, though that family allus fancied itself somethin' special." Gus slipped the folder onto the table beside her. Hy held up the article, backed by discoloured cardboard and wrapped in Saran Wrap. Hardly archival. The newspaper clipping itself was yellow and decaying.

"Can I hold onto this for a bit?"

"As safe in your hands as mine." Gus picked up a quilt patch and started embroidering. White on white. Hard on old eyes. But it was only a crib quilt. Finished soon.

"Did they have money?"

"Not even when that house was built. Made out of bits and pieces, like a quilt."

"A pretty nice quilt."

"I'll grant you that. He did all right, that one. Daniel Sullivan. Before my time." Gus broke off a thread on the quilt patch with her teeth, fished it out of her mouth, and dropped it on the floor.

Hy steered her back to her question. "In your time – was there talk of a legacy?"

Gus put the patch down on her knees.

"Mebbe. Mebbe there was. We didn't pay much attention. We were too busy getting by day to day to worry about legacies – especially other people's."

"Think, Gus."

Gus looked out the window, as if searching for the past through the glass, in the empty spaces where all the buildings used to be, where village life had once passed by her in a constant stream.

"I don't think it was money. They never had a penny, not two to rub together."

Hy wanted to know what it was, not what it wasn't.

"Jewels?"

Gus slapped a hand on her thigh, knocking the patch onto the floor. She laughed.

"No one ever had jewels in The Shores. Not more'n a string of fake pearls or a weddin' ring." She looked at hers, pointed at Hy.

"You should get yourself one of them."

Hy screwed up her face, and looked down at her hands. Not a ring of any kind on them. *Long, slender, fingers*, thought Gus. Not red and thickened by work like her own, her wedding ring embedded in her flesh, unable to be removed.

"Now, you watch it. Remember that woman last year."

Suki. Ian's old flame from college. She'd moved right in on him the same night her husband was killed. It had looked suspicious.

"That Jamieson, now, when she comes, she'll be living right close to him. Not a bad-looking woman. A bit pale. A bit scrawny."

"Thin, Gus, thin. It's Moira who's scrawny."

Gus smiled. "Happen you're right. Still too thin. Put a bit of beef on her, and she'd be right easy on the eyes. He's seen it. I seen him see it."

So had Hy.

She didn't want to talk or think about that now. She steered Gus back to a more pleasant topic: murder.

Rose could tell by the way Fitz drove the truck, weaving into the lane, that he'd already been drinking on the way back from town. He'd run out of liquor and had been sober for two days. Now he was drunk and he'd be all over her, no matter whether she wanted it or not. She hadn't wanted it in years. Not since Jamie was born, and he had tried to do it to her while she was in labour. The midwife had come in and put an end to that. A huge woman with the strength of a heavyweight fighter, she'd hauled Fitz off Rose and dumped him on the floor.

"She should be glad I can't knock her up right now," he grumbled, getting up and fastening his pants, unsteady on his feet. The midwife, who thought she'd seen everything, had never seen anything like this before – the child, fighting to get out; the father, fighting to get in.

She'd pushed him out of the room with her sausage-fat arms, hairy like her black moustache, and turned to the mother. The child slipped out only minutes after the door slammed on his father, straight into the midwife's waiting hands. She held the baby up so Rose could see, and then quickly, efficiently, wrapped the infant tightly in flannelette.

"A son," said the mother, taking the swaddled infant in her arms. "Just like his father." *Not like Fitz, she thought secretly, not at all like him, she hoped, but wasn't that what new mothers were supposed to say?*

The midwife had looked at her quizzically, then at the baby. *Like his father? Not at all.* The child was like the mother – her hair, her eyes.

"Yes," she'd said, to humour Rose. New mothers took fancies.

Gus had a satisfied set to her mouth as she watched Hy cycle up the lane. All the way up. Gus could see her clearly the full distance. The trees that used to line the driveway were gone. They had been beautiful spruce trees, with full branches all the way around, not scrawny and half-dead like others near the shore. But they were gone.

"I cut them trees down because I could see nothin', not a person, not the cars goin' by," Gus explained to anyone who asked. She hadn't been able to see Ian's house, or Moira's house, and had to stand up and crane her neck to see who was coming and going from the Hall.

"I can see trees out back when I want."

But she couldn't, not on her own land. She'd had her husband Abel cut them down, too, to be clear of them, hiding her view of all the new cottages going up.

He must have done it in the dark, thought Hy, as she passed the stumps on the way up the lane. No one had seen him do it. No one ever saw Abel. She was beginning to think he was a figment of Gus's imagination and the rest of the village was humouring her. Then how the eight children? Hy had never seen them either. It was odd. It was Christmas. A time for family.

At least Gus had one.

Hy did not.

Sometimes Rose thought about killing Fitz, about how she'd do it. He was stronger than her, so she'd probably have to suffocate him with a pillow when he was passed out drunk. When he really made her angry, she could see herself doing it. Drowning out his snoring, which filled her with rage, and made her want to kick him. Kill him. How else would she do it? Her thinking usually stopped there. Some chore, Fitz himself, or little Jamie would interrupt her. She would be doing it for him, Jamie, not herself. He worshipped his father. She was waiting for the day that illusion would shatter, wondering if she'd be able to pick up the pieces. It wouldn't be long. A few years at most.

She sighed, a deep sigh, as she continued unpacking, flitting from one thing to another, trying to find the broom to sweep the kitchen. Her back ached. She arched it, hands on her hips, and, slim as she was in every other way, her belly swelled, like a Third World child suffering malnutrition. She hadn't been eating well. Fitz always took the most and best of everything.

Rose always sacrificed what little she had to keep Jamie healthy and growing.

She looked out the window and saw him running around with Freddy. He was certainly healthy, in spite of the life they led. And growing.

The tent. Where was the tent? Her mind skipped away, as it always did from the troublesome thought.

Time enough. Time enough.

For now, she had other things to think about.

Back and forth to the truck she went, with Fitz nowhere in sight. Jamie was still playing with the dog in the front yard, and she hadn't the heart to ask him to help – he'd been cooped up so long in that boxcar. That filthy, smelly boxcar. It was still in her nostrils.

The broom was sticking out of the pile on the truck, and she grabbed it and went back inside. She sighed again. It was something she was good at. Fitz entered, just in time to hear it. It infuriated him.

"Bitch," he muttered under his breath, well-scented with rum. The rum he had brought back from town instead of the Warfarin.

"I've put Jenny away," he said, standing smack in front of the old wood range and blocking the heat from getting into the room.

"Did you get the Warfarin?"

He slapped his hand on his forehead, a gesture Rose knew well. It meant that the next thing she heard would be a lie.

"Jeez, I forgot."

He had not forgotten. Money was tight. It had been a choice between a mickey of rum and the rat poison. He chose his own poison.

She sighed again and turned from him.

"The shed in the back's in pretty good shape. I'll fix it up so it's a solid shelter for Jenny soon as I get the chance."

Rose, her back to him, wondered when that would be.

"What about us?" she said. "The tent. Where's the tent?"

"Patience, woman. I'll get it. Soon as I warm up a bit." He pulled the rum from his back pocket, and sat down on one of the rickety chairs. A leg broke. He picked up the chair and flung it across the room. Sat down on another.

He took a slug.

Rose crossed the room, picked up the chair leg, and fed it into the stove. She shoved at the wood with the poker, and the thoughts returned. She saw herself smashing Fitz across the head with the poker, sticking it in his eye, thrusting it down his throat, red hot, warming up the rum as it went down.

But that was another Rose. Not her. She'd probably miss – and then what would happen to her and Jamie?

Chapter Four

Oliver Sullivan was Buddha-fat and bald, his fingers weighted with rings. He was twisting the ones on his left hand in sequence, starting with the thumb, down to the little finger, and then from the little finger back to the thumb. Unlike most Buddhas, he did not have a beatific smile or Mona Lisa calm. His forehead was agitated into furrows, several V-shaped funnels diving down between his eyebrows – thick, white, bushy, containing all the hair his head did not – rising and falling as he sputtered into the phone.

"Nothing? How nothing?" He stared at the cards spread out before him. He was sitting in the lotus position, his legs hidden under his robe, so that he looked less like Buddha, and more like Humpty Dumpty.

The Magician...myself? The Castle...that would signify the house.

He reached out a hand, the rings encrusted with precious stones, large and colourful like the cards, his robe, and the room around him. Rubies, sapphires, emeralds glinted in the flickering candles in their ornate silver candelabras, sending shadows shooting across the ceiling, which was domed and painted with the night sky, like an old ballroom he'd seen somewhere once and had recreated. He used it, not as a ballroom, but as a massive library, full of arcane knowledge.

He tapped the cards prophesying Knowledge and Wisdom and Wealth. They were there every time he consulted the Tarot.

It was a sign. Surely it was a sign. And it was obvious, wasn't it? That's where the legacy should be. The Sullivan legacy. In that house, as he kept insisting to this low-life he'd hired to conduct the search while the house was still empty.

The cards had told him it would not be for long. He'd seen tragedy and death in them as well. His own? He tried not to think about that, but he'd seen death all around the Magician.

"Have you looked everywhere? No? Well, then, keep looking. I'll pay you when you find it."

So far, he hadn't said how much he'd pay, just that it would be "commensurate with the value of the object." Jared didn't know what commensurate meant. He was as stupid as his father had been and his father before him. That's why they'd been stuck in that backwater, while he was living the life of Riley. His lip curled at the thought that someone called Riley could inhabit his lifestyle.

He looked down at the cards again. He knew the Tarot was trying to tell him something important – the cards from the Major Arcana kept showing up in the read in significant positions, the same cards appearing again and again. The Magician turned up in every reading. He flipped it over and laid it down in the second position in the layout of brightly coloured cards on the black silk cloth, the cloth he would wrap them in after the reading and bind with a velvet ribbon – all part of the careful and mindful relationship he nurtured with the cards.

He also liked to think of himself as The High Priest. That card came up often, too, but not today. He laid out the now-familiar pattern, in only slightly different sequence from the reading a half-hour before. The pentacles were there. This must be a matter of money, wealth. Justice was there signalling what was to come. He took it to mean he would find gold, jewels, the Sullivan legacy.

Whatever it was.

Not that money mattered. Oliver's bank account was as abundant as he was.

Hy had left Gus's house with plastic bags stuffed in her bicycle basket. There were blueberry muffins – "they won't be good beyond today" – some preserves and two loaves of bread for "those poor souls up there."

Hy was a great preserver of gasoline, because it was a forty-kilometre trip to town to get it. The way her old truck used gas, she'd burn a third of a tank on the way home. It helped that there was no snow this year – she'd been able to cycle right into December.

As she rode past Ian's house on Shipwreck Hill, she was torn by her curiosity to see how the Fitzpatricks were making out at Wild Rose Cottage and by the desire to drop in to tell Ian what she'd found out about the Sullivans. *Him and his history.* Sanitized, architectural history. Whereas she had a story of murder.

The hill was a long, low incline, and Hy was gasping by the time she got to the top. After that, it was an easy coast down to the house.

A mess of weeds was growing up between broken clamshells, laid along the driveway fifty years before. A spire of black smoke was belching from one of the four chimneys.

Hy wondered if it was safe to have a fire in there.

She leaned her bicycle up against the house, took the offerings from Gus out of her basket, and, because these people were new to The Shores, knocked before she went in, yelling out a greeting. That was hardly necessary. The door opened right into the kitchen. Hy couldn't believe what she was looking at.

A tent. A large tent set up in the room, too close to the wood range, its flaps open to the heat.

Rose was stoking the range. She interpreted Hy's look immediately.

"We've done this before. It's obvious we had to do it here. You can't live in any of the rooms, and it makes sense to conserve our heat. It's a single storey here, and the roof leaks."

Hy looked up and down. Wet spots on the ceiling. Wet spots on the floor. Yes, she could see.

She held out her offerings, and Rose beamed, taking them into her arms.

"Thank goodness. Jamie and I are starving. Fitz was supposed to bring food back from town, but he didn't. He forgot. I don't know where he is now." That wasn't true. He'd be out back with that donkey, drinking and singing to her. She was the only one who would put up with him in his state.

"Let me fetch you something more. You can't have bread and jam for supper." That wasn't true either. Hy often did.

"Oh, we'll be fine." She didn't look fine, her face pained as she put her hands on her hips and arched her back.

That's when Hy noticed the swollen belly. An unnatural lump on a thin frame. A tumour? The woman looked sick, pale, drained.

"You'll need something nutritious."

Rose put her hand on her stomach. She dropped it. "Grumbling stomach." A weak smile.

For a moment their eyes met. Rose's flickered, but revealed nothing.

"Are you…?" Hy didn't know what to say next. *Ill? Pregnant?* None of it was really her business.

"It doesn't matter." Rose shrugged her shoulders.

Four or five months. I'd say she's four or five months on, from the look of her. There I go – thinking like an Islander again.

Hy looked around. Rose couldn't have the baby here. If there were a baby.

It could be that Rose was simply very, very ill.

Chapter Five

Oliver had laid out the cards more than twenty times, always
getting the same satisfying signals, but not the answer. The
pentacles were there in abundance, signifying wealth, but Oliver
was a polished practitioner of the Tarot, and knew that might
mean actual wealth or an abundance of some other kind. It
might mean the very opposite – poverty. The cards indicating
spiritual advancement were few. Oliver didn't care – he didn't
associate the cards with spirituality. They were Black Magic to
him. Spirituality he associated with religion, and he had no use
for religion.

He tapped each card with two fingers.

And then it came to him. A book. The answer would be in a
book. He of all people should know that. Something he had in
abundance. The source of his spiritual and material comfort.

Oliver was an antiquarian book dealer, but he bought more
books than he sold. He couldn't bear to part with the treasures
he'd accumulated. They surrounded him in bookshelves stuffed
with leather-bound words. Dull browns, faded greens and dusty
blues, the occasional soft red. He hadn't read them all. He considered some acquaintances, others companions, some close

friends. Those were frequently pulled from the shelves, held lovingly, the dust smeared by the soft caresses of his fingertips.

Money couldn't take them away from him. He parted with a book only if someone proved to have a greater passion for it than his own. Then he would let it go – often for nothing. He didn't need the money, for he had once found the book that had made his fortune. A book the Catholic Church had bought from him, along with his silence. Money well-invested that left him, as he often said, comfortable. Comfortable as a minor monarch. His silence wasn't cheap.

He felt that he'd got the better of the deal. The book, that book, he wouldn't have kept in his house. Even thinking about it brought despair seeping into his blood, a physical as well as mental despair. He rubbed his hands whenever he thought of it, trying to get rid of its stain on him. And talk about it? Never. He had no desire to talk about it. They needn't have paid him for that. But they had, and the thought brightened his mood until he was smiling like the Cheshire cat.

He got up and rolled across the room. He was fat, but fluid in his movements. He pulled out a book. A first edition of Hesse's *Gertrude.* A folded paper slipped from it, and fell to the floor. White, the cat, dashed at it, took it in his mouth, and jumped up on the shelf, having retrieved it for him. Oliver took the paper, stroked the cat, and gave him a treat from the depths of his silk-lined pocket. Ginger, the other cat, less nimble, wound himself around Oliver's feet, and Oliver tossed him a treat, too.

He opened the paper, as he had done many times before. It was a love letter from the past. He had found it tucked into the book. It had become more valuable to him than the book itself. A love poem that had never been sent? Never responded to? The mystery of it impelled him. He had fallen in love with the woman who had written it.

my soul is with you

thank god.
I thought I had lost it
still – how to recall it?

my god
it's with you
where I dare not go

it is quite easily forgotten
you know

once I yearned for it
when my life was painful
now it is not –

time
give me time
I must decide
if I want it

or not

But the woman – and it must have been a woman who had written this – was long dead. The poem wasn't dated, but the paper, yellowed with age, brittle with sadness, told Oliver it was an ancient tale. He liked it that way. It suited him to love a woman who didn't exist. It was bittersweet. That was the most Oliver expected from love, or life.

He filled his life with searching for precious things, and the results became his emotional fulfillment.

A particular book, or print, a map, or small, exquisite piece of ephemera or art – these were the things Oliver wanted to possess. Not another human being. And now it was the mystery of the Sullivan legacy. The mystery, more than the actual legacy. He was determined to solve it.

A book. The answer might well lie in a book. Would that character he'd hired have the sensibility for such a search? He knew the answer to that question.

He would have to go himself.

Hy grabbed the old placemat from the pile of books and sticks of wood stacked by the range. She recognized the satellite photo right away. She hadn't seen it in years. Ian had probably never seen it. The photo had been shot and reproduced on placemats before he had taken early retirement and moved to The Shores. There had been a big fuss about it that had lasted a year or more. *Imagine. The Shores seen from space.* That Hallowe'en there had been several miniature astronauts knocking on doors for treats.

Everybody bought several of the placemats, some sent to friends and relatives off-island, providing proof that The Shores, the forgotten little village, truly did exist. Carpenter Harold MacLean and his wife Olive had been the last to use the mats daily – he, out of a fascination with space, she out of a sense of economy: they'd bought them and had better use them. Now the mats were all tucked away and forgotten like the community itself.

"Can I have this?"

"What is it?" Rose was tearing up books and stuffing them in the range. They were damp and the fire was smoldering and giving off more smoke than heat. She looked over. *Plastic. That wouldn't burn.* She waved a hand in dismissal.

"Sure, go ahead."

Hy looked at the shining star in the cobalt sea. This would appeal to Ian's scientific self. Maybe it would jolt him to get onboard with the rest of the community and light up his house.

Armed with the placemat and the information from Gus, Hy made her excuses to Rose, trying to hide her eagerness to go, and slammed out the door, hopped on her bicycle, and sped up the hill to Ian's.

It wasn't long before he was googling the satellite photo. It had appeared in a few papers across the country, a novelty photograph at Christmas.

Ian thought it was terrific, but it didn't change his attitude.

He picked up the placemat and poked his finger on the urine-stained surface, aiming straight at the "star."

"If Canada's tiniest village in Canada's tiniest province can do that..." He poked again. "Multiply that by thousands and thousands of larger cities around the world – "

"And you think that one string of lights on your house is going to make a difference?" Hy felt argumentative because her tactic had failed.

"It's impressive, Hy, but it doesn't change my mind."

"Have a look at this, then." She shoved the Saran-Wrapped newspaper clipping at him. Creased and torn in its protective wrapping, yellowed with age, brown spots obliterating words, its message was still clear.

Fire Burns Sullivan Cottage
Valiant villagers battle raging blaze to save magnificent Victorian country home...

"Where'd you get this?"

"You google. I 'Gus.'"

"Gus gave you this?"

"Yup." She tried to keep the smirk out of her tone. "Gus thinks it was murder."

"Gus always thinks it's murder."

"That's not true."

"Well, she thinks Jared MacPherson's a murderer."

"I know...I know." Years before, Jared had hit and killed an old woman crossing the highway for her mail. He got off with two weeks for careless driving. It was ruled an accident.

"She's worse now." Ian's posture was stiff, his mouth set. He didn't like Hy to uncover something before he'd had a crack at it, always a technological one.

Hy had to concede that Gus was seeing crime and murder around every corner since the killings on the Labour Day weekend a year ago, on top of what had happened the year before at Jared's cookhouse on the shore.

Ian turned back to the clipping. He scanned the article. "So what's the story?"

"Well, it's all there."

"I mean Gus's story."

"She thinks the brother who started the fire set it deliberately."

Ian waved the clipping. "It was ruled accidental."

"As in, he was accidentally carrying a can of gasoline, unclosed, past the back of the house…it slipped from his grasp, and the cigarette dangling from his lips fell into it and ignited the gasoline."

"He had no idea his brother was taking a nap in the back room," Ian's eyes grazed over the paper.

"As he did every day at that time."
Ian scanned for that detail. He looked up.

"Not here."

"Gus. That's why Gus says he killed his brother. He knew his brother would be napping."

"They said there wasn't enough evidence to make a charge. The facts bore out what he said, more or less." He gave the clipping back. "The neighbours must have known."

"If they did, they didn't say. The house came to him, which is what he wanted all along."

Ian went to the computer, and started clicking on links.
"Wow."

"What've you got?" Hy slipped across the room and looked over his shoulder. Her eyes widened at what she saw on the screen. "But…"

Ian looked at her with glee.

"You're right…but…that wasn't the only murder at Wild Rose Cottage. I was just googling the article, and this one came up. Also two brothers."

Hy looked at the screen, as Ian read bits from an historical article and commented.

"Sam and Henry Sullivan. Sam, a bachelor, had money, from where it isn't clear. The other, Henry, had a family, no cash, but had farmed the family land. When the parents died, Sam bought out their joint inheritance, promising Henry he could stay and work the farm. But Sam sold the harvest and kept the money himself. Henry put up with it for a few years, until, his family starving and in rags, he killed Sam. Shot him in the outhouse."

"Through the head, in the head," Gus would say when she told the story, cackling, slapping her hands on her knees and rocking back and forth.

"Henry was hanged." Hy reached the end of the post just before Ian.

"Right – and his widow was left with the land and a log house. She married again. An architect – "

"Who built the Rose cottage."

"Yup. Called that because of all the roses, naturally."

"Nope. Because her name was Rose. The first of the Roses to inhabit the house. The one who planted all the rose bushes." She had that from Gus, too, who only had a sniff of the actual scandal, so long ago it had been. But the roses were community memory, the kind of information you couldn't google, thought Hy.

"The architect only lived long enough to finish the house." Ian had clicked on a related post. "Technically, it never was finished. He had plans for an even more magnificent home, complete with a ballroom with an arched ceiling painted like the night sky. It never happened. He died of typhoid."

"Then, seventy years ago, it happens again. Brother kills

brother."

They'd come full circle.

Hy had slumped down in a chair. Danish Modern. Rickety. She yanked at the arm that was always falling off and laid it on the floor.

"Twins," she said. "Tom showed up in the world a couple of minutes before Allen. That made him the heir. When the house was left to Tom, Allen went nuts and threatened to burn it down, with Tom in it."

"He very nearly succeeded." Ian grabbed a couple of logs, and stuffed them in the woodstove. The fire had burned down to red coals. The logs rapidly ignited, shooting the brilliance of their flames across the room, highlighting Hy's copper curls.

He passed a hand over his thinning crop.

"Tom died of smoke inhalation, but the men and women of the village organized a bucket brigade and contained the fire to that the back."

"And here's the really weird bit." Hy stretched out her legs, so that the fire warmed her toes, still chilly from Wild Rose cottage. "There was a Rose living in the house at that time, too. Tom's wife. She was out for the day. Maybe Allen was in love with her. Maybe they plotted together – "

"If you want to start sleuthing, think about who's there now. Another Rose."

"Do you think?"

"C'mon Hy, I was just kidding. It's coincidence. Family name. Family home."

"You're right. How likely is it that there would be another murder there?"

"Or here. The law of averages would tell you it's not likely."

"Knock on wood."

She did – and the other arm of the chair fell off. Ian didn't notice. His eyes were fixed on the flames playing in her hair.

Chapter Six

Oliver had seen the book, the diary, when he was a child. He had found it in the library of Wild Rose Cottage, a warm, inviting room back then, with wood paneling, built-in benches and window seats, and shelves full of books. He'd been exploring them. He'd pulled down a sheaf of papers, and his four-year-old eyes had opened wide at the beauty of the architectural plans for the house. He had stared, entranced, at the plans for the ballroom – with its arc of a night sky as a ceiling. The image had stayed with him, until one day he'd had enough money to create his own. He had built it, but no one came. No one was invited. It was never used, except on the occasional night when Oliver, heavy with drink and some posthumous affection for a woman who had lived and died before he was born, would burst through the great doors, and, accompanied by only his own substantial voice, would dance. Dance, as if he held someone in his arms, singing words of love to a woman who wasn't there. Never would be. This he knew. It was why he ached, and the ache was, to him, love itself, most pure.

More than the ballroom, the diary had burned into his child brain. It had lain on the desk. It was nearly out of reach, but the tips of his tiny fingers had managed to pull it into his plump grasp.

It was old, very old. He caressed it. It fell open too easily, the book broken along its spine with use. The pages, some ready to peel out from the binding, were alternating writing and blotting paper. It had been written by more than one hand. Even Oliver could tell that, though he could only just read, and not grown-up handwriting. He passed a chubby hand over the open pages, reverently. He had never seen anything so beautiful. He wanted it. His need for it was physical. He felt it in his stomach, like a hunger, of a different kind. This would not be assuaged by a donut or cookie.

Smack! A heavy hand hit the back of his head, and another yanked the diary from him. He reached up for it, now in the hands of the adult towering above him. An uncle of some kind, he wasn't quite sure.

"Don't touch! You mustn't touch the book!"

Oliver looked up at the fierce face of the man, covered in black hair. His own big blue eyes, cushioned in his pudgy face, were washed with confusion and unspilled tears.

In that moment was born a desire to possess books – and one in particular. He'd longed to see the book again, and had lurked around the library, until one day he'd managed to get in again. Once more he saw it. He had forgotten that day, and the book had been lost. Not just to him, but to everyone. After that day, it was simply gone.

But that ancient family treasure had set his path in life.

Books. It was all about books from then on for Oliver. A book in one hand, a cookie or piece of pie in the other, his eyes glued to the latest manuscript. Of course, the food would be absent when the book he was holding was an old treasure. So many were.

There were a few additions to this scene over time. Two cats. One white and elegant, the other ginger, friendly and a bit paunchy. The two, White and Ginger, when they weren't poking around for mice or basking in the sun, were likely to be found slithering somewhere on Oliver's body, large enough to accommodate both of them at the same time.

And then there was the rat.

When she left Ian's, Hy went back to see Gus to tell her about the murderous history of Wild Rose Cottage and the family living in a tent. It was hard to know which to start with.

"In a tent?"

"It's all the house is good for."

"Reckon you're right. So help me – if Eleanor Sullivan could have seen this day." Gus shook her head slowly, back and forth, back and forth. "That would be Rose Sullivan's mother. Did you ask?"

Hy bit her lip. "Actually, no. I forgot."

"Forgot?" Gus looked shocked. These connections had to be established. You needed to know who was who, where they came from, and who their people were.

To distract Gus, Hy told her about the state the house was in. Hy's eyes shone with glee as she described the rats and mice scurrying around. Hy grinned at Gus, with her eyes opened wide, her jaw dropped. Gus shuddered.

Hy shifted in her chair. The seat was hard. All the seats, including the big purple recliner, were uncomfortable. It was surprising visitors stayed as long as they did. They stayed for Gus, to see Gus's wide-eyed look of wonder when told a choice piece of gossip, as Hy did now, handing Gus the printouts of the posts she and Ian had googled.

Gus read, silently for some time, then waved the papers at Hy.

"How'd you get all this?"

"Googled it."

"Googled?"

"A computer search engine."

"Engine? Does it use gas?"

"Nope. Just electricity."

"Could I find out all about my family on one of them things?"

"Yup. You could even speak to them."

"What, them as is dead?" Gus rolled her eyes.

"No, just the live ones, Gus. You could speak to them."

"Speak to them? Why would I do that?"

"You could see them when you speak to them."

Gus shook her head.

"And me just gettin' used to the phone." She shook her head again, dismissing the idea. But Hy had seen a spark of interest, and wondered what she and Ian might arrange to connect Gus with her kids. Christmas was coming. Family time.

Mountie Jane Jamieson was frowning. Murdo didn't have to look at her to know it. He could feel it.

Stuck in a backwater, that's what she'd be thinking. But what a magnificent backwater. He scanned the approaching shore. The frosty caps on slate-grey waves were muted through his poor eyesight, and, if possible, more beautiful for it. He darted a look at Jamieson, her eyes fixed on the road, her hands curled into fists, where all her anger appeared to have gathered. If she'd been driving, she'd have sunk her emotions and her foot into the accelerator. That's why she'd handed him the keys.

Stuck in a backwater. Jamieson's own thoughts echoed Murdo's. Would she go adrift with this posting?

Ever since she'd come to Red Island, Jamieson had been trying to get away. Now she'd been assigned permanently to The Shores, the most isolated area possible. The unusual posting was a result of a number of separate incidents over the past couple of years. Three murders. Two manslaughters. On her watch. Now, it really was her watch. Until now, there had been only a community liaison officer, in the form of handsome, well-intentioned, but not very bright, Billy Pride. He'd been the only one who'd volunteered. He had made an accidental drug arrest so there was no question of replacing him. But he couldn't be in charge. Thankfully, Murdo Black, her regular partner, had been sent out with her.

She didn't know that Murdo had engineered it. It was partly self-serving and partly because he knew how hard this assignment would hit Jamieson. He was a kind man. Jamieson would have been furious if she'd known that he had done it, and how he had done it.

"A woman – out there all alone," Murdo had appealed to his superior's outdated but charming chivalry, and also to his view of The Shores as a barren, uncivilized outpost.

"On a trial basis," had been the decision. They had few enough officers to let two go out there for a few hundred people. It was all those deaths last year that did it. And the fact that Murdo knew something about the superior officer that he wouldn't want his wife to know. It wasn't mentioned, but it was in the air.

Murdo had come out beaming.

His motives weren't entirely selfless. April Dewey, the plump little cook who'd captured his heart and stomach last year, would be just minutes away. She was married. She was Catholic. Well, Murdo was Catholic, too. He imagined his intentions were honourable. In a way, they were.

The closer they came to the causeway that joined Red Island to The Shores, the more excited Murdo became. He began to speed – rocketing across the causeway that usually made him nervous. A few years back, a storm surge had severed it – sea ice had sliced through the roadbed, and flung houses into the water. Cars were tossed into the sea, and boats onto the road – people had died. The province patched the causeway, threw a river ferry into service, and left The Shores to fend for itself.

Until now. It was an unusual agreement with the RCMP to provide police presence.

Jamieson had been so caught up in her bitter thoughts, she'd hardly noticed they had crossed the causeway. She hadn't noticed much as she'd brooded all the way from Winterside, but as they crested the last hill, the black cloud hanging over the village below moved off, and it was bathed in sunshine. The neat white shingle houses with their green and black roofs, the Hall with the greenest roof of all. The patchwork fields in the soft velvety greens and yellows of late fall, cut through by the red clay and neat lines of evergreens, lay like a giant quilt blanketing the landscape. The meadows tripped down to the sand, and the grey sea with its foaming waves clung to the shore. The pond was shaped like a large tadpole, its run of fresh water curving across the sand and flowing into the great Gulf of St. Lawrence.

Jamieson felt her spirits lift. The sun, she thought. But she was wrong. It was The Shores. It might not be Toronto or Halifax or Montreal. It might be a backwater. But it was her backwater, more than she knew. She felt odd. Better than she thought she would. To her surprise, as they descended the long high hill that dropped down into the village, it felt like she was coming home. But the feeling was mixed with disappointment. Jamieson was ambitious. So much had already happened here that nothing would ever likely happen again. Nothing to propel her to promotion and the big city. Any city.

There had been too many deaths here. How had it happened – in this quiet place, where people were supposed to live and die the way they always had? Where people from away, like McAllister, came to find peace and solitude. And others came – for what? Running from demons they hoped would not pursue them here. But it seemed they did.

Jamieson had her own demons. She knew how they followed you, no matter where you went. She could feel them at her back, always.

Having exhausted the topic of Wild Rose Cottage, Hy asked the question she'd been meaning to ask Gus for days.

"Any chance you'll be in the Women's Institute skit this year?"

Gus pressed her lips together. In more than sixty years she had only ever once appeared in a skit at the annual Christmas pageant. Just a few years back, her performance, of one line, the punch line to the piece, had been received with a genuine standing ovation. She had decided to quit while she was ahead.

"Oh, c'mon Gus."

"And what part could I play?"

"I fancy you as the fairy godmother."

"The fairy grandmother, more like."

"Well then, the queen."

"There is no queen in that story." Gus smiled a smug smile.

"There could be."

Hy always wrote the Women's Institute skit for the Christmas pageant. This year she'd written "Shores Ella," a spoof on "Cinderella," and was still trying to cast it and rehearse in time for the show on Christmas Eve. It wasn't easy. The women took it as their duty to act in the show because the proceeds went to maintenance of the Hall and village life. The Hall was the only public building still standing in the village. But the Institute women were no actresses. If Hy weren't so determined to do a good job, she'd realize that's what made it so entertaining.

"I'll just make my squares," said Gus. The highlight of every event in The Shores was the bake sale. But the Christmas show had a special appeal. It wasn't just squares and muffins, nor April Dewey's lemon cake. It was the Institute women embarrassing themselves, the children losing shoes and lines and courage, and always, always a little magic. There had never been a Christmas show without it. So far that magic was missing.

"And I'll be making something now." Gus stood up and smoothed down her apron. "For those poor souls as think they can live in that place this winter. P'raps I'll do them a quilt. The Log Cabin or the House on the Hill. What do you think?"

"How about the tent?"

"No such pattern."

"You could create it."

"Oh, not me. You know me. I can copy it, but I can't make it up."

"You might surprise yourself."

"I wouldn't want to do that."

Gus didn't like surprises.

"No, I think I'll do the Log Cabin. Lots of small pieces and they don't have to match."

She shuffled off to her back room to see what material she had. More than she'd ever need the rest of her life.

Chapter Seven

The new police house was one of Abel's rentals. It was on Shipwreck Hill, just above Ian's. It was the oddest little house in The Shores, called the Lego house because addition after addition had been attached to it in no logical pattern. A series of rooms had been added on willy-nilly to the main structure, some of them larger than the original house. It could not be said to have a shape at all. Geometry couldn't describe it.

Jamieson soon carved it into shape inside. She sectioned off an office area, quarters for herself and Murdo, and common areas. When they were settled in, she went out to establish herself in the village, walking the beat, knocking on doors, providing police presence, as she'd been instructed.

Murdo took the opportunity to snoop through the house. He remembered the one time he had been to Jamieson's apartment in town, to pick up a uniform for her during a disastrous murder investigation. The place had been clean, organized, sterile. Nothing personal. It was the same here, too. Bed made within an inch of its life. Sheets and bedspread starched, pulled taut and tucked in tight. Nothing on the dresser. In the closet, uniforms, and just a few civilian clothes that looked like uniforms, too – white shirts and black pants and skirts.

In the living room were the furnishings provided with the rental. The only books were Murdo's detective novels and Jamieson's forensic reference books. A photo of a bloated body, on the cover of a book called *Drowning for Dummies*, graced the coffee table. There were no knick-knacks, no magazines or photographs, no cushions, no feminine touch.

Jamieson had brought her own pots, pans, dishes, and small appliances. Everything was white. Murdo didn't care. He'd eat off any colour.

Jamieson didn't have any personal items. She had her graduation photo from police college, framed, but it was stuffed in a drawer. She didn't like to look at herself staring back from a photo. There was a reason Jamieson had so few things, but she hadn't told anyone about it. She didn't like to think of it. She didn't want them to get the wrong idea about her.

Hy had gathered most of the Institute women at the Hall to discuss their skit and hand out the parts. There were thirteen of them, an unlucky number the women were always trying to change. But as soon as they got one new member, another would leave, get sick, or die. The aging membership meant that most monthly meetings included time spent signing condolence, sympathy, and get-well cards.

"I'd like to be Cinderella," Moira Toombs piped up.

"Shores Ella," Hy corrected, buying time. *Moira – Cinderella?* Ludicrous with her tightly permed curls, pasty skin, and height – almost as tall as herself and Annabelle. And Shores Ella had to at least be likable.

"How about the prince?" she offered in a panic.

Moira took a moment to taste the possibility. The second most important part, or so she thought. And maybe she could upstage Shores Ella.

"All right. I'll do it." She said it as if she were doing Hy a personal favour.

Hy chose Gladys Fraser, a bulldog of a woman, short and square and surly, with never a smile on her face, belligerent by nature, as one of the ugly sisters. And because she was so short and Hy's friend Annabelle so tall that they would look ridiculous together, she chose Annabelle as the other ugly sister. Annabelle got it right away. She laughed. That's why they were friends.

Annabelle was not ugly. She was tall and glamorous, with blond hair that tumbled in loose curls past her shoulders. She wore plunging necklines, high heels, and had perfectly manicured fingernails. In the off-season. She fished with her husband Ben, Abel Mack's much younger brother, and at the opening of the season the hair went up and under a baseball cap, the nails were cut off, the high heels traded for rubber boots. She still, somehow, looked glamorous.

"April, I'd like you to be the fairy godmother."

April Dewey blushed with delight and bashfulness. She was pretty, pleasantly plump, with a characteristic streak of flour on her cheek. It would be perfect, thought Hy. Fairy dust.

She also thought that any one of the women might make a perfect wicked stepmother, but chose Estelle Joudry, Gus's neighbour. Estelle was thrilled. She was addicted to her "stories," the soap operas on afternoon TV, and delighted to be given a real acting part. If she could only memorize the lines.

Everyone was waiting to find out who would be Shores Ella, looking around now to see who was left.

There was only Madeline.

Not Madeline. For a moment, something like vulnerability passed across Moira's face. Her teeth clenched. Her left eye twitched. Her hands closed in tight fists.

Madeline? It was a communal, unspoken question.

"Madeline," said Hy. Tiny, shy Madeline Toombs, overshadowed and under the thumb of her big sister Moira, looked at Hy like a frightened deer. Hy smiled.

"I'd like you to be Shores Ella."

Madeline started shaking her head before the words came out of her mouth.

"Oh, no. I couldn't. I...I...I..." Madeline had always helped, usually handling the curtains – heavy red velvet ones on a pulley – but she'd never acted.

Moira's pasty skin had turned an unhealthy red. Madeline. Shores Ella? Not if she had anything to do with it.

"Just say yes for today, Madeline," Hy coaxed. "We'll see how it goes day by day. We won't force you onstage."

Madeline nodded dumbly, unable to say no to anyone. Moira was already hatching a plan to keep her offstage. She'd learn the lines and step in to save the day when Madeline welched, as Moira knew she would, especially after she'd finished with her. Every day, for the next several, she'd ask Madeline if she was sure she was up to it. That would put an end to it.

When the meeting was over, Hy and Annabelle were alone in the Hall.

"Do you think that's going to work?'

"What?" Hy knew exactly what.

"Little Madeline."

"I don't know. I thought I'd try to bring her out of her shell. Let her be the centre of attention."

"I'm not sure she wants that."

"We'll see. Anyway, I've got news. They've come."

"Who?"

"The Wild Rose Cottage people."

"Jesus, Mary, and Joseph."

"No – Fitz, Rose, and Jamie."

Annabelle let out a guffaw.

"Tell me all about it." She started to stack chairs.

Finally, thought Fitz, Jared had found out what they were supposed to be looking for.

"A diary."

Fitz spat some tobacco off his tongue and onto the ground. A fucking diary. Jeez.

"A diary?"

"A real old one. Family thing."

"Worth money?"

"I dunno. I don't think so. Can't see much in it for me."

Fitz's hand came down hard on Jared's back.

"There must be something in it for somebody, else he wouldn't be sending you on this chase."

Jared chewed the inside of his cheeks. He hadn't thought about it. Why hadn't he thought about it? He'd just seen it as a few easy bucks. Suddenly, it was getting complicated – but maybe more worthwhile than he'd thought.

"Tell you what." Fitz lit another cigarette. "I'll help you find it. You'll connect to the geezer, and we'll split the payoff."

"Wait a minute…"

"You wait a minute. You ain't finding that thing without me. If it's in the house, well, you can't go in the house unless I let you."

When Jared left, Fitz went back inside.

"A book?" he said to no one in particular, eyeing the pile in front of the stove. Jeez, a fucking book. There were dozens of them. More – hundreds. Some he'd already got rid of, burning them in the stove just to keep warm. They weren't much good even for that. They were rotting, rat-eaten, and mildewed, and didn't burn well. He was supposed to look through them for a fucking diary? He wasn't even really sure what that was. It made him think of tough times on the toilet after a night out.

Jared probably didn't know what it was either.

Fitz planned to outwit him.

Moira Toombs was disappointed when she cleaned up the police house after Jamieson and Murdo's arrival. There was nothing to be found. Moira was a snoop. She liked turning up people's secrets. She didn't use them, just hugged them to her like something precious. It was perhaps the only thing that gave her joy, knowing something about someone else that they didn't know she knew.

She knew a lot about Ian – especially since she'd learned to use a computer herself. She cleaned for him and was also in and out of his house frequently, whether he was there or not. She'd check his email – received and sent. She'd check his History, Bookmarks, and visit the sites he'd been visiting.

Oh, yes, she knew a lot about Ian – things even Hy didn't know. Things she might use, someday, if she thought it would bring Ian closer to her, or push Hy away. She was waiting to find the right thing, snooping the Internet, following him around electronically. There was bound to be something. Someday.

Today, it seemed she would find out nothing about Jamieson and Murdo.

Until, at last, she found it in a small pocket of a suitcase in a back closet.

A newspaper clipping.

Moira read it with interest. It should have saddened her, but she came away smiling. A plum piece of information.

By the time she got home, she was frowning. As she walked down Shipwreck Hill, she spied Billy Pride and her sister Madeline kissing on the front stoop.

Kissing, where everyone can see. Disgusting.

Bristling with sanctimonious outrage and burning jealousy,

Moira quickened her pace, marching forward toward the guilty pair who didn't notice her. Marching, then nearly running. When she was within shouting distance:

"Billy Pride!"

He pulled away from Madeline, both of them flushed red, a combination of the excitement that had been building up from the kiss, and the fear of what Moira was about to do – or say.

"Get you home, Billy Pride. Leave. Now."

Billy, well over six feet of muscular male, physically dominated the stoop and the two women on it. But that did not make him brave when confronted with Moira's rage. He'd been brought up by his mother to cower before women. Perhaps that's why he was attracted to tiny, fearful Madeline. No one could cower before her.

His shoulders dropped, he turned, and, miserably, made his way over to the Hall, where he had parked his Smart car, inherited from an uncle. To see big Billy squeeze into that tiny car was like Cinderella's ugly sisters trying to negotiate the glass slipper. But he made it, curled up, and sped by the two women as Moira was hustling Madeline inside the door.

And then it began, all her spite and jealousy spitting out of her:

"You won't marry him, you know. You won't go living in that house with his mother."

Madeline had seen the house – and the mother. She didn't want to live in it or with her.

"She won't have it. She won't have you. And Billy won't leave his mother."

Then, triumphant:

"And you won't leave me."

Madeline didn't say anything. She couldn't say anything. She had nothing to say. Nothing, because she knew Moira was right.

"And I won't have him here. You and him getting up to all sorts. It disgusts me. I won't have it in my own house." It occurred to neither that it was Madeline's house, too.

A tear spilled down Madeline's face.

She had no idea – not yet – how strong she could be if pushed to it. And she had no idea that her sister was weak, bitter, spiteful, jealous, and a much lesser woman than she was.

She would find out, but it would take time.

Until then, Moira bullied her. Her and Billy. The only two people over whom she had any power. Faced with the rest of the world, Moira became uncertain, unsure.

For now, she had power over these two, and she wielded it. She tolerated Billy's presence, because he was handy around the house and she got work done free.

It was the only reason she put up with him. Physically, he was much too much man for her. That knowledge was one of the things that made her rage.

She smiled a tight-lipped smile of satisfaction when she went into the kitchen. Billy had not spent all his time here smooching with Madeline. The six cupboard doors that had refused to close properly were now tightly shut.

Billy had done as she had told him. He always did.

He always did at home, too. Home was even bleaker than Moira's house – grim in its lack of ornamentation and mean sobriety. When Moira washed the floor, she'd lay layers of newspaper down over top so it wouldn't get dirty. If company was coming, she'd lift them off. When company left, the newspapers would go back down again. Since Moira and Madeline rarely had company, the newspapers covered the floor most of the time.

When Billy got home, he asked the question he always asked: "How are you?" You'd think he'd know better.

"How am I? How am I?" Pearl Pride responded as she always did. There was no winning. If he hadn't asked, she'd have shoved that in his face – along with the empty mug of tea that sat in the tray in front of her.

"I'm parched. You leave your poor old crippled mother here

for hours, without so much as a bit of tea to wet her lips."

Billy took the mug. In the kitchen, he filled the kettle and plugged it in, stuck his head back into the front room. It was decorated for Christmas.

Pathetically decorated.

An aging garland hung across the fake fireplace mantel. The bough was losing its needles and turning from green to brown, hung with a few skinny pieces of tinsel, and a half-dozen glass balls, colour chipping off them. In the centre was a nativity scene – two bakelite figurines, Mary and Joseph, and a cradle, all turned yellow with age.

"Biscuits or bread and cheese?"

"A bit of both," his mother replied. "And quickly, or I'll starve to death. What are you doing in there? Growing the tea leaves?"

Billy sighed and turned back into the kitchen. He could never leave his mother. And he couldn't bring Madeline here.

Oliver was frowning, having just come off a conversation with Jared. The man was getting difficult. He had assumed there was something of value in what he was looking for and was angling to get some, or all of it, for himself.

Oliver had swatted larger flies than Jared. He'd killed a man once. It had been necessary. That's what he'd told the judge, without guilt or shame.

Murdo answered the first call that came to the police house when Jamieson was out on her rounds.

"Domestic." It was Jamieson.

Just one curt word, the address, and she hung up.

Murdo knew he was meant to get his ass over there right away. Jeez. They hadn't been here two minutes and she'd already managed to find trouble. Or create it?

He looked at the address he'd scribbled down. Then looked at it again.

April's house.

He pulled on his jacket, raced out the door, and jumped in the cruiser. He didn't have far to go – down the hill, past the Hall and Gus Mack's house on The Shore Lane, and right next-door was April's.

April was lying in the driveway behind her husband Ron's cherry red Ford Fairlane.

Jamieson and Ron had been trying to get her to stand up.

She had her plump little arms folded across her chest, and her chin stuck up in defiance.

A domestic? Murdo looked confused. He looked at Jamieson. Raised an eyebrow.

"Well, I thought…" she began defensively.

"The way the kids was screamin'," put in Ron, "I don't blame you."

Ron had been shouting at April to get out of the driveway. He'd slammed himself into the car and edged it backward an inch or two as a threat. The kids – all six of them – had come running and begun to scream and cry. Ron had started yelling, too, just as Jamieson was coming around the corner, prompting her to phone Murdo with the dreaded word: domestic.

It was more like a domestic comedy than a tragedy.

Murdo squatted down and whispered a few kind words to April.

"He's leaving me," she said.

"Good riddance, I'd say." Ron was a well-known womanizer.

"He's leaving the children."

"They're better off without him, too."

"He's leaving us." Her hands scrunched up her apron and now pulled it over her face, depositing flour on her nose and hair.

Murdo found her nearly irresistible when she looked like that. Other men did, too.

"Let him go." He dared to brush some of the flour off her forehead.

"But the children need a father."

"They need their mother right now." He took her by the elbow, and helped her sit up. Then he got her to her feet and led her over to her children. The moment they were off the driveway, Ron jumped in the car and backed up with a screech. He looked straight ahead as he sped down The Shore Lane to freedom and his blowsy, bleach-blond mistress in Winterside.

Chapter Eight

Hy and Annabelle were in the Hall, untangling the Christmas lights. There were boxes full of cheesy decorations, each of which had a specific place it belonged, locations Moira Toombs knew by heart. She'd picked them all. She would be over soon to boss them into doing it her way.

Normally, the decorating would have been done by now, but there had been a memorial service for The Shores' oldest resident, 105-year-old Agnes Cousins.

"She could have picked a better time to die," Annabelle grumbled. It was something she'd only dare say to Hy. She was usually good-natured and easy-going, but she was behind on her Christmas baking, shopping, and her own decorating.

"She did pick a time."

Agnes Cousins had died shortly after midnight on the day of her 105th birthday. She had lived to be the oldest resident of The Shores.

The lights were untangled and ready to hang when the door opened. From where they were in the main room, Hy and Annabelle couldn't see who'd come in. They assumed it was Moira.

"Ah. Indulging your heathen practices."

Jamieson – competing with Ian as Grinch of The Shores. Hy was no more a believer than they were, but she enjoyed the holiday season, even as a heathen.

"Why not enjoy it, even if you're not a Christian? The lights at the darkest time of year, bountiful food, when there might not be much in the next few months."

"That was then," said Jamieson.

"It could be now – if the snow comes and the causeway floods and freezes over."

The causeway provided a very tenuous link between The Shores and the rest of Red Island. It had never been satisfactorily fixed after a storm surge that sliced it in two. In the winter The Shores was sometimes stormbound – bad weather making it impossible to cross the causeway. Ian, for a while, had circulated a petition for a *fixed* fixed link to The Shores, but people had just laughed at him, and he put it away.

They made do with the inconvenience – just one more thing that set The Shores apart from the rest of Red Island. People like Ian had computers and high-speed Internet, but the ladies of the Women's Institute in the village still wore only dresses, summer and winter. They had not given in to what they still called slacks.

And then there was the weather – as brutal, as benign, as varying as in other places along the Atlantic seaboard, and more so. Last year there had been a fog of which Gus said she'd "never seen the like." The Shores had been in a shroud of invisibility for two days.

No surprise that many, like Hy, had stores of preserves in their cellars, some root crops and freezers full of fruit and vegetables from their gardens.

"It could be us," Hy repeated. "Easily."

Jamieson conveyed contempt and disbelief in one twist of her mouth. A city girl, though she'd experienced the perils of the causeway, she didn't believe it could seriously interfere with modern life.

"There hasn't even been any snow yet."

"It's going to snow. It's winter. How can it not snow? And it will…" Hy predicted, "…by Christmas Eve. I have faith."

"I thought you didn't."

"For Christmas I do. Light. Food. Good will toward men."

"And women," said Jamieson.

"Amen to that," said Annabelle.

Jamieson seemed to have come in for no reason, but she'd recognized Annabelle's car and Hy's bicycle outside. Might as well start community policing with people she knew.

Jamieson said nothing more, just stood there and watched as they strung the lights, all along the shrill pink tongue-and-groove wainscoting covering the lower half of the walls, also pink, but thankfully paler. The Institute women had all agreed on the colour as soothing, and, they thought privately, flattering – but treasurer Olive MacLean, wife of Harold the carpenter, had picked the colour. Or rather, the price. The paint she'd bought was on sale for a reason. It was garish. It wasn't soothing or flattering, but it was the right price for Olive, who was as mean with the Institute money as she was with her own.

The lights in place and tested, Hy and Annabelle began to dig into the boxes. There were feathery angels, stars made by every child who had ever attended The Shores' school in the past eighty years, until it had closed. Many of the ornaments showed their age. They were yellowed, flaking, but still put up every year.

"Can't we get rid of Conrad Kelly?" Annabelle held up a tattered star that had only two limp points left.

"Of course not." Moira slammed the Hall door shut. She marched in, steel wool hair lacquered onto her head, pasty face with just a smudge of colour – caused by her irritation. Conrad Kelly had been the conservative MLA for The Shores fifty years before. He'd got her father his garbage job. Her loyalty to him and his tattered star ran deep.

Moira frowned at Annabelle and Hy digging in the boxes. She

began taking things out herself, with care, holding them tenderly, mumbling, "famous photos grouping…the War Dead…Harvest Festival."

She was naming specific locations around the Hall where particular ornaments would be tacked to the wall or hung on the lights attached to the wainscoting. The "famous" photos, in dusty frames donated from village attics, hung haphazardly at the back of the Hall. They included Gus shaking hands with the current premier. Gus shaking hands with a former premier. A photo of Gus shaking hands with Shania Twain, both looking a bit puzzled. Shania had only stopped in during her tour of the island hoping to use the bathroom. As it turned out, the toilet had been out of order, and moments after the shot, she'd gone dashing into the bushes behind the Hall. Or so the story went.

"The War Dead." Moira said it with capital letters. It was a gilded document of the brave men of The Shores who'd given their lives in the two world wars. The Harvest Festival was a group of ten "Best Float" awards. That had taken on new meaning since the causeway had collapsed. One of the winning floats, tricked out by Annabelle's son, Nathan, and his pal Dooley, was a boat with car wheels and wings. They'd called it The Shoresmobile.

Jamieson said nothing, but stood watching them unpack the Christmas treasures. There was the suggestion of a smirk on her face at the Santa Claus made out of jelly beans, glued onto a piece of faded construction paper. The jelly beans were faded, too, and many of them lost or stolen. Not exactly a case for a police investigation, Jamieson thought.

Hy shot Annabelle a look and mouthed, "Why's she here?" Annabelle shrugged. They had a good laugh later when they figured out this was Jamieson's idea of community policing. Jamieson didn't know how to start an unofficial conversation. Hy did – or so she thought until she tried to chat with Jamieson to break the uncomfortable feeling in the room.

"Will you be spending Christmas with the family?" There was

a long pause before Jamieson answered.

"I don't have a family." It wasn't quite true.

Both Annabelle and Moira looked up. No family? That was unheard of in The Shores.

"I thought you had a sister. She got married last year. You showed up here for that murder investigation in a bridesmaid's dress."

Jamieson did not like to be reminded of the dress or the disastrous investigation.

"She'll be away." She was always gone at Christmas. Jamieson knew why. She understood. She didn't want to celebrate with family either.

"You must have parents."

"I don't have parents." Was this community policing? If so, Jamieson didn't like it. Much too personal.

Dead, thought Hy. *Her parents must be dead. Like mine. But I'd never say I didn't have them.*

"Passed away?" Hy didn't like the phrase. It was avoiding reality, but she was trying to use a soft probe.

"I wouldn't call it that."

The conversation was over. Hy knew it. Jamieson was not prepared to say anything more, her lips shut tight in one long, disapproving line.

Shortly after, Jamieson left.

Annabelle took a big breath and exhaled on a deep sigh.

"Man, she's a piece of work."

"Yup," said Hy, placing Conrad Kelly's star where it always went, next to the wall hanging the Institute ladies had quilted to celebrate one hundred years of the W.I. The star was right above the new recycling bin. Hy tacked it loosely to the wall, hoping it might fall in.

Chapter Nine

"Who's the man lives in that shed just outside the village?"

It was Jamieson's community policing day again, and she'd stopped in at Hy's. She'd decided that every second day she would go on her rounds until she knew everyone in the village, their backgrounds and relationships.

An hour or two with Gus would have told her that, but she'd have been dizzy with the tangled web of brothers and sisters, uncles and aunts – a web so large and intricate that Gus sometimes confused herself.

"Don't let Abel Mack hear you call it a shed."

"I've never met Abel Mack." Jamieson made a mental note to do so.

"He built it for Buddy."

Buddy meant nothing. It was a name for anyone.

"Buddy – that's the man?"

"Yup. Buddy."

"Buddy –" She expected more. "Buddy who?"

"That's it. Buddy."

"No last name?"

"Not that we know. He didn't have a first name until Abel gave it to him."

"The name and the shed?"

Hy nodded.

"I went up there to say hello but he ran off."

"He's shy. A bit simple, but good-hearted and hard-working. C'mon." Hy grabbed her jacket. "I'll take you up to meet him."

Jamieson went, somewhat reluctantly. What good meeting this Buddy would be, she didn't know. Then reminded herself: *community policing.*

They trudged up the long low incline to Buddy's. He was outside, splitting wood. There was a pair of very stiff long johns hanging from a single clothesline slumped between the house and a spruce tree. The long johns and the clothes pegs had turned the same shade of grey.

Community policing was also getting to know the troublemakers. Jamieson sensed that she was looking at trouble. She stopped and turned to Hy.

"How well do you know him?" Eyes now squinting at the scene.

"Pretty well." Hy was shaken by the question. She knew Jamieson well enough to know that she was, if not on the hunt, in stalking mode.

"How long?"

"Since he came."

"And that was when?"

This was turning into an interrogation. Hy stiffened, defensive.

"A while."

"A while?"

"A few years."

"Then you don't know anything."

Jamieson started up again, looking at the clothesline with distaste. It offended her fastidiousness, the long johns especially. An article of clothing unattractive at best, and the way they looked now made her turn her head away. But she had to look at Buddy, his face crumpled in a smile, saliva leaking from a side of his mouth, which, when he opened it, foamed with moisture.

Unfortunately, some of his saliva hit Jamieson in the face when he said something she deciphered as "hello," and stuck a fat hand out to her.

She didn't take it. She couldn't. She wiped the saliva from her face with the sleeve of her uniform, and looked at it with distaste.

His smile drooped. His bright eyes lost their shine, and he looked at Hy, an appeal for help. He didn't speak well, but he knew how to communicate his feelings.

"You might want this," Hy said to Jamieson, handing her a crushed Kleenex that she had in her pocket. Jamieson looked at it with distaste as well.

"It hasn't been used. Promise."

Jamieson wiped her sleeve, and took a step back from Buddy.

"This is Officer Jamieson, Buddy. She's one half of the new police presence in the village." Hy spoke to Buddy as she spoke to everyone else. She didn't patronize him, and he seemed to understand what she said.

"Half. Half." He repeated, pointing at Jamieson and smiling again, a big broad smile that pushed his eyes up into a squint, laughter in them.

"Half. Half." He said it again, now laughing. Then he raised his arms as high as they would go.

"He means you're too tall to be half of anything," said Hy, and Buddy nodded furiously to indicate she was correct. He kept laughing at his own joke.

Jamieson scowled.

Buddy began nodding his head, and gestured to the women to go into the house. Jamieson was reluctant, but Hy gave her a little push forward.

It was small, cramped, and stuffed with newspapers.

"He reads?" Jamieson asked Hy, as if Buddy were not there. Again, his face drooped.

Buddy didn't read. He collected newspapers – no one knew

why. Not even Buddy. He couldn't remember that his parents had kept him in a cage until he was five years old, sitting on layers of newspapers they would peel off when the top ones became too foul. Buddy had learned where to do his business now – in the outhouse behind his shed, but he still went around the village asking people for newspapers. He burned them in his woodstove, but not all. He used some for insulation, stuffed into the cracks between the baseboard and the floor. Others were stacked in piles everywhere. Apart from the newspapers, there were only a simple single cot, a small table, a chair, a few bits of crockery, and an old rusty potbellied stove smack in the centre of the room. Jamieson gave it a good look. *Definitely not code.* A couple of pairs of pants and a jacket hung on hooks on the wall.

The one-room shack smelled of bachelor, newspapers, and wood smoke.

A firetrap, thought Jamieson, looking at the chimney pipe. Near the top were a few pin-sized holes in the pipe. Metal fatigue.

Suddenly, she was overcome with a desperate feeling of entrapment.

Buddy opened the door of the stove, and shot in another small log. An ember fell out onto the floor, smoking. Buddy snuffed it with his boot, grinding the charcoal into a black mark on the floor.

Jamieson felt as if she were choking. She began to shake. She had to get out.

Hy reached out to her, put a hand on her sleeve. Oddly, Jamieson did not shake her off as she normally might have.

"Buddy, the officer needs air. We'll be going now."

"Go?" Frown.

"I'll be back later." Hy hauled the door open and Jamieson burst outside. Buddy wrinkled his brow. "Back." Smile. He waved and sat down on a stack of papers.

Outside in the clear, crisp air, Jamieson was perspiring. Drops of sweat were running down her face. It was washed of all colour.

"Are you okay?"

"I'm fine." Jamieson wiped the sweat from her forehead with the Kleenex Hy had given her, realizing too late she had swiped Buddy's spit across her face. She cringed.

"What's wrong?"

In answer, Jamieson shook her head, took several deep breaths and one look back at the shack.

"Nothing." She began to walk away from it. "Nothing's wrong."

But it was obvious that something was wrong. Very wrong.

They walked back down to the road. Hy wanted to drop in at Ian's, but felt she should walk Jamieson to the police house. When they got there, she went in with her, forced her to sit down, and made them both some tea.

Jamieson was an interesting one, thought Hy. She was determined to find out more. She looked around the main room as she brought in the teapot. Nothing in here to tell her anything. No photos, no certificates, no knick-knacks.

What's Jamieson's story?

Hy would find out. *Not today. But soon.*

When Hy left, Jamieson lay back on the couch, her arm shielding her eyes from the light, and tried to fall asleep – something she never did during the day and couldn't manage now. Jamieson had a vivid imagination that often led her down the right trail in an investigation. She tried to suppress it, because it wasn't logical, but she saw Buddy's shack bursting into flame. She saw herself, not him, inside it. It played in her head over and over until finally, exhausted, she fell into sleep. There was no relief there. The images wouldn't let go. She dreamed of fire, the imagined one and the one from long ago. She woke up in a sweat, stumbled to the bathroom, shed her clothes onto the floor – something else she had never done. She had an unusually long, hot shower. It didn't stop the shaking. She was still shivering when she got out. She toweled down, threw on her bathrobe, picked up her clothes – and, instead of hanging them up as she normally did, tossed them on her bed. She opened a suitcase in the back cupboard. Inside was the one thing she had kept. One thing. A newspaper clipping. She unfolded it, and began to cry. That was another thing she never did. If she had known that Moira had found and read this, she'd have been furious. She might have been forced to resign her job.

After that experience, Buddy gave Jamieson the creeps. She steered clear of him whenever he was around. It was irrational, she knew, but she didn't like the man, didn't trust his lack of sense, didn't trust his disability.

Jamieson herself had always been able.

The village always began its Christmas celebrations early, on the Feast of the Immaculate Conception. It was strangely Catholic for the mostly Protestant community, but the Institute President, Gladys Fraser, liked the sound of "immaculate," as did many of the local women. So, every December 8, they had what Hy called "The Feed of the Immaculate Conception," to kick off the holiday season. They pulled out the lobster they had stored in their freezers from the height of the season, and cooked up a true feast. This year, however, the villagers had used up the lobster in a "198 and Counting" celebration in the early fall. The Shores would be two hundred years old in a couple of years, and they'd begun celebrating early, on the premise that, as Gus put it: "You only turn two hundred once, so you might as well celebrate it at least twice."

How to get some lobster?

Somehow, it had become Hy's problem.

Actually, she'd volunteered. She had looked around the table at the twelve other members of Institute and realized they all had families to make Christmas preparations for, and she did not. Gus didn't either, it occurred to her later. *She has family, but you never see them at Christmas. Why is that?*

She shelved the thought, and concentrated on getting hold of some lobster. It wouldn't be easy in the off-season.

It turned out to be impossible. It was Fitz, of all people, who provided the solution.

Hy was having tea with Rose inside the tent.

"You need to get out," said Hy.

"Where?"

"Well, you should join the Institute, for one thing."

"Oh, well, I…"

"Don't be shy. They'll love having fresh blood. And that will make us fourteen."

"What does that matter?"

"It's not thirteen," said Hy.

"Superstitious."

"Yup." Hy took a sip of tea. She put down her mug.

"You can help me organize the Feed of the Immaculate Conception."

"What's that?"

Hy was just telling her about trying to find lobster when Fitz peeked into the tent. Hy shifted, feeling uncomfortable that he had come up on them like that, silent as a…mouse? No, the mice in this house made more noise than he did. You could hear their constant scratching.

"I can help you there," he said.

Hy looked up with suspicion.

"Met a fella last night. Got a ton of frozen lobster he wants to unload. Good price."

Hy didn't know what to say. She didn't want to insult Rose –

"Is it legal?" Rose asked for her.

For once, it was. Fitz had been looking for an angle to make some money on the stuff, and here it had dropped right in his lap.

"Yeah, it's legal. Lobster belongs to him. A restaurant contract fell through. He needs to unload it to make room in his freezer."

"How much does he have? How much does he want?"

Fitz hesitated.

"Well there's clams, too. We'd have to take the clams with it."

"Clams? What will we do with clams?"

"I make a cracking clam chowder, don't I, Rose?" He smiled and winked at his wife, the friendliest he'd been in days.

Hy raised her eyebrows. Rose nodded and smiled at Fitz. For a moment, just a moment, Hy saw the spark between them. Fitz looked almost handsome. She could imagine him younger, with all his teeth, a real charmer.

"He does. I'll give him that. Doesn't lift a finger in the kitchen any other way, but his chowder's a dream."

The moment was gone when Fitz slipped into the tent on a cloud of tobacco smoke and rum, mixed thinly with fresh outdoor air. Rose poured him a mug of tea. She was glad he didn't pull out his mickey to top it up. They had to live in this community. She was hoping Fitz's offer might put them in better standing. Then maybe she could join this Women's Institute with a clear conscience.

"You'd do that?" Hy's eyes opened wide. Fitz? A cook? "Can you make enough for everyone?"

Fitz's eyes narrowed. "What's everyone?"

"Well, about a hundred people could show."

Fitz whistled, surprised the tiny village could turn up that many.

"Sure." He pulled out a pouch of tobacco and some cigarette papers and began rolling. His fingers were stained orange.

Hy felt her upper lip curl involuntarily with disgust. Was she doing the right thing?

"Done it before. Plenty of times."

"He has." Rose's eyes appealed to Hy. It was Rose, not Fitz, whom Hy couldn't resist.

Hy pulled out the Institute money, carefully peeled off one bill at a time by treasurer Olive MacLean earlier that day. She'd rubbed each one to make sure it wasn't two sticking together. Crisp twenties from a bashed-up metal box. "No need of a new one," she said every time she produced it. For once, Hy agreed with her. No one would think there were hundreds of dollars in that rusty old box. Olive kept the key on a chain around her neck at all times. Even in bed, Gus would say with a chuckle. Gus said it was "the key to her heart."

"I'll need a receipt," Olive had said when Hy had turned to leave.

"Of course," she said, "I'll bring it back with any change."

"No. From you." Olive was already writing it, and Hy flushed red as she signed. That her honesty would be questioned. She knew what it felt like, suddenly, to be Fitz, always questioned, never believed. In a rush of generosity, Hy shoved the money at him.

"Whatever that'll buy us."

Fitz took it, hands shaking. He willed them to stop, to conceal his excitement.

"Lobster for all and a killer of a clam chowder." It was the money he could smell, not the food.

He promised to deliver the next day.

Hy crossed the problem off her list, but again asked herself: *Am I doing the right thing?*

It began before anyone finished eating.

Germaine Joudry started it. He'd had a roast beef sandwich before he came to the Hall, afraid the "pickings would be meager." He stood up suddenly, his belly scraping the table, and sent the plates tipping onto the diners opposite.

"I got half a side of beef stuck in my tooth," he announced, his plump finger digging at the inside of his mouth.

That set it off.

Ben Mack was the first to go. His vomit arched across the table and landed on Germaine Joudry's plate.

As Annabelle attempted to clean Ben, Hy saw her face screw up in distress. She went dashing for the bathroom, hand clasped over her mouth.

There was soon a long line-up behind her.

Ian went pale and dashed outside, his parrot Jasmine on his shoulder, making retching sounds.

Olive MacLean took her turn over the pink porcelain toilet bowl. She flushed as she vomited, and her dentures went flying out of her mouth and down the bowl.

"Do you know how much good teeth cost?" she slurred, as she tried to fish them out. No one answered. They all knew Olive had spent as little as possible on those dentures.

Two more people heaved into the toilet, and then no more could. Olive's teeth had clogged it.

Instead of trooping out, as they usually did, smiling, making jokes and gossiping, the villagers left the Hall, cleaning themselves off, holding hands over mouths in a desperate attempt to keep the food down.

Ben, at the back of the line, burped.

Everybody took off.

But it was only a burp.

Chapter Ten

Neither Jamieson nor Murdo had gone to the village dinner. Jamieson's idea of community policing didn't go that far, even though Murdo had tried to nudge her into it.

"We can't get too close," she'd said. They both knew she was warning him about April. He held back his response to a mumble.

The two were gazing out of a picture window almost as large as the cube of a room that contained it, an addition to the Lego house that functioned as a front room, with a perfect view of the village centre.

April Dewey. Dewy, thought Murdo, as he stared wistfully at the Hall, wishing he were there with her.

"Jesus," said Jamieson. Murdo's eyes, poor at best, opened wide, as the villagers streamed out of the Hall. And wider still, when Gladys Fraser sicked up on the sandwich board sign announcing the dinner.

"Not good advertising," said Murdo.

"Hmm." It was noncommittal, but Murdo caught the twitch of a smile on Jamieson's face.

"Just as well we didn't go." She turned away from the window. "I can cook better than that."

Murdo opened his mouth to say something, but thought better of it.

Jamieson, like Hy, couldn't cook.

The village pumps and septics were getting a good workout the morning after what the village children referred to as "The Toss Up." And it remained a toss up as to where to lay the blame. The evidence was fairly clear, but facts never got in the way of a good story in the village.

"There was something wrong with that fish," said Harold MacLean, the carpenter. It was difficult to know if he meant the lobster or the clams. He called anything that came out of the ocean "fish," whatever they were – shrimp, scallop, clam, or lobster.

There might have been something wrong with the "fish," but there had also been that potato salad. Someone – who? – had taken it out of the fridge to make room and forgot to put it back. It was concealed behind a stack of paper plates on a table, where it sat for hours with the heat up right where Gus liked it – an even eighty-five degrees Fahrenheit. She still used Fahrenheit because she claimed she couldn't get warm in Celsius.

Since Institute President Gladys Fraser had made the potato salad, no one dared accuse her. Whatever the evidence showed, they were inclined to think it was that fella Fitzpatrick and his bad clams.

No matter how many times Hy pointed out that Ian had been sick and hadn't eaten the chowder, it just didn't sit with some. The shut-ins had received potato salad that hadn't sat overlong in the Hall kitchen and none of them had been sick.

Hy went over and over it in her head, wondering if there was anything Fitz had done in the cooking that wasn't sanitary. She couldn't think of a thing.

No, there had been nothing wrong with the cooking. Had there been something wrong with the clams? Hy pedalled furiously up to the Fitzpatricks' on an empty stomach.

Fitz was splitting wood behind the house.

"So – where *did* that fish come from?" Hy liked the feel of Harold's all-encompassing word on her lips, his economy of speech.

"Like I said. Fella supplies restaurants."

"And why was he getting rid of it?"

"Deal fell through."

Rose had come to the back door, and was standing in the doorway, propping the door open with her body.

"Well, they were all sick as dogs, Fitz. They weren't thawed and re-frozen, were they? What's the story?"

Fitz brought the axe down hard, too hard, on the piece of wood. Bits splintered and flew off at Hy and at Rose.

They both jumped back. Rose let the door slam shut.

Fitz dropped the axe, turned, and went off toward the shed.

Rose opened the door again, and motioned Hy in.

"I'll get him to tell," she said.

"Don't worry. It's not worth it." Talking about it made Hy feel as if it were happening all over again. A wave of nausea rose from her stomach to her throat. She turned quickly, and said, "I have to go. Sorry." She didn't want to vomit in front of Rose, or on her.

Olive MacLean's sister, Beatrice, a retired domestic science teacher, had watched the villagers with disdain and made her pronouncement. *Mild food poisoning.* Her only regret was that she hadn't brought her microscope along to do a salmonella count. Hy had never experienced anything like it. She wasn't sure she could cycle home, but she did. She burst through the door, up the stairs to the bathroom, and threw up again, even though she had nothing to give.

Curse Fitzpatrick.

Curse Gladys.

Curse Christmas.

Running out of things to curse, Hy went into her bedroom, flopped on the bed and fell asleep. She woke an hour later, feeling much better. She ate a big bowl of porridge, had a bath, and while she was soaking, realized someone would have to clean the Hall.

Bah. Humbug.

Chapter Eleven

Fitz and Jared were laughing out loud, partly because it was funny and partly because they'd just smoked two giant spliffs.

Jared had been pissing in the bushes when the villagers began spilling out of the Hall. He lit out of there, peeling off in his truck before someone could blame him for whatever it was that had happened.

Fitz frowned, a cloud covering his face, malevolence in his eyes.

"They're sayin' it was me. I'm sayin' it was that Fraser bitch. I've a good mind to – "

He didn't know what he had a good mind to do. He'd better think carefully. What he needed was cash. He'd made a nice bit from the lobster deal by inflating the price and skimming off the top, but he'd placed a big order with Jared. This was the sampling session, and he liked what he'd been smoking.

If they could just find what this Oliver guy was looking for. If he could only get Jared to do most of the work.

By the time they'd finished another reefer, they had both fallen asleep, heads slumped forward on the table, nesting in their arms, the bag of primo marijuana on the table between them.

Fitz woke first. He eyed the pot. Grabbed it. It was his. He hadn't paid for it yet, but that didn't bother him. As silently as he could over the pizza boxes littering the floor, he slipped out of the house.

"Interesting creatures, clams. Who knew?" Ian was googling when Hy stopped in before going to the Hall. The mention of clams made her feel ill. So did the prospect of facing the clean-up.

"Some clams are hermaphrodites. The quahog starts out male, then may become female."

"May?" Hy edged closer to the screen.

"It's not easy to tell the males and females apart, so I guess they don't always know for sure." He scrolled down. "Oysters alternate sexes – male one year, female the next."

Hy scanned the screen.

"Look at that – a giant clam that weighed 734 pounds. Nearly four feet long." She gave Ian a shove. "That could kill you even if you didn't eat it."

He grinned.

They spent a pleasant half-hour surfing the sex lives of ocean creatures, concluding that it had nothing on human sex, and Hy finally, reluctantly, left to go down to the Hall.

She had prepared herself for an overpowering smell of sick when she opened the Hall door. What she wasn't prepared for was the sound of the television.

There had never been a television in the Hall.

Still the theme to "Hockey Night in Canada" filled the room. A soft breeze played with the lace sheers at an open window, the smell of sick gently wafting through the Hall.

Then it was "Jeopardy."

"Entertainment Tonight."

Not a television. The piano.

Chopin.

A delicate, tentative touch, followed by sure, strong rippling across the keyboard, then soft again, tiptoeing on the notes, rising gradually to a swell, heartachingly beautiful, heartachingly perfect. Played by a ten-year-old gypsy of a boy. Jamie.

That piano had never been played like that, not by anyone, Hy was sure. It had been owned originally by a local music teacher, whose style was to pound on the keys, arms rigid, back ramrod straight, producing jarring sounds. Only accuracy moved her. Her soul was not the least musical. She had willed the piano to the Hall, and, since then, generations of youngsters had banged away at it – most so pathetically that the women of the Institute had given up tuning it.

But even on the old out-of-tune piano this boy was managing to coax beautiful music. It ended sharply. Then it was back to "Hockey Night in Canada."

When Hy stepped into the room, Jamie stopped playing and turned, the ancient photographs of Queen Elizabeth and Prince Philip looking down on him. The photos were fifty years old, and the only ones in the Hall that had been professionally framed. They usually looked judgmental. Today, Hy thought, they appeared to be approving in a restrained British way.

Hy came up, placing her hands on the stage. "You're good."

Jamie smiled, shrugged his shoulders and slipped off the bench. The shoelaces of his sneakers were untied.

"Don't stop."

"That's all I know."

"Hockey Night in Canada?"

He nodded.

"Jeopardy?"

"Oh, yeah, that stuff. I can play lots of TV themes. Some pop songs."

"And Chopin?" Her pitch rose in curiosity.

"Is that who it is?"

"Oh, yes." Hy hoisted herself up on to the stage and sat on the edge of it. He dropped down beside her. "Who taught you?"

"No one. I learned on my own."

"Piano at home?"

"No. Just whenever I could, wherever there was a piano. I played what I heard."

"You figured it out, note by note?"

"No, I just played what I heard."

"Hang on, I'll be right back." Hy got up and went out the side entrance of the stage, back into the Institute room, where the W.I. held its meetings. It was the kitchen. There was a radio on the counter. She turned it on to CBC Radio Two.

Chopin.

"That's the same one." Jamie recognized the musical signature. "I like her."

"She's a he."

Jamie frowned. "Doesn't sound like a he."

"Why not?"

"Well, all kinda…"

"Sensitive?"

"Ya."

Hy smiled when she heard herself say: "Men can be sensitive, too."

"I guess…" Jamie dragged out the words, sounding unconvinced.

"But you play that music. You like it. And you're a boy. Does it make you any less of a boy to be able to play that music?"

Jamie appeared to think about it for a moment. He squirmed, and smiled up at her. "No. The music? Course not."

"Now listen," said Hy. "Listen and play it to me after. They listened for a few minutes. Hy shut it off.

"Well?"

Jamie got up, sat down at the piano and began to play.

Note for note, subtlety for subtlety, fingers tripping across the keys, their touch intensifying as the music rose to a climax.

Jamie had heard, and played, it all – even the parts while they'd been talking.

A child prodigy. Hidden away in Wild Rose Cottage with a brute for a father – capable of charm, but a brute – and an ineffectual mother, faded, demoralized, and possibly, Hy suddenly thought, ill. Very ill? Did either of them know how talented their child was?

Her answer came charging through the door, leapt up on the stage, and slammed the piano lid down. Jamie whipped his fingers out just in time.

"What the hell are you doing in here? Fiddling about while I'm waiting on you to get back."

Hy placed a hand on Jamie's shoulder.

"We'd like Jamie to play in the Christmas Pageant. A few pieces. At intervals through the show."

Fitz flashed a big grin.

"And what about me?" He leapt up in the air, flipped backward off the stage, spinning cartwheels and somersaults down the length of the Hall and back up onto the stage again, landing inches from Hy.

"I can walk the tightrope if you like. We could hook up a trapeze..."

Hy put up a hand. "Whoa," she said. But she grinned with delight. Between Fitz's acrobatics and Jamie's music, this year's show would easily outdo Moira Toombs' directorial efforts last year. She wouldn't mind putting Moira in her place. She was always trying to edge in on Ian. Hy wasn't sure she herself wanted Ian as more than a friend, but friends can be jealous, too, she always told herself. Moira had done some pretty nasty things in the past, trying to get close to Ian and push Hy away.

"Where'd you learn that?"

"The circus. Din't I tell you I bin in the circus? In the family. Circus performers going way back. Rose, she was my spotter. Jamie was turnin' into a right real performer."

Jamie responded by doing his own series of flips down the room and back.

Fitz smiled – with pride? Again, Hy experienced a moment, an opening to the man he might have been – or was once?

He frowned. "But circuses aren't popular anymore."

"There's Cirque de Soleil."

"Cirque de Soleil. Yup. They courted me after I qualified for the Olympic gymnastics team."

Fitz Fitpatrick claimed he'd been a star of the professional circuit.

Hy wondered if it were true. Any of it. Still, he was obviously talented – and would be an asset to the show, as long as he was sober. She could smell rum on his breath and marijuana on his clothes, and it wasn't noon yet.

More overpowering than the smell of Fitz's breath was the stale smell of vomit in the Hall. Hy got out a bucket and mop. Fitz and Jamie left – Fitz slapping the boy on the head to move him along as they went out. Rose had been whining about more wood for the woodstove. He'd come to get Jamie to collect it.

Hy was mopping and grumbling under her breath when Annabelle swept in, wearing her work clothes, sleeves rolled up, and began to mop alongside her.

Another reason they were friends.

"You're making him supper?" Annabelle's eyes opened wide, the edges of her mouth curved up in a suppressed smile. They were putting away the mops and brooms, preparing to leave the Hall. Annabelle had invited Hy to supper. She'd said no, she was making supper for Ian.

"Yes." Hy was defensive. "No big deal."

"But you don't cook."

Hy grinned. "Not often."

"The way to a man's heart..."

"Well, yes, with Ian it would be his stomach. But I'm not after his stomach. Or his heart."

Annabelle had never been able to figure out what was going on with Hy and Ian. And then it came out. Just came out. The question she'd never dared ask before.

"Are you sleeping with him?" All this time she'd held back, and there she had gone and just blurted it out.

"No, I'm talking with you."

Annabelle sighed. "You know what I mean."

Hy said nothing. She must be, Annabelle thought, or she'd just outright deny it, and not be so coy.

What would it matter if everyone knew?

Maybe they still didn't know themselves.

She was right.

"If you must know…" Hy paused, a long pause.

Annabelle held her breath. Was she finally going to admit it?

"I'm going to try out a recipe on him. I'm thinking of making Christmas dinner."

"For who?" Annabelle wished she hadn't asked that the moment it came out of her mouth. Here, Christmas dinner was about family, and Hy didn't have any family. Only friends. But the friends all had family. Except Ian.

"Well, Ian. Buddy. Maybe Jamieson."

"Jamieson?" Disbelief in her tone. Buddy drooled. What must it be like when he ate? Annabelle winced. "Has she met Buddy?"

"Well, yes, she has." Hy told Annabelle about Jamieson's visit to the shack and how desperate she'd been to get out.

"Perfectly normal," Annabelle pronounced it. "I've never been in there," she said, "because the idea alone gives me claustrophobia. I bet it's dirty and stinky."

Hy shook her head, slowly, thinking. "No. There was something more to it. Something more."

"Well, that dinner won't be a tough test of your skills. I'm sure Buddy's happy with anything you put in front of him. I expect

Jamieson would be eating canned soup otherwise. And Ian, give him any food, he takes a bite and says, 'Delicious.'"

"Precisely why I'm testing it on him. And in his kitchen."

"In his kitchen?"

"Well, it is better equipped than mine." Ian's kitchen was the best equipped in the village. He didn't cook, but he had the latest and the best of everything – stainless steel fridge, stove, and microwave. In his cupboards was every labour-saving appliance ever advertised on late-night TV, most unused.

With a wave, Hy crossed the road and took off up Shipwreck Hill.

She didn't cook dinner. Ian had just set up his new computer. His old one – two years old – sat forlorn in a corner of the room, its wires all neatly wrapped, its screen black.

It was then Hy got the idea.

"What are you going to do with that?" She pointed at it.

Ian, his hands stroking his new keyboard, looked up.

"What?"

"That." She pointed at the abandoned iMac more forcefully.

"I don't know. Do you want it?"

"Yes."

He beamed. Ian was always thrilled when someone took an interest in his equipment.

"Well, sort of. I have an idea."

When she explained to him, he agreed, and said he'd take care of it.

"Elmira Fraser is dead." Those four words telegraphed through the community with the speed of a grass fire in a high wind.

Everyone was shocked. Elmira had been so busy dying for years, they'd given up hope it would happen.

When someone was so foolish as to ask how she was, she would sigh, "I've not long now."

Elmira dragged her skinny, pallid self to every village event, where she would belabour the number and extent of her aches and pains.

And yet she lived on…and on…and on.

Gus always said, with disapproval, "She'll live forever." Gus had been determined to outlive her. Now she had.

Everyone noticed how Elmira had knocked back the clam chowder, lobster, and potato salad at the Hall dinner with an appetite almost as big and healthy as Ben Mack's. But between bites, she had bemoaned her terrible health. Health that, she claimed, had been so bad since she was born, it had almost killed her from the start. She'd been eighty-eight, and perhaps had earned the right to complain.

Gus heard the news about Elmira from her neighbour Estelle, who phoned with a sober glee. Estelle wasn't thrilled because Elmira was dead, though she'd never liked her, but at being the first to impart the information to Gus.

Gus shook her head and eased down onto her rocker recliner. Elmira Fraser was what Gus called a tough old bird. If she could go, what hope was there for the rest of them? What hope for her, inching toward her mid-eighties? No, not inching – propelling with a speed she was incapable of when it came to doing anything else.

She sighed. Elmira Fraser. Dead. *Of what?*

Chapter Twelve

"My badada salad? *My* badada salad?"

Even Jamieson felt a trill of discomfort, confronted by Gladys Fraser's bulldog face, balled fists, and belligerent stance. She always looked pissed off, and usually was. She had looks that had once actually stopped a truck.

"I'm not saying it was the potato salad. But that's what everyone ate – except for the few who weren't sick at all."

"And the lobster and the chowder," said Gladys, jutting her chin out. Stubborn. Defensive.

"Well…" said Jamieson. *How to be diplomatic?* "Not everyone."

"Wha'? So you *are* sayin' it was my badada salad."

"No, not until it's tested. Do you have a sample?"

"Happen I don't," said Gladys, folding her arms across her chest, smug smile set in triumph, eyes daring Jamieson to continue the conversation.

She dared.

"Well, we have some of the lobster and chowder, so we can test that."

Gladys's rock solid posture slumped.

"Well, she was a cousin, anyway."

Jamieson raised an eyebrow. *What did that mean?*

Elmira wasn't actually Gladys's cousin. Only by marriage. Elmira was her husband Wally's cousin. And when he came home, he agreed with Gladys. If…*if*…the potato salad had been bad, it was best it had killed one of their own.

Gus had dozed off in her chair for a light afternoon nap, but it had been deeper than she thought. When she woke up, she thought she was still dreaming. There were fish – colourful tropical fish, swimming around under the window. Had she had a stroke? She sat up. Blinked her eyes. Blinked again.

Nothing wrong with her eyesight, other than the usual.

She was still looking puzzled when Hy came stomping into the mudroom, shaking her boots, kicking them off, and padding into the kitchen. The only thing that made the room a kitchen was the stove – a throwback to the time when the woodstove had been both the centre of the kitchen and the home. Gus cooked in here, but the food preparation, the fridge, and the sink were in the tiny pantry next door. Here in the kitchen were a sofa, coffee table, and Gus's big purple chair.

Though Gus kept the heat up, the floor was cold, and Hy was glad she was wearing her fat wool socks. Socks that Gus had made her.

"All I'm good for anymore," she gestured to the squares of her log cabin quilt on the floor. "Can't seem to get it finished."

"You're just spooked," said Hy.

"Yes, and I am. By that." Gus nodded at the swimming fish.

Hy smiled.

The fish were a screen saver Ian had especially chosen for

Gus. He thought she'd like them. Ian had done what he'd said he would – given Gus his old equipment as soon as he'd set up his new kit. An early Christmas present to himself. And a very strange gift for Gus.

"Nice fish," said Hy.

Gus settled back in her chair, relieved.

"You see them, too."

"Yes, that's Ian's old computer. The fish are his screen saver."

Gus wrinkled her brow.

"Screen saver. Now what's that?" She raised a hand. "No, don't tell me. You'll be wasting your breath. What did he give it me for?"

"So you could speak to your children on it."

"On *that?*" Gus pointed, eyes wide open. "Why would I be doin' that?"

"Well you can Skype them."

"They've already escaped me. Sons is good for nothing. Seven of them I had. Just the four left. Only the one girl. And her all over the world." She shook her head. So did Hy.

"No, no. You don't understand. Skyping is a way of communicating – through the computer."

"I can do that with the phone, and I know how to work it." She flipped open the arm of the chair, where a phone nestled, still wrapped in its original plastic.

"Or I did." She shut the compartment. The real phone was in the next room, on the wall, its heavy black receiver at the end of a long misshapen cord that hung nearly to the ground and stretched right into the pantry. "Mobile enough for me," Gus always said.

"Yes, but this way you can see *and* hear."

"Well that would be somethin'. Because right now I don't see or hear much of them at all. I don't see how them fishes is gonna change things."

Abel, thought Hy. Maybe Abel would help Gus figure this out.

He was handy. But where was he? Gus didn't seem to see or hear much of *him*, either, Hy thought, as she put the kettle on for tea.

Ian was smiling at his new computer. He stroked the screen, lightly, so as not to smudge it. His trailed his hands around the frame, loving the cool, fresh plastic feel of it. Those same hands had touched his old machine almost as lovingly, when he'd set it up at Gus's. There had been something of reluctance in his touch, then, reluctance to let it go. He'd managed to finish without waking her, and smiled as he left, thinking Gus was in for a surprise. It never occurred to Ian that it might be an unwelcome surprise. Who wouldn't be happy to receive, gratis, an iMac, just two years old, frequently but tenderly used, and maintained, in tiptop shape?

As this one was going to be. He had checked all the systems, all the apps, and having done that, he checked his email.

His smile turned to a frown.

Wild Rose Cottage and its inhabitants, Fitz above all, were under what Gus called "a cloud of suspicion." There was no question of Rose joining the W.I. now. There were no more visitors up the road, bringing welcoming gifts for the new family.

The gifts had been mixed with more than the usual curiosity, once the word had gone out about the tent in the kitchen. No one believed it, until they saw it. And when they saw it, they talked about it for days.

Rose was always home, so no one had to leave an offering at the door. All had it opened to them – and there, in plain view, was the tent in the kitchen. It gave rise to some exaggerations by those who had been there. And even some who had not.

A campfire, right there on the floor. Roasting marshmallows, they was.

The dog eating the same food as the humans, right alongside them.

Rats and mice all over the place.

That last, at least, was true.

It was not the lobster. Nothing wrong with the lobster, the report said. Only a sample from one lobster, Gladys had made sure to point out. There had been a hundred served. The chowder – inconclusive. No clams left in it. And the potato salad? In the heat of that kitchen. The most likely culprit.

But it couldn't be tested. It had been thrown out, and the dogs had eaten it and barfed it up. Yes, thought Jamieson, it had been the potato salad.

But what was the charge?

Was there a charge?

Was it manslaughter?

Probably so.

The woman who died – the victim? – was eighty-eight, for God's sake, Jamieson.

She'd been talking to herself more and more, alone in the police house. Where was Murdo? He was getting to be like Abel Mack, never around.

Was that what happened to men in The Shores?

"What's this?" Hy had an annoying habit of hitting the space bar on Ian's computer whenever she came in the house. She'd come up to Ian's to thank him for giving the computer to Gus. What she saw on the screen blew that right out of her head.

"Uncle Ian? *Uncle* Ian?" She stared at the screen, without reading any more than those two words.

Ian was fiddling with the woodstove.

He flushed.

"You have a nephew?" She advanced into the room. "A nephew?"

He nodded, a look of resignation on his face.

She flopped down in the high-backed Danish modern lounge chair – the sturdiest piece of his furniture. It wobbled.

"My brother's boy."

"Brother? I didn't know you had a brother. What other skeletons are there in the family closet?"

Ian stood up and shook his head.

"None. That's it. The nephew and the brother. Younger, by two years."

"And a sister-in-law."

"Nope. Absconded long ago. They haven't heard from her in years."

"But why do you never speak of them?"

Ian sighed – a long intake of breath, but the exhalation unburdened him only briefly. He sat down in the chair with the arm that always fell off. It fell off.

"I haven't spoken to them in years. My brother and I are… estranged."

"Why?"

"If you must know –"

"I must."

Ian got up again. Went into the kitchen. Came back with two glasses of Chardonnay. He took a slow sip.

"It was because of my mother."

"She had Alzheimer's." That much Hy knew. Ian had spoken of it. Once.

"He never came."

"What – to see her?"

"He said later that he couldn't bear it. She asked for him when she was lucid. I told him that. Still, he didn't come. To the last, when she didn't know me and wouldn't have known him, though he was her favourite."

"And? You argued? Fought over it?"

Ian shook his head. "Not that passionate. He came to the funeral. We didn't speak. I buried him with her. Haven't seen or talked to him since."

"And now?" Hy looked over at the computer, wishing she'd read more than "Uncle Ian." "Why the email?"

"Redmond has it himself."

Redmond. As if she read Hy's thoughts, Ian's parrot Jasmine squawked: "Redmond? Redmond." She liked both the name and upward inflection. "Redmond?" she squawked again.

"Early onset Alzheimer's? Like your mother?"

"Correct."

"How bad?"

"Bad."

"What are you going to do?"

Ian looked down into his glass, as if the answer lay there.

"I don't know."

"What does he want you to do? Your nephew?"

"David wants me to see Redmond, make it up, I guess, before it's too late."

"And will you?"

"I told you." His tone was hard, then melted in indecision.

"I don't know. I don't know."

Sobered by what she'd found out about Ian, Hy cycled home, down Shipwreck Hill, around the corner at the village centre where the Hall stood, and the empty lot where Abel Mack's General Store had been. Before Hy's time. Gone, too, was the school, where she had taught briefly. She cycled onto The Island Way, the main road through the village. The province had made it a provincial scenic route to draw tourism. The murders and deaths over the past two years had done a better job of that, attracting nosy sightseers to the crime scenes on the shore and the capes.

The village had suffered more than its share of killings.

Hy shifted gears, and her gaze, down to the Macks' house. Gus was in her rocker recliner, head down, working on the quilt. On fine summer nights, Gus would stretch out her quilt in the building by the side of the house. It was just big enough to frame a large king-size quilt.

"Them big beds," Gus would complain. "Jus' more work, if you ask me. A double is good enough. Time was it was three-quarters." Then she'd get a twinkle in her eye, and say, "Don't know how they make babies in them big beds. You could sleep the whole night and never know you had a husband."

No one ever responded to that. There were some people who hadn't seen Abel in years. Hy was one of them. *Odd*, she thought – she was over there so often. When she asked Gus why he was never there when she was, Gus had shrugged. Gus couldn't say what she knew to be true: Abel was hiding from Hy, the woman from away whose height and opinions scared him.

Abel had built Buddy's house, just ahead on The Way. Buddy had shown up in The Shores, a big grin on his face, looking for work, "missus," as he called Gus. She wouldn't let him in the house. Who knew what would come in with him? But she gave him soup and some of her fresh-made bread out there on the stoop, and then he offered to repay her – pointing at the hill-shaped pile of wood that Abel hadn't got around to stacking yet.

Buddy couldn't talk properly. He had just a few words that he'd grunt out between heavy breaths and drool spilling from the corners of his lips.

He was a special person, said Gus, when she got to know him. She let him do chores around the yard, chores that Abel always seemed to be too busy to do – especially when he was in the store, smoking with the other farmers and fishermen, all unable to work on any given day because the weather wasn't "just right" for whatever it was they were supposed to be doing. Gus let Buddy sleep in the barn for a couple of weeks, until Abel built him this tiny house on a scrap of land no good for farming.

Abel had built it, but it was Gus who made him do it, making use of the cozy size of their simple double bed to nudge him in the ribs one night until he gave in.

You couldn't do that in a king-size bed, Gus smiled, smug, whenever she told the story.

Buddy was outside his house when Hy passed by. He was splitting wood, his height and strength making it as easy as carving up balsa. He paused and gave her a big grin and a wave. Then he made the motion of fiddling. She nodded her head.

"Tomorra…" he mouthed.

"Yes," she called up. It wouldn't be "tomorra." Hy knew that. Buddy didn't. He couldn't keep track of the days.

No one knew Buddy's real name or where he came from. But they did know he was a mighty fiddler, who entertained in homes through the long winter nights, in exchange for offerings of food and clothing.

No one need be homeless in a place like The Shores. Hy was comforted by the thought. The village took care of its own, and some who weren't, like Buddy.

"What if he were mine?" Gus asked. "Wandering around the world with no one, like a stray cat." She would shudder. "No. No. He has no people of his own. Someone has to take care of him."

No people of his own, thought Hy. *Did they kick him out – or did he wander off?* He seemed happy enough, but he had no one.

Alone at Christmas. Like her, but not like her. Somehow Buddy was facing a lonelier Christmas, in her mind, than even she. The warm feeling she had been experiencing dissipated. She felt sad. Sad for Buddy, and, self-indulgently, for herself.

But Buddy was happy, content as he split the wood, eyes shining at he thought of fiddling tomorrow, or whatever day tomorrow was. He didn't know he was supposed to have people. He never remembered Christmas from one year to the next. It was all new to him, every time. He couldn't remember most things between one day and the next.

Remembering was difficult for him.

All of them were dead. Hy was home and sipping a glass of red wine – her third, counting the one at Ian's. There were a couple of photograph albums, worn, discoloured, on the coffee table – a steamer trunk. The albums had been in the trunk; they smelled moldy. Hy had unearthed them and had tipped from feeling joyful about Christmas to feeling maudlin. Gus might not see her family, but at least she had one. Most of Hy's had died when she was an infant, and she had very nearly died herself.

Her grandmother had been her family. Bitter, brittle, standing ramrod straight by the white picket fence. The fence that embodied restraint, not the comforting circle of family life.

The grandfather. Studio shots for work and passport. Driver's license. Only one candid shot of him, with his hand on his bush plane, caressing it, a hint of a smile on his usually forbidding face.

Ray, her father. She didn't even know his last name. She'd been called by her mother's family name. Ray. Ray who? She'd never known him. She was half in love with him. A tall American boy, no more than twenty. Long legs, crossed at the ankles, propped on the desk he gave up for a life in the woods. Her mother, tall, too, long-haired, doe-eyed, easily swayed by the American draft dodger into a new exile, a life of freedom from the white picket fence.

Hy fingered the coffee-table book, the new edition of her mother's work that had come out just a few years before. *A Life in the Woods* had been written in ink and on paper her mother had made herself. One reviewer had called it "the bible of the back to the land movement." Her parents had lived and died by that religion. Her father, out trapping in winter. Her mother, when she flew out of the woods in the single engine plane piloted by Hy's grandfather. It went down in a lake, and only Hy survived.

Her grandmother had brought her up, bitter at the loss of her husband, and at having to care for an infant at her age.

Hy snapped the photograph albums shut. Shoved them across the table. Leaned back onto the couch, eyes shut, glass in hand.

She hadn't loved her grandmother, hadn't even liked her. She hadn't shed a tear when the woman died. Hy had been only nineteen and left alone in the world.

She was usually okay with that, but not at Christmas.

I'm the last one.

Every Christmas, Hy tortured herself with the thought. She knew that she would never have children. Too late now.

There will be no one after me.

A choice – or a mistake?

Chapter Thirteen

Moira Toombs had unhooked her computer in what had been the parlour of the family's modest one-and-a-half-storey home. It had been turned into a bedroom for her dying father, and then her mother. A little more than a year ago, Moira had started cleaning the cottages mushrooming along the capes, and turned the room into an office. She'd bought a computer for the modest little business she called "Nice As You Please." She didn't really need it, but it had won Ian's interest for a few weeks.

Now she'd stashed the computer in the small room at the top of the stairs. She had hoped to get Ian's help, but he hadn't answered his phone. Instead, she'd made use of Billy. He had muscled the desk and file cabinet up the stairs, and shoved a bed and dresser into the room downstairs.

Seeing the money some of her customers were making from renting their cottages, she'd decided to get into hospitality herself, although there was nothing hospitable about the Toombs' home, or the name she chose for her venture: Toombs' Stop. Hy had smirked when Moira told her the name she'd chosen.

Moira had advertised online, but got no customers. Maybe because of the name, maybe because it had been late August. She'd left the posting up, more out of forgetfulness than savvy, but the previous morning she'd received a request for a downstairs room. She hadn't prepared one. That's why it was moving day.

When it was done, Gus dropped by to give her opinion. She wasn't in the B&B business anymore, but hers had been the first tourist home in The Shores.

"My land, this won't do." Gus was shocked by how Spartan it was. The bed cover and curtains were a stark white. There was a simple bed and dresser, white walls, and old linoleum. Still good, but a drab colour somewhere between navy blue and black, worn, not from use, but from constant cleaning. It was covering up a good wood floor.

Moira pursed her lips. She didn't really want an opinion from Gus. She'd expected praise for how neat and clean it was. Moira inhaled the fresh scent of Pine-Sol, which she preferred to roses. There was a slight undertone of tobacco. Both her parents had been smokers.

"Clean and tidy," Moira pronounced it.

Gus screwed up her face. "What's wrong with your mother's good quilts?"

"Nothing – "

"Well…?"

"They're put away."

"For what?"

"For keeping."

"Quilts is for usin'." Gus knew she'd find them in the cupboard at the top of the stairs. She puffed her way up and pulled out the best one. "Apurpose," she would tell Hy later.

"This'll do." She mumbled to herself and tried to conceal her glee.

Moira watched, lips set in a thin line, as Gus descended. She said nothing. Next, Gus went looking for a hooked rug, took the best one out of the dining room, and tossed it on the floor of the bedroom. She turned round and pointed at the hall floor.

"You'll be taking that off before your guests arrive."

Moira looked down at the newspaper. Not just a single newspaper. Newspaper all over the floor, neatly layered and overlapped.

Gus gazed at them. "Well, now, there's somethin' I didn't know." Moira flinched when Gus picked up a copy of *The Guardian* from the floor.

"Mabel Allard, dead at 83. How'd I miss that?" Gus checked the obituaries every day. Gus claimed she was related to half of Red Island. She scanned the paper for the date.

"Six months gone, and me only findin' out now." She looked at Moira, who was fidgeting, anxious to get the paper back where it belonged – on the floor. There was real hardwood under there. Here and in the dining room. She only removed the newspaper "for good" – when she had the Women's Institute in, or at Christmas. She hadn't thought about bed and breakfast guests. *Tramping in and out as they did. Surely they wouldn't object.*

"Well, she was only a distant cousin of Abel's. I don't think he ever knew her. Still, finding out this way…" Gus shook her head and dropped the paper to the floor. Moira leaned down and set it back in place.

"I wouldn't be doing that. Them newspapers got to go." Gus folded her arms across her chest in eloquent disapproval.

Moira caved in.

"Yes, of course." That it hadn't been certain, Gus knew. Moira had decided that her first paying guests might merit this sacrifice, but the others? She glanced back at the rug and the quilt in the bedroom. She could take them out after Gus left.

In the end, she didn't. She thought they looked nice. The brilliant colours of the log cabin quilt, small rectangular pieces, intricately nested into each other, pulling the eye along a myriad of pleasing colour combinations, the mismatching creating a wonderful whole. The hooked rug was of two comical cats, her mother's last effort. Puffed with a proprietary pride – her guest certainly wouldn't have better things home – Moira left them there. She was to regret that when her lodger arrived.

It was raining when Hy took Rose and Jamie to Charlottetown. They had an appointment with a music teacher, known for his work with gifted young pianists. Hy had seen Tchaikovsky Ferguson's photograph once in the newspaper, but it didn't prepare her for the real thing.

So slight. More like a woman. But still masculine – the shadow over the lip. If she hadn't known this was a man –

"Transgendered," said the odd creature as if it were his – her? – name, crossing the room, arms outstretched, old-fashioned black academic gown billowing out with his – her? – brisk movements. "Publicly I am known as Mr. Tchaikovsky Ferguson. It will remain that way until the transition is complete."

Jamie looked at Rose and Hy. His forehead wrinkled. *Transgendered.* He mouthed the word. Such a strange word.

"Then I will be Miss Tchai Ferguson. You may call me Tchai."

Jamie looked puzzled. "You're a boy – and a girl?"

Hy looked at Rose. Rose flushed, and shrugged, hoping the moment would pass.

Hy assumed she didn't want a facts of life conversation now, and didn't blame her.

Jamie's attention was suddenly diverted. He cocked his head to one side when he saw the Heintzman grand piano, reflected in a huge mirror, so it appeared to be two pianos.

Jamie flew across the room. Tchai tripped lightly behind him, the sleeves of the gown billowing out, so that with her short black hair she looked a bit like a bat.

Jamie flopped down on the bench, opened the lid with reverence, and took a couple of tentative pokes at the keys.

Tchai gestured at the sheet music. Jamie flushed.

"He doesn't read music." Hy offered from across the room.

"Then how does he play?"

As if on cue, Jamie began to play his new medley of classical hits – CDs Hy had lent him to listen to on the Hall's ghetto blaster – Chopin, Beethoven, Brahms, Tchaikovsky.

He could have gone on much longer, but Tchai stopped him.

"And where and when did you learn these?"

"This week. At the Hall."

"This *week?*"

"Yup. Can I play that?" Jamie jumped off the bench and ran across the room to an antique harpsichord, Tchai's prize possession.

But the teacher was still stuck on what Jamie had just said.

"This week? This week? But surely – " That a child should be playing any of this, much less all of it within a week... The sound of the harpsichord catapulted Tchai across the room, waving her hands, making the gown billow again with that odd bat-like effect.

"No, no, no – " And then she stopped. The sound took over. Jamie's pressure on the keys was exacting, intuitive. This child was too good a musician to harm any instrument. Tchai turned back to Hy and Rose, forgotten in the front of the room.

"I will take him."

Rose beamed. Hy hugged her, and Jamie darted across the room and gave them both the high five.

But Rose's smile had turned to a frown.

"How? When? We haven't..."

Tchai waved her objections away. He knew she meant money. He also knew there was something special about this child – more than just the music.

"For this child, I will work free. His progress will be my reward. After Christmas," he said," nodding his head. "After Christmas, we will start."

On the way home, they celebrated by eating fish and chips in the truck. Jamie ate and grinned at the same time, stuffing the food into his open mouth, cheeks bulging, hands and mouth shiny with grease.

Hy could have touched Rose's pleasure, so strongly did it emanate from her.

When they got back to the house, Rose invited Hy in for tea. Hy didn't want to accept, because she could see Fitz was home. Rose saw her hesitation. Her face fell, so Hy accepted. Rose went straight in, while Hy and Jamie dumped the take-out in the compost bin. It was almost empty. Even the scraps were eaten in this house. Sometimes there were only scraps.

Fitz was pacing the kitchen, around and around the tent, in a rage. When Rose came in, he grabbed her and began sniffing her, like an animal. He wanted to know where she'd been, and if she'd been with someone else. A man.

Fish, she smelled of fish. Half the population of The Shores smelled of fish. That couldn't narrow it down. She'd been doing it.

"Where have you been?" It was an accusation. He grabbed her hand, and secured it behind her back. He pushed her up against the wall. He stuck his face right up against hers. She could smell the cigarettes and the rum on his breath. His lips spread in a sneer, and all she could see was his nicotine-stained teeth.

"Where did you take my boy?"

A heavy weight of despair flooded Rose's brain and flowed through her blood. The giving up. She could feel it as a physical part of her being. She would never be rid of it. She would never be rid of him.

She slumped to the floor, so she wouldn't have to smell him or see him. The nasty grin, more like a grimace, that she knew too well. She buried her head in her hands and wished she were anywhere but here, anyone but herself. She could cope with anything but this.

Hy was shocked when she opened the door. She turned and

pushed Jamie back outside. *The child should not see this.* She pulled him back to the truck.

"But – " he protested.

"You stay here, and I'll make sure everything's all right."

It wasn't. But it was not violent. Not yet. Hy slipped back in and felt in her pocket for her cell phone. Perhaps she should phone Jamieson.

Fitz snorted his contempt, and aimed a kick at Rose. It just missed. "Where is my boy?" he repeated.

A mouse skittered by Rose, underlining her degradation, and something swelled in her, something that thrust her up off the floor, her face shoved close to his.

"He's not your boy."

His expression – nasty, sneering – turned ugly, darkness on his brow and in his eyes. He couldn't speak. He knew it was true. They both knew that Jamie was his mother's son. The bright, open face. Hers. Clouded now, after her years with Fitz. Not fresh and accepting, the way it had been when it had drawn him to her.

"I'll kill you, bitch."

"When?" she taunted him.

"In your sleep."

"I never sleep when you're around."

Now *she* sneered. Her hand slid to a knife on the counter. What she'd said about Jamie was the one thing she could say that would cut into him like a knife, twist his insides. But what she really wanted to do was shove a knife into him. In and out. Not once, but many times.

"I'll kill you," she said through clenched teeth. "Sometime when you're too drunk to know what's happening to you."

She was becoming just like him.

Fitz flung himself out of the kitchen, shoved Hy out of the way, and slammed through the door.

At least Jamie hadn't seen that.

But Hy was wrong. He had seen it. He had gone in the front

door and through the house to the room next to the kitchen. He'd seen – and heard – as much as Hy had.

They were both wondering the same thing: what had Rose meant when she said *He's not your boy?*

Hy asked her outright when she came back in the room and put a kettle on to boil. Rose didn't answer at first.

"What did you mean?" Hy insisted as she found some clean cups and a box of cookies. The cardboard was shredded in one corner. *Mice.* Hy put the box back, without opening it.

"Well, look at him."

Jamie lay down inside the tent, crying softly. Rose tried to comfort him, but he pushed her away. His breathing began to change as he surrendered to exhaustion brought on by the excitement of the day and the scene he'd witnessed.

"He looks like you."

"Exactly. Jamie's *my* boy. That's what I meant."

"And did Fitz mean it when he said he'd kill you?"

"No, he says that all the time."

"And you? Do you?"

"I've never said it before."

"You didn't mean it." Hy's tone and eyes begged for confirmation.

Rose took a quick look in Jamie's direction. The child was fully asleep on the floor of the tent.

"I did," she said softly. "I meant it."

What a life, Hy thought as she poured the water into the teapot. Sensing her disapproval, Rose said one more thing.

"If you only knew."

As they sipped their tea, Rose, with a quiet strength, refused to answer Hy's questions about what that meant.

But Hy was pretty sure she knew what it meant. As she climbed into her truck in the darkening late afternoon, she thought about the ugly, brutal life Rose and Jamie were living. *It doesn't require details. Let Rose hide behind a veil of mystery.*

That's all it was. A veil. Anyone could see through it.

The rain continued into the night. If the temperature would only fall, there would be snow, glorious white fluffy snow that would make the village, with its lights, look enchanted, something out of a fairy tale.

Not now. The lights dripped with water, tree branches drooped, overburdened with the weight of decoration and dousing. Red clay splattered on cars, houses, people; sump pumps grated in cellars flooded with water.

A moonless night fell. Dispirited lights did their best to twinkle. Santa and his reindeer should have been cheerful atop the Hall roof, but looked ridiculous and out of place.

Hy was drying out in front of Ian's woodstove after the dramatic scene at Wild Rose Cottage. Even though she was now dry, she shivered at what she had seen.

"She was holding a knife. He threatened to kill her. And she him. I thought of alerting Jamieson. But I didn't want both of them, certainly not Rose, charged with uttering threats."

Ian picked up the brandy and refreshed her glass. He sat down on the floor beside her, feeling it in his legs. Why she always sat on the floor, he didn't know.

"You did the right thing," he said. "You don't want to get in the way of a domestic dispute."

"What if either of them does something?"

"It's not your worry. I wouldn't worry Jamieson with it either." Ian thought of Jamieson. That sleek forbidding look of hers. He'd like to get that black hair down out of its bun and run his fingers through it. He loved hair. Perhaps because he had so little of his own.

Ian liked Hy's hair, too. That red gold colour. But it was so curly, you couldn't run your fingers through it. Not that he'd tried. All he'd ever done was pick up a stray curl and wind it around his finger.

He did that now.

The lights in the living room automatically dimmed. Ian had them on a timer, and right now, the timing was perfect. Quite accidental, but perfect.

Hy leaned into him.

It felt good to both of them.

Chapter Fourteen

"I have come."

No one stranger had ever knocked at Moira Toombs' door.

Oliver Sullivan was wearing a fur coat – and cats. One, sleek, white, almost Egyptian, was draped around his neck, drawing warmth from the folds of fat that circled under his chin and all the way around the back of his head. The folds formed a ledge that the slim cat had attached himself to, winding, with the fat around Oliver's neck. The other cat was a big ginger, lazy, smiling and purring. Oliver held it in his arms, supported by his vast belly.

As soon as Moira opened the door, the cats became alert. The ginger jumped down and strolled into the house as if it were his. He began to sniff at the baseboards. White unwound himself slowly from Oliver's neck, eyes half-open, stretched, first front legs, then back, licked a paw, and melted down Oliver, slithering across his belly and onto the floor, landing as silent as a fly.

"Mice?" Oliver asked a shocked Moira.

Cats, thought Moira. He'd asked if there were any cats. She assumed that meant he didn't like them, or was allergic to them. He'd booked for his "small family." When Moira emailed back: "How many children?" he'd responded, "None." So she'd thought he was coming with his wife.

"No," she answered, her back stiffening, offended by the question. "No mice."

"Good," said Oliver, setting down his suitcase. "Oscar hates mice."

Moira rang a bell on the small table and Billy appeared. They'd rehearsed this. She made a gesture and he picked up the suitcase and reached for another small one still in Oliver's hand. Oliver resisted.

"Which cat is Oscar?" Moira asked as if she were interested. She hated cats. She hadn't thought to put a "no pets" condition in her online ad. It would be the next thing she did, as soon as she got this one into his room.

Oliver smiled, a big, benign Buddha smile. He chuckled. He opened the small case in his hand. Whiskers and a pointy nose appeared, sniffed in every direction, and the pet jumped out of the case into Oliver's arms.

"This is Oscar," he beamed, tickling the whiskers.

A rat. Moira and Billy were horrified. You didn't bring rats into the house. That was just the wrong way around.

"Oh, I know what you're thinking, but Oscar won't bother you. Member of the family. White and Ginger love him." As if to prove it, White jumped up onto Oliver and nuzzled Oscar.

Moira understood now why Oliver had asked if there were cats in the house. Most would think Oscar was a meal.

"I'll keep Oscar caged – as a courtesy. It's not really necessary. I'll take him with me when I'm out, although he doesn't like the cold. I found Oscar in the bookstore I purchased. Heard him scratching in the Wilde section, and removed a book – *The Importance of Being Earnest* – to find a white rat. A rat with breeding and good taste. Wilde is my favourite author. Thus the name." He tickled Oscar under the chin and stroked his whiskers.

Moira wasn't listening. She was thinking about her mother's quilt. How would she be able to get it off the bed without his seeing? And the rug. Would the cats pee on it?

She'd just have to swallow it – him and his menagerie. He was her first customer. He was paying well – full, not off-season rates – and his stay might be lengthy. She could use the money over Christmas.

She showed him to the room.

"Delightful. Charming," he said, the cats circling around his feet. "What a wonderful quilt." The Log Cabin pattern, not in the usual dismal greys and browns, but soft old shades of red and green and yellow. White and Ginger showed their approval by jumping on it and kneading, circling, finding a spot, deciding on another spot, beginning the kneading again. Ginger jumped down and began clawing at the hooked rug. Moira winced.

Oliver set Oscar down on the bed, and removed his fur coat. Underneath he was dressed in a navy blue silk robe.

A man in a dress.

What next, thought Moira.

When he pulled the jeweled sandals out of his suitcase and slipped them on, she had her answer.

Nathan didn't get much call for taxi service in winter. His eight-seater was used mostly in the summer, taking tourists to and from the ferry. Most tourists didn't drive over the causeway. They liked the ferry. It satisfied their notions of the laid-back east-coast life. It was an old river ferry borrowed from another province and it only took eight cars per trip, so there was always a wait. Visitors relished that, too, as part of the Red Island experience, an experience no longer available from the mainland, since the train tunnel had replaced the ferry across the Sunderland Strait.

Two of Nathan's businesses were dependent on the ferry – a snack, coffee, and souvenir stand at the docking area and the ferry shuttle service. His other businesses were seasonal, too: lawn-mowing and snowplowing. Without snow, he had nothing much to do. For Nathan, that was agony. He was always on the move, always up to something. He burst with excess energy, his feet constantly tapping, his hands drumming tables, the steering wheel – anywhere they landed.

He was relieved when he got some pre-Christmas business.

"A fella staying at Toombs is going to pay me fifty bucks an hour to be on call," he yelled in the direction of the kitchen.

No answer.

Nathan went into the kitchen. No Lili.

"Did you hear me?" He yelled in the direction of the living room.

"Ommmmmmmmmm."

Probably not.

Nathan peeked his head around the door frame. Lili was pretzeled on the living room floor, slim legs in the lotus position, slender back straight, long neck swept by a neat bob of black hair that required monthly trips to Charlottetown. Her hands were resting on her knees, thumb and index fingers lightly touching.

"Ommmmmm." It was a big deep sound from such a tiny frame. It vibrated and circled the room. "Ommmmmm." The volume rose. So did the vibration.

"Ommmmm."

Nathan felt a bit lightheaded.

Lili lifted her arms above her head, palms together, and, elbows bending, brought her arms down and nestled her hands in prayer position against her chest.

"Namaste." She bowed slightly as she said it.

She unwound effortlessly from her position, shook out her legs, rolled her head gently, and stood up. Her eyes were glazed. It took a moment for her to register Nathan's presence. When she did, she smiled, the smile he always thought of as a promise of happiness.

He wanted to hug her, but he'd learned not to. It would be an intrusion so soon after her meditation. She hadn't made a big fuss about it the first time he'd invaded that space, but she had made it clear he must keep his distance. He'd learned to observe it. It was never long before she was his again.

"Tea?" she asked now, her voice deep and slow, almost slurred. If you didn't know her, didn't know what she'd been up to, you might think she was drunk.

She plugged in the kettle.

"Make mine a coffee," he said and sat down at the table.

Soon they were having tea and coffee, along with muffins, made with spelt flour and healthful seeds. Nathan chewed his manfully, but it was just like eating a muffin that had been dropped in the sand, the grit jamming in between his teeth.

"You were saying…?"

He'd begun to tell her about the call from the stranger, when he'd stopped to allow his tongue to search for and excavate a poppy or sesame seed. *Maybe some genuine sand.*

"I was saying…" Nathan made one last tongue-check, and slurped down the remainder of his coffee. "The guy's gonna pay me fifty bucks an hour to be on call."

"All the time?"

"No, just certain times. Like if he goes visiting somewhere, I'm to wait to bring him back – or be available to bring him back. I get paid for the waiting time."

"How long is he going to be here?"

"I don't know. He said at least a week."

"You could make a nice bit of Christmas money."

"I could." He stood up. "I gotta meet the fella now."

"Who is he?"

"No one I know. He said Oliver Sullivan."

"Oliver Sullivan," Lili echoed as Nathan went out the front door.

And then she said it again, frowning.

"Oliver Sullivan."

Oliver Sullivan seemed to roll into the Hall, easing along like a slinky, one bit after another finding the ground and moving forward. He walked with fluidity, in spite of his short legs hidden by his fur coat and the robe underneath, so all you could see was a round head, a round torso – and feet, like Humpty Dumpty.

"Santa Claus!" yelled out Millie Fraser, halting her stumbling step dance when Oliver entered the room.

Oliver whipped off his hat, and bowed with a flourish. "At your service, young miss."

She screwed up her face and turned red.

"You're not Santa," she screamed. "Santa has hair."

Oliver unwrapped his muffler.

"And a beard. No, I'm not Santa, as you correctly deduce."

"Do doos? Mummy, he's talking dirty." She shoved her face into her mother's skirts and clung to her.

Hy sighed. She'd have to coax Millie into a performance now. Little Millie was, as her mother Fiona and grandmother Gladys were constantly repeating, "a sensitive child."

Hy climbed down from the stage.

"We could use a Santa, if you're offering."

It was Ben Mack's job, but Hy knew he wouldn't mind skipping it. He did it more as a duty than a pleasure, and he felt ridiculous in the outfit that was too small for him. The W.I. had bought the largest Santa suit they could get, but Ben was still too big, bigger than anyone else. The pants only just skimmed the top of the boots. The sleeves stopped at his elbows, and the buttons of the jacket strained at the front.

On Oliver, the suit would probably pool on the floor, although his girth would take up some of the slack.

Oliver said nothing. He'd often been asked to play Santa. He never had. Maybe this time he would. But not in that dreadful costume. In his own clothes. The Magician from the East. The cards had brought him here, and perhaps for this purpose. He extended his hand.

"Oliver Sullivan."

Hy was immediately alert. Sullivan. The Sullivan legacy. Did he have something to do with it?

After the rehearsal, Hy went up to Ian's. She clicked on his keyboard. He'd been googling Jamieson. There was nothing much on screen. Just her status as a Mountie, and a reference to a seaweed bust in *Frank*, the satiric Halifax magazine. It referred to the thieves as "slime buckets" and the cops who failed to crack the case as "wet and weedy."

"Oh, God, does she know about this?"

Ian shrugged.

"I hope not." There was more. A duck decoy roundup in Emerald. "She'd be mortified."

Why was Ian googling Jamieson? Was he interested? Hy sat down on the floor in front of the woodstove. As she gazed into the fire, she was reminded of the visit to Buddy's shack, about Jamieson's reaction to the ember falling from Buddy's stove.

"There must be more," she said, jumping up. "There must be something we can find out. Something that makes her like she is."

Ian joined her, and they began googling a series of word combinations including "fire" and "Jamieson," scrolling down the suggested links well past the first screens, until they found it. In the Toronto Public Library's newspaper archives. Funny, thought Hy, unable to resist taking a poke at Ian who worshipped at the shrine of the Internet.

"Amazing, isn't it?"

Ian grunted, his attention almost fully absorbed by the screen, as if part of him had melted into it.

"The Internet. Just amazing," Hy shook her head. "Here it's gone and taken us to the old-fashioned library archives."

"Mmmm." Ian was scrolling the archives, but floating in the

ether.

"Yes, but it's a lot faster," he said, coming out of it as he found what they were looking for. The front page of the *Toronto Star* from 1978. The photograph took up almost all the space the headline didn't. Just a few lines of the grim story and then over to page three.

The photo was of a wood frame house engulfed in flames, two small children being carried out in the arms of firefighters. "Christmas Tragedy in Thunder Bay," the headline read. And then the awful subhead: "Parents Die in Fire. Children saved by foolhardy firefighters."

"They never should've done it," the Fire Chief was quoted as saying. "We're glad they did, but there could have been four more lives lost, instead of just the two."

"Just the two?" The phrase caught Hy as it had Jamieson. It had haunted Jamieson for years. *Just the two.* Her parents. At six years old, she'd learned to shut down her emotions on that day. They were just too painful.

It wasn't until later, when she left, that Hy thought again of Ian's googling Jamieson. He googled everyone, but he hadn't googled her, Hy, until she'd let him – given him permission, in a moment of anger, to poke into her past.

What they'd found out about Jamieson, Hy found very interesting. But she also found it interesting that Ian had wanted to know more about her before Hy arrived.

Just how interested is he in Jane Jamieson?

Do I care? Ian's a friend. I shouldn't feel possessive about a friend.

Protective?

Yes.

Jamieson and Ian?

It would be disastrous.

Chapter Fifteen

Gus had watched Oliver arrive at Moira's, from her vantage point in the purple rocker recliner next to the big picture window that framed the village centre. Her neighbour Estelle Joudry was busy packing Germaine's suitcase for his hospital trip to Halifax, and her daughter and son-in-law had arrived to drive him over. With Estelle thus occupied, Gus had the satisfaction of knowing that she was the first to see Moira's visitor when he arrived.

Imagine, a man in a fur coat.

She'd thought it then, and she thought it again as he came out of Moira's door.

Oliver was, perhaps, the most unusual sight she'd ever seen through this window, challenging the time her husband, Abel, had propelled through the window of his General Store when a propane tank exploded. He didn't hurt a hair on his head, she never tired of saying. Except they all went white after that.

Oliver seemed to be rolling down the path, two slippered feet just barely visible under his coat, two cats – cats! – wrapped around his neck. If he were coming here, as it soon became apparent that he was, he would have to leave them outside.

Gus watched Oliver get in Nathan's cab, and relaxed. *Not here, then.* She was relieved and disappointed. And she was wrong. Nathan pulled a U-turn, glided along a couple of hundred feet and turned into Mack's lane. Oliver emerged from the vehicle like a furry marshmallow popping out of a bag, two cats clinging to it.

Had Gus known there was a white rat up Oliver's sleeve, she would have gotten up and locked the door. The Macks' door was almost never locked, especially when there was a thunderstorm, in case anyone needed shelter. If they had, they would have found Gus sitting rigid and upright in her chair, coat on, handbag in hand, ready to exit at the first lightning strike.

Oliver was not happy about the four concrete stairs. Carrying twenty pounds of cat didn't make it easier. He shook them off his neck, and they jumped down to the ground, immediately sniffing the neighbourhood dogs, Toby and Newt, on the stoop.

Oliver had been too young when he'd been here last to know the drill. He knocked on the door.

No one knocked on the door in The Shores.

"Come in," Gus called out. "But leave those cats outside."

Oliver's round head peered around the door.

"Oh, but I can't do that, Madam. They're not used to it."

Gus sighed, easing herself out of her chair. Every day her limbs seemed stiffer than the day before. She shuffled over to the mudroom, holding the inner door, ready to slam it shut if need be.

"Then bring them in here," she said. "But leave them in here."

Oliver let the cats in the front door. They were about to dash into the kitchen, but Oliver held up his hand, in a command to stay where they were. White tried to jump back on him. Ginger wrapped himself around his legs. Oliver disentangled them and gently closed the door.

The cats began to scratch the door. Oliver rolled his eyes. All this could have been prevented if she had just let them in.

He turned to Gus.

"Oliver Sullivan, ma'am." He made a little bow. It never occurred to him to shake hands, not with a lady. It would never have occurred to her either.

The cats stopped scratching. Gus and Oliver sat down, he in a rocker recliner like hers, only moss green.

"Our Sullivans? Up the road?" Gus's eyes burned with interest. She might get more information to add to her history of the village.

"The very same."

"And so you'd be Eleanor's sister Edie's son."

"Correct."

"Rose Sullivan's cousin." Not a question. A statement of fact. Gus was on sure ground now, building herself a bridge of linkages.

"Yes." The path Gus was on was less certain for Oliver, more like a rope bridge than a fixed link. "What do you know of my family?"

Gus shook her head.

"They moved away. They all moved away to the Boston States. They came back home – it would be only once, I think, with you, as a young 'un."

Oliver nodded. "Four years old."

"Yes. I saw you with ice cream all over your face at the Strawberry Social."

Oliver didn't remember that. Not at all. Odd, how other people held parts of your life in their memories, things that you didn't recall yourself. Oliver would have been impressed at how many memories Gus held of her own *and* others.

Gus saw something move inside Oliver's sleeve.

She looked at her own hand. It trembled, always, unless she supported it. But he shouldn't have the shakes, a man of his age. No more than fifty.

She looked back at his twitching sleeve.

A set of whiskers emerged.

Followed by a pointy white face.

She shrieked and jumped up, moving faster than she had in twenty years, and went to fetch the fly swatter.

Gus was trying to keep her eye on the rat, once Oliver had calmed her and got her to sit down again. He'd even tried to get her to make "friends" with Oscar. That didn't work. Gus kept her eyes fixed on the sleeve from which the rat had emerged. Her pleasure in having a good old gossip with a visitor who had history at The Shores was dampened by the knowledge of the four-legged creature up his sleeve. And wondering what the cats might be up to in the mudroom. Would they relieve themselves in Abel's boots? She smiled.

"Well, I've taken enough of your time." Oliver pushed himself out of the chair. He'd found out what he'd come to find out.

There was a Rose Sullivan living in Wild Rose Cottage.

Jamie was at Ian's – again. He stopped in at Ian's every time he went to the Hall. The cookies at Ian's were good.

"Moira makes them," Ian had told him, jerking his head in the direction of Moira Toombs' house.

"You should marry her," Jamie said, mouth full, crumbs sticking to his chin. He passed his sleeve across his mouth, and Ian, the confirmed bachelor, never even noticed the crumbs spilling to the floor. He sat down on the couch. Jamie was staring at the computer. It had never happened before, but Ian had not been on his computer for more than a day. He couldn't answer the email from his nephew and he couldn't do anything else if he didn't. He was as frozen as the screen.

Jamie clicked on the keyboard. The email came up.

Unashamed, Jamie read it. Ian, electronically paralyzed, was unable to stop him. "Your brother's in hospital?"

"Yes."

"Are you going to see him?"

"I don't think so."

"Why not?"

What could he say to this child?

"We haven't spoken in many years."

"What?" Jamie's eyes popped open.

"If I had a brother, I would always talk to him. Why don't you talk?"

Ian ran a hand through the strands of hair still clinging to the top of his head.

"We had a fight."

"Who won?"

"Well I guess no one won."

"I guess not," said Jamie, pulling his eyes off the computer screen.

"It says he's got Al...al...al...who? Is that a person?"

"Alzheimer's. It's a disease."

"Oh. Is it bad?"

"Yes."

"So why don't you visit him?"

"It's a long story." Ian hoped that would put Jamie off. Instead, the child plunked himself down beside him, placed a hand on Ian's knee, and said, "Tell me, please."

"For a start, it means he wouldn't even know who I was."

"Does that matter?"

They sat like that for a long while. The child's simple approach stirred something in Ian. He couldn't do anything about Redmond yet. Not yet. But sometime, maybe.

They ended with Jamie teaching Ian the latest games and tricks on his own computer, and Ian wondering how the child had learned his way so well around the technology.

Ian had a secret wish he'd been born into this digital generation. He wasn't, like Jamie, a native. He was an immigrant. Well-educated, but not a natural. Not like Jamie. But Jamie was like few others, he suspected. A child genius perhaps.

They stared at each other.

Rose – and what looked like Buddha on her doorstep. A worldly Buddha, with a fur coat and hat. She appeared to him a worn-out Madonna, but the inside of this house was not a stable. It was a pigsty.

A small rodent skittered by Oliver's feet and out the door.

One less. Rose shrugged her shoulders. "Mice," she apologized, holding a hand out to him.

"Oliver Sullivan," he smiled as if he'd made a great joke.

She smiled back. "Rose Fitzpatrick."

He raised his eyebrow. "Not mice?"

She smiled again.

"Not Sullivan?"

"Well, yes."

"Are we related?"

He smiled. "I hope so."

She smiled, even more broadly.

Jamie had come to see who was at the door. He liked to see her smile. She looked pretty when she smiled. Then he grinned, a big, startled grin, of shock and delight, as White emerged from Oliver's fur collar, jumped down, stretched across the threshold, and began sniffing the floorboards.

"Mice," said Rose again, the smile gone, her eyes drawn to the dinginess of her life, exposed to this fabulous stranger. Ginger emerged from somewhere in the folds of the coat and hopped to the floor, then sauntered after his brother.

Soon both were sitting upright in a corner of the room, eyes unswerving, staring at a hole in the wood trim, a genuine mouse hole shape.

"Oh, dear," said Rose, "I'll have to plug that up."

"I'm not sure it will make much difference, my dear."

Oscar's beady little nose and whiskers appeared from Oliver's sleeve.

Rose's hands flew to her mouth, but didn't manage to stifle the shriek. A rat. A white rat.

Oliver's pudgy forehead folded into its "V" of wrinkles.

"Just a pet, my dear. No need to be afraid."

That's what Jamie had been telling his mother about getting a snake, a boa constrictor that would eat all the rats in the house. Rose had explained that the snake wouldn't eat more than about one a month – and what good would that be?

Now Jamie was glad there was no snake. He stepped closer to Oliver, and reached out a hand toward the rat.

"Jamie, be careful."

"He's harmless. Absolutely harmless. But I'll keep him out of your sight since you find him distressing."

It wasn't the word Rose would have used, and she wanted to keep the rat *in* her sight, but Oliver had already tucked Oscar back into the folds of his fur coat. Rose didn't ask if he'd like to take it off.

Oliver had no intention of removing his coat. In spite of his layers of insulation, he felt the cold. Poor circulation. He stamped his feet and flexed his fingers.

"Here, come sit by the fire." Rose indicated a chair, small and missing a couple of rungs.

But the tent had caught his attention.

"My dear, how unique."

"That's not the word I'd use. Tea?" She avoided the seating problem, then was surprised to see Oliver accordion down to the floor in the front entrance to the tent, smack in front of the wood range.

How will he ever get up? He read her look.

"My dear, I do this all the time. It surprises people because of my – "

He looked down at the mountain of body collapsed around him – "girth. But I've always been flexible. This is how I sit for my readings. I have no problem getting up, come the time."

"Readings?"

"Tarot." Oliver slipped a hand into his coat pocket and pulled out the cards.

"I can read your fate in here, my dear."

"Please don't."

Oliver basked in the warmth of the range, watching Rose busy herself with the tea. He had the heady feeling of being in love. In love with Rose. He was imagining her as a young woman, a vibrant, untouchable being, like all of the women he fell in love with, women he couldn't have. Women in books, usually. Either fictitious, long dead, or happily married.

The sound of several rounds of gunfire startled Oliver. Rose made no response to the gunshots. Fitz finding dinner. A rabbit or a squirrel.

Another shot rang out. *Thud.* A bark, strangled into a whimper. A child's cry of shock.

Rose whipped around, still clutching the kettle, spilling boiling water down her dress, wincing, bringing Oliver to his feet; the cats, White and Ginger, on high alert, sitting straight up, ears cocked, eyes fixed on the danger. Oscar peeked out from Oliver's sleeve, sniffing for information.

Rose threw the kettle to the floor, the hot liquid stinging at Oliver's ankles as he followed her through the door.

Fitz had his rifle aimed at Freddy. Jamie had his arms around the dog, protecting him. Fitz had a wild look in his eye that made Rose and Oliver freeze, in spite of their desire to go to Jamie.

They didn't have to. Fitz never saw Nathan coming. He'd been asleep in his truck waiting for Oliver. The shots had punctuated his dream and had woken him up. When he saw what was going on, he jumped out of the truck, hurled himself at Fitz, whipped the shotgun from his hands, and used it to pin him to the ground.

Then he sat on him.

Fitz struggled to free himself, but Nathan was too strong.

"That fuckin' dog." Fitz's speech was guttural. The gun was pressing on his neck, making the bicycle chain dig into him.

Oliver winced at the language.

"That fuckin' dog went and ate the rabbit I wuz after."

"The dog has to eat, too," said Rose. "We can't afford to feed her anything."

Freddy was pitifully skinny, shivering from fright and cold.

"We can't afford to let her eat our food."

Nathan relaxed his hold just a bit.

"If I let you up, you won't go for the dog again?"

"Nah."

Nathan stood up. Fitz got up, too, and dusted himself off. He grabbed the rifle from Nathan. He grinned, an ugly grin, more like a sneer.

"If she wasn't skin and bone, we could kill her and eat her."

"No!" Jamie leapt up and ran at his father. Fitz held him back with a hand on his forehead. Jamie flailed helplessly at his father, trying to land a punch.

Fitz laughed, a mean and heartless laugh. He dropped his hand, took up his rifle with both hands, and strode back toward the woods.

"That mutt better not be here when I get back," he yelled behind him. "Or I will make dog soup of her."

Jamie was weeping. Big tears rolling down his face, he patted Freddy, who leaned in close to him, shooting helpless looks at the people around her. She nuzzled him. How could she make him feel better?

Nathan put a hand on Jamie's shoulder.

"I'll take her," he said. "Lili and I will take her until your father calms down. You can come and visit her at our house. We're just the next one down the hill there."

Nathan had traded it with Abel in exchange for a lifetime of snowplowing and lawn-mowing. When he had made the deal, the villagers had been more interested to know how Abel was looking than in Nathan's acquisition of the house, though the terms and money exchanged were mulled over frequently on long winter nights.

Nathan patted Freddy, and she looked up at him with adoring eyes. So did Jamie.

Nathan smiled.

"We'll keep her inside so she doesn't run into him."

In that moment, Nathan became Jamie's hero. His eyes shone with relief and gratitude. He wasn't used to kindness from strangers. People avoided his family.

Rose expressed her gratitude in the only way she could:

"Can I offer you a cup of tea?"

"Don't mind if I do," said Nathan. "Just let me get the dog in the truck, where she'll be safe."

Jamie followed Nathan like a puppy himself. His eyes went big when he saw the inside of the vehicle.

"Wow, I'd love to drive this."

Nathan chuckled.

"I can drive, you know."

"I'm sure you can. A tractor? A ride-on mower?"

Jamie's head dropped.

"Well, yeah…"

"I'm sure you could drive this, too." Nathan's voice softened. "As soon as you're tall enough. Right now your foot wouldn't reach the gas pedal or the brake."

Jamie frowned.

"But as soon as it does…" Nathan winked. "…you can take her for a spin."

He was still young enough to remember how exciting driving was to a young boy – tractors, mowers, anything with a motor – but the real thing, an actual road vehicle, that was the prize.

Freddy hopped into the truck and nestled into an old blanket

Nathan kept for his parents' dog Toby. Freddy sniffed at it, gave Toby's smell her approval, and flopped her head down on her front paws. Nathan and Jamie went back inside to find Oliver and Rose in deep conversation. They looked up, and Rose blushed, the blush rising high on her cheeks. Now she really did look like that glowing young woman Oliver fancied she had been.

Oliver meant to keep the attraction a close secret, but on his next visit, he was frank about his other interest. The diary.

"I don't suppose your husband has mentioned it," he had said. "Or Jamie?"

She had sniffed dismissively. "Jamie's too busy visiting Freddy, playing the piano or computer games."

At the moment, Jamie was playing cat and mouse. When Ginger and White jumped off Oliver, he'd taken off with them around the house, encouraging them in their mouse-hunting, and clearing up their kill as they went. They didn't eat the mice. Jamie would have liked to play with Oscar as well, but Rose wouldn't allow it. Oliver had to keep his pet rat out of her sight.

"Fitz wouldn't pay attention to a book unless he thought it was useful. And these are only good for burning."

She nodded at the pile of books tossed in an untidy heap by the wood range.

Oliver looked horrified.

"It's okay. I've checked them all," said Rose. "No diary." She picked up a couple, opened the stove door, and tossed them in.

Oliver winced. They were beyond saving, but the idea of burning books sent a sharp pain through him, as if he'd been stabbed. He turned away. He couldn't look. He left the room and hit a wall of cold. Cobwebs hung in the corners of the doorframe, filled with dead flies and moths.

He hauled himself up the stairs, planting one foot first, his hand on the banister, pulling the next foot up, keeping his feet wide apart for balance. When Rose came out into the hallway, she left the door open. It was usually closed to contain the heat inside the kitchen, but she wanted some of the heat to drift up to Oliver.

By the time he reached the top of the stairs, Oliver's breathing was laboured. He had to stop, still clinging to the banister, his chest heaving, his mouth half-open.

Rose glided up the stairs and placed a soft hand on his back.

"Are you all right?" Her eyes full of concern. It warmed his heart, calmed its beating. But then it swelled to aching again, full of the warmth of her. Oliver was in love with a living female. Not in a book, not created out of a book, but a woman in the flesh, a woman he knew could never love him back. That much remained the same.

She took him by the hand – *ecstasy!* Together, they went into the library. Oliver's step was now quick, his eyes bright from Rose's touch and the prospect of finding the diary. He knew he could, with Rose here.

Rose looked around the room in despair. Books strewn everywhere, covers yawning open or ripped off, pages chewed by rats and used as urinals. She shuddered at the thought of touching any of them.

How would they find anything here?

They wouldn't.

It would find them.

Chapter Sixteen

"The kid's a genius."

Hy looked up. Surprised that Ian knew. Surprised that he'd met the boy.

"Yes, a prodigy. I'm putting him in the Christmas show."

Ian looked puzzled. So did Hy.

"The piano," she said. "You've heard him play?"

He shook his head. "I'm talking about the computer. He's been here to play games and surf on mine. I'd gone up to see if I could help them set up theirs and if they could connect to high-speed."

Hy snorted.

"You can say that again. No electricity. A tent pitched in the kitchen. Nothing resembling an electronic device."

Hy smiled.

"You went up because you were snooping, and you didn't believe what I told you."

He grinned. "That, too. Man, what a desperate way to live."

She nodded. "So you took Jamie to your place."

"Yeah, showed him a few things, and he caught on faster than I've seen anyone do. Told him he could come and use it anytime."

"I said the same thing about the piano. I think I'll have it tuned."

"That good, is he?"

"That good and more." I took him to Tchai Ferguson in Charlottetown, and he – she – is willing to take Jamie on."

"He? She?"

"Transgendered. Coming out. Doing the surgery. Guy to a gal."

Ian winced.

"But what good will it do him living in that place with that father, and the mother so beaten down?"

Beaten. The word caught in her mind. Was there domestic abuse going on at Wild Rose Cottage? She had nothing to prove it. It was just a thought.

Fitz had her pinned up against the wall, his angry teeth bared at her. Rose was used to it. It didn't even frighten her anymore.

"So what're you and that fat slob up to? Somethin' you won't do with me?" He pressed his body hard against hers. She felt her gag reflex swelling, held it back. It wouldn't do to vomit on him, as he had done to her so many times.

"That fuckin' fag." His hands tightened against her wrists.

"He's not – " She broke off. Maybe he was, but what did it matter?

His face came even closer. She could smell the rum on his breath. Another thing she was used to.

"What's he doing here?"

What could she say? She grabbed at anything.

"He reads the cards." It was a lie. She'd never let him. She was too afraid of her future.

"Pah!" He splattered his contempt on her face. Spit on her. She tried to move an arm to wipe it off, but he clamped even harder.

"And there's a book," she said finally, tired of this. Fitz wasn't interested in books. The real secret was safe. Besides, the book was safe, wasn't it? Somewhere no one could find it. If it existed anymore.

Fitz's grip on her loosened. "A book?" Was that a glint of interest in his eyes? It couldn't be.

"A diary." She expected contempt. If he even knew what a diary was.

"A diary." He said it slowly, drawing the word out. He relaxed his grip on her, and she pulled herself free.

"A diary," he repeated, lingering on the word. Rose wondered why he was acting so strangely.

"Well, maybe I'll let him keep looking." He grabbed her arm as she tried to slip away. "And maybe I won't. You just better tell me if he finds it."

Buddy watched. Buddy was always watching. He watched Hy, just across the road, all the time. He watched over her, that is. Ready to come to her defence. It had never been necessary.

Now he watched Wild Rose Cottage. The lay of the land, the way it swept downwards, gave him a view of the house on the far side of Shipwreck Hill.

He watched, not just from his shack, but closer up, too. From in the woods, where he spent his days wandering and looking for kindling for his stove. He'd gather it up in piles, sticking one branch upright on top, and no one else would touch them. They would know they were his.

So he could hear the angry voices coming out of the house.

Buddy had heard the gunshots, too. He'd seen the child and the dog, their love for each other. He often watched Jamie go down the hill to Nathan's. Sometimes he followed, but carefully. Careful not to be seen. He worried about the woman and the child. He stopped watching Hy, and began to keep a constant eye on Wild Rose Cottage.

Like Oliver, he fell in love with Rose. From a distance. Always from a distance. The child, too. The child with the golden hair. He wanted to touch it, but he knew he couldn't. They'd think he wanted to harm the child. It had happened before.

Rose could hear them upstairs, flinging books, and themselves, around the library.

"We'll look at the ones on this side of the room first," Fitz had said, scraping his boot along the floor, moving books, dung, and dust across the room.

"We'll pile them over there." He pointed to one end of the room. "Then we'll work on the other side after."

"Sounds like a plan," said Jared, ambling over. "But first – " He pulled a joint out of his pocket. Fitz grinned. No hard feelings then about the grass he'd stolen. *Not stolen. Just hadn't paid for it yet.*

Jared had been furious to find the pot gone, but he contained himself, for once. There could be some money in this little search, and he needed to stay tight with Fitz. Besides, there was plenty more. He grew his own supply in a clearing in the woods. Well-protected. Hot. And hidden. Harvested and dried in his barn. Stashed in urns meant for human remains, urns that had "fallen off a truck."

They leaned up against a wall that had a tiny door in it, crooked and jammed shut with age. They'd tried to open it but couldn't. The house had shifted, tilted it, and jammed it shut. They smoked. One joint. They began to riffle through books and toss them to the end of the room. Suddenly, Fitz stood up straight and smacked his forehead.

"That fat fella. He's the one." That Oliver. He was the guy who'd been making promises to Jared. "He's the one you bin talkin' to. He'll pay fer it." A wide grin. "Oh, he'll pay fer it."

Two joints. They stopped the search and each breathed in forgetting with the pot. Each forgetting a different thing. Fitz – his children. The things he had done to his children. For one moment the agony sliced through his mind, and then he let it go. Let it be buried, because he couldn't think of it now, couldn't think of them now. What he had done.

Jared was forgetting…nothing. What he had to forget was so well forgotten that he couldn't find it anymore.

Fitz slapped Jared on the shoulder.

"Screw the fuckin' diary."

The diary was in a dark place. It had been there for a lifetime. That was nothing. The diary had been around for longer than one lifetime. No one had approached this place – because it couldn't be seen. And it wasn't remembered. Oliver didn't remember it. He didn't remember that he had brought it here himself. Hid it himself. The diary was waiting for Oliver, waiting for him to find it again.

"A diary?" Hy was intrigued when Rose told her what they were looking for.

Now that she'd told one person, it was easy to tell another. Besides, Oliver can't have meant what he said. Surely the more people who knew about it, the more likely it was to be found.

Hy put down her teacup.

"Well, let's go look."

They were just on their way when Oliver arrived. He came up behind them and tugged himself up the stairs.

Hy tripped over the pile of books Fitz and Jared had shoved up against the wall. Her hand came down on something sticky, and she pulled it away, disgusted. Oliver came to help her up. And then they saw it. The door. The tiny door into the eaves. They looked at each other, silent, but tingling with expectation – why, none of them could have said.

Hy stood up and dusted herself off. Oliver reached for the doorknob.

The door was stuck shut, and he had to tug at it repeatedly. Just as he was about to give up, it gave in, and he went flying back onto his ass. His legs came up, and he lay there helplessly on his back, legs in the air. Hy and Rose helped him up. It wasn't easy – they pushed and pushed again until he was rocking back and forth, until finally his feet tapped the ground and he was able to sit up. From there, it was easy. Rose watched with the amazement she always had at how Oliver brought himself up from the floor with ease.

He opened the door, and reeled back at the smell. Rose squeezed her nose shut and peeked in. She, too, reeled back.

The eave was filled with raccoon shit, ancient and current, as well as urine, which gave off the powerful smell. Oliver slammed the door shut.

"What's that?" Rose called out just as he did so. When he didn't respond, she insisted. "Open it again."

A shaft of sunlight through a hole in the fascia illuminated a book in the far corner of the eave.

"Is that it?"

"I think it is." Oliver's voice was soft and slow. "Maybe it is…" There was wonder in his words. He didn't know why he said it, but somehow he knew it was so. But they couldn't reach it. Hy, the slimmest, tried, but couldn't get through the tiny door. They'd need Jamie.

Until then they wouldn't know if they'd found the diary. But Oliver was already sure of it – a memory of childhood tugging at his mind.

"The diary," he said, in a reverent whisper. "The key to The Sullivan legacy."

He had found it. They had. Jamie, all boy, had delighted in squirreling into the eave, oblivious to the raccoon scat.

"Careful, careful." Oliver peeked in after him, his sensitive nose wrinkling at the odour. Jamie had grabbed the book and begun to shuffle out when Oliver was assaulted by memory. The memory of another young child putting the book in that very place. Himself, at four, finding the diary after the adults had snatched it away, and hiding it from them. Their reaction – shouting and hitting – had frightened young Oliver into forgetting. He had denied knowing where the diary was, so many times, he no longer remembered.

It was in his hands again. He stroked its suede leather exterior, murmuring soothing sounds as if it were a baby. With a soft touch, he turned the pages, alternating writing and blotting paper. The text, and on the facing page, smudges of ink blotted dry.

So absorbed was he in the book that he might have been alone. He'd forgotten about Jamie, Hy, and even Rose. Soon he was alone. Touching a finger to her lips, Rose corralled the other two and eased them out of the room.

He began to read it. The penmanship was elegant, feminine, but, even so, he was surprised to find it had been written by a woman. It was not until he had read several pages that the writer revealed herself. And not for many, many more pages was there anything said about a legacy.

Moira had become used to Oliver's strange ways – his caftan, his embroidered bejeweled slippers, even his cats. Not that damn rodent, though. Moira had never used the word "damn" in her life, and she used it now only mentally. It would take a lot more than a rat to make her say it out loud. Hyacinth, for instance. She could see saying it about her.

In spite of the rat, she was catering to Oliver devotedly. Her focus on Ian seemed to have shifted to the corpulent guru occupying the back bedroom. It wasn't a romantic interest – not like her feelings for Ian – but it was a devotion that could turn slavish, were it not checked. The checking point was the white rat.

The shift had occurred when Oliver gave Moira a Tarot reading.

Black magic, she had thought, when she had first seen the cards laid out on what she always thought of as her mother's good dining room table. Word for word, that's how she always referred to it.

"Mother's good dining room table" was never seen. It was covered by a protective board, overlaid with a white linen tablecloth – also too good to do its job without protection. The linen tablecloth was covered by thick plastic. When Hy had seen it on the occasion of a Women's Institute meeting, she wondered what could go over the plastic to protect *it.*

Oliver was using the table to lay out the colourful cards of the Major Arcana. He was still attempting to find clues to the Sullivan legacy. Moira tiptoed into the room – in part not to disturb Oliver, but also in fear of releasing the evil that might be in the cards.

"Nothing to be afraid of," Oliver said, without even looking at her behind him, able to sense her trepidation from her hesitant tread.

"What are you doing?"

"Amusing myself, my dear. Just simply amusing myself."

Moira flushed. No one had – ever – called her "my dear." It quite flustered her and made her blush red, which was not unbecoming on her usually pasty face.

She edged closer. She reached out a hand and touched a card. Turned it over. It was The Lovers.

"Ah, now I know the nature of your question."

Moira pulled back.

"I was just touching – "

"We touch the cards that have meaning to us." Oliver picked up the cards, one by one.

"Sit down."

She sat down beside him. He shuffled the cards.

"Cut them."

Moira looked bewildered.

"But, I have no scissors."

Oliver chuckled again.

"No, no, my dear. Split the cards up, take a portion. Think on your question, concentrate, as you cut the cards."

Oliver picked the first card.

"The nature of the question," he said, laying it down.

It was The Lovers.

"See," he said, winking. "The cards know."

The Lovers was upside down.

"The Lovers," he said. "A time of choice." *But the choice would be negative.* He would not reveal that.

He laid a card on top of it.

"This covers you. This is what favours the situation."

Staring up at them was the Queen of Wands. Moira smiled. That must be a good card. That must be her. The Queen of Wands, well, mops and buckets, anyway.

"Ah, the Queen of Wands," said Oliver. "A card of the emotions. This is a romantic question, your silent question."

Moira flushed, just a bit. It made her look almost pretty, thought Oliver. Almost. This card, too, was reversed. It meant jealousy, deceit, infidelity. *What could he say?*

"It is a card of success," he lied. But not reversed, the way it was. Reversed, the emotional prognosis was not good.

He laid a card across the two. "This crosses you. This is what will oppose you in the situation." *She's opposed before it's even begun, and this won't help.*

He was looking at The Fool. Some interpreted this card of the Major Arcana positively – but to Oliver it had always meant folly – the young man standing on the edge of a cliff, oblivious to the danger. *What could he say? Folly – The Fool – was staring right at them.*

"Don't look dismayed, my dear. This means only that if the object of your affection does not reciprocate, he's a fool."

She smiled tentatively.

More fool you, he thought.

The reading continued, and it didn't get better. Most of the cards were reversed, which was usually not good. Oliver put the best face on it, and Moira was quite gratified by the reading. The accuracy of it. The nice things he'd said about her. At least somebody appreciated her. If Oliver saw that, maybe Ian would, too.

By the end of the reading, Moira was a devoted follower of Oliver. She had fallen under his spell, hypnotized by his art.

So grateful was she that Moira now laid out tea at four o'clock every afternoon in the dining room. Moira liked the idea so much – so refined – that she had taken out some of her mother's linens and silver plate. The pot dispensed tea that tasted of silver polish. Oliver, drinking out of a china cup, could taste the metallic cleaner. The cucumber sandwiches were limp and had crusts, but he didn't notice. He was lost in the diary.

Moira wrinkled her nose and curled her lip when she saw and smelled the musty old book. But he was an antiquarian, so she supposed she'd have to put up with it. Moira thought having an antiquarian in her house lent it a certain dignity that would rub off on her "establishment," as she had begun to call it.

The diary of Rose Sullivan, that was, was a treasure. As Oliver sipped his metallic tea, he thought that perhaps the diary was the legacy. It drew a picture of life on the tree-covered island, a wilderness hacked out with few tools and no help from the landlords. The Sullivans had spent the first winter in a six-foot by four-foot log house, with a loft for sleeping.

Oliver shivered when he imagined four people in such proximity, even if two of them were children. Then he smiled. An effective method of birth control.

Oliver turned the pages impatiently, looking for a clue, a sign. It was a marvel of history. The book was valuable, not just in a monetary way, although it would fetch a bit, but in its portrayal of Island life as far back as there was island life, white human island life. This Rose Sullivan was the east coast's Susannah Moodie, and it would be Oliver's pleasure to introduce her to Canadian literati and historians.

He turned the pages, brittle with age, carefully, right to the last page, where, in a different hand, the words jumped out at him: "the Sullivan legacy." He shifted his half-moon spectacles securely onto the bridge of his nose.

Chapter Seventeen

"What a bitch!" Hy was preparing for the rehearsal of "Shores Ella" without a leading actress or actor. She'd been furious about it since she'd received an email from Moira, withdrawing herself and her sister Madeline from the Christmas skit.

"I should be glad she's not taking part." Hy was shoving chairs to clear the stage at The Hall. Annabelle was in the kitchen, preparing sandwiches and a tray of squares, a "lunch" for the actors. She said nothing but let Hy rant on.

"I don't care about Moira. I'll find a prince."

Annabelle stuck her head out the door from the kitchen. She winked: "Really?"

Hy wasn't in a mood to grin, but she couldn't stop herself. "You know what I mean." Then she frowned again.

"I'm really angry about Madeline. Moira shouldn't speak for her."

"She didn't want to do it, anyway, Hy."

"I think she should be given the chance to shine. Not be pushed around by that domineering sister of hers."

Annabelle came through the door, put a hand on Hy's shoulder. "And she should be pushed around by you?"

Hy thrust a stubborn chin at her friend. Then they both grinned.

"Yeah, okay. So who's my Shores Ella?"

Just then, Jamie came into The Hall.

"How about me?" The sun shone onto his soft golden hair. Hy and Annabelle stared at the boy. Hy thought, *Why not?* She clasped her hands together and beamed.

"It's positively Shakespearean," she said to Annabelle. "Boys always played girls. Might raise the tone a bit."

Jamie smiled his wide, partly toothless, smile.

"Are you sure you want to do it?" Hy took in Jamie's dirty jeans, covered in mud and ripped at the knees. "You'll have to wear a dress."

He screwed up his face.

Hy was about to suggest dungarees, when he nodded.

"I could do that."

"I wanted you to play the piano."

"I will."

"I mean for the skit."

"We can figure that out," Jamie responded in a remarkably adult way. And they did. Hy, Annabelle, and Jamie worked Shores Ella's musical abilities into the plot.

"But remember," Hy warned Jamie, "the part does belong to Madeline if she wants it. You're just the understudy."

Jamie nodded, leapt up, and kicked his heels, looking very much the little boy and very far from a princess. Hy sighed.

They still didn't have a prince.

...They say the Sullivan legacy is murder, and that may be. Some say these things run in families as they have run in ours. But there is a greater legacy, fully unrealized as yet, but someday... someday. Nimble fingers hold the key to unlock the family's hidden

wealth. The secret is not in this book, but in the world, where it has always been.

There was no more. Impatient, Oliver had skipped to the end, hoping for a conclusion, but the diary ended with the secret untold. Had the writer merely been fueling a dull life? Leaving a secret, in fact no secret at all, for future generations to puzzle over. That's what it seemed like. He'd found the tendency in journals and diaries before. A grabbing out at the future, exercising some control, however trivial, over what was to come. Or over people like himself who ponder the past.

But if he took it seriously?

Oliver looked at his own sausage-like fingers. Not nimble. Why nimble? To unlock the secret. But where was the key? A new search. He went to the cards. They told him nothing. The Pentacles, wealth, were there repeatedly. The Magician, The Priestess, and The Fool.

Was he The Fool to think there was anything in this? He gazed out the window. The secret was in the world, where it had always been. He turned and opened the book again. Nimble fingers.

Could it be Jamie? Jamie, with his nimble fingers? The key – the keys of the piano? A special piano? Or could playing the notes of any piano bring forth the clue to the legacy? Did the fingers have to be nimble, because the sequence of notes was difficult to play? Would the clue spell out words by the names of the notes?

Oliver was so excited his stomach was churning. A rush of energy had him standing upright, pacing the room. This was better, even, than deciphering the tarot. The trail of clues led directly to Jamie and the piano in the Hall. How close was he to discovering the great family secret? He rushed out of the room as fast as he could go. He would find Jamie. They would go to the Hall. Jamie would play for him and all, all would be revealed. Surely.

Oliver's excitement fueled him all the way to Wild Rose Cottage. He never thought of calling Nathan. He arrived, out of breath, perspiration sliding down his forehead so thick it clouded his vision. His cheeks were an unhealthy high colour of red.

"Jamie?" he gasped when Rose opened the door.

She shook her head. "At The Hall." She looked concerned. "Come. Sit down."

"No, no," he said. "I may have found the secret to the Sullivan legacy, but I need Jamie's help."

"Jamie's help?"

He slipped the precious book out of his coat. He had it wrapped in fine linen – one of Moira's mother's napkins. It was theft, but it couldn't be helped. He would recompense her. He opened to the passage about the Sullivan legacy and showed it to Rose.

"What does it mean?"

"I'll have to work on that with Jamie. He has the nimble fingers. Perhaps the cards will help, too. I will consult them. But," he added, "only after I see Jamie. In the meantime, take a look at this. It belongs to you. It could be worth quite a bit. I shall return."

He would have liked to call Nathan now, but he couldn't. *No phone. No electricity. That poor woman. And the child. And the child to come.*

She hadn't told him that, but the cards had.

Hy was auditioning the Institute women for the role of prince, whom she'd scripted as a buffoon. Jamie was playing the role of Shores Ella. In worn-out jeans, a plaid shirt and socks with holes, he hardly looked the part, but he delivered his lines perfectly, flashing the long eyelashes that women always said were wasted on a boy.

Rose Rose, the minister's wife, was hopeless as the prince. She was much too feminine – soft voice, graceful movements. Estelle Joudry was a complete ham – all fluttering eyelashes and clasped hands. *More like a diva past her best-before date,* thought Hy. Olive MacLean was stiff and unyielding, only able to say the lines word by word. The remaining women were too old, too ill, or going away for Christmas. Community spirit wasn't what it had been.

But community policing was, in the form of Jane Jamieson who, seeing so many cars outside, stuck her head in the door and herself into their dilemma.

The moment Hy saw her, the idea struck, as a lot of her ideas did, suddenly and without forethought, and came spurting out of her with no hesitation.

"Our prince. Will you be our prince?"

"Oh, yes!" Jamie jumped up from the chair onstage, eyes glowing. Playing opposite a real cop. Even a girl cop.

Jamieson jerked her head back in surprise.

"Prince? What prince?"

"In our Christmas skit. We need a prince, and you'd be perfect."

"Well, I couldn't…I'm a police officer…"

"You'd be off duty."

"I'm not sure when that is."

"It must be sometime. Like Christmas Eve."

"That's one of the bad nights in policing…"

"Not at The Shores. What could happen here?"

"What hasn't already happened?" Jamieson's tone was grim.

"Well, yes," said Hy, thinking of the deaths and murders over the past two years. "But that was unusual. We've had more than our share."

"Indeed," said Jamieson. And none of them to her credit. People had been killed on her watch. Repeatedly. Some people thought she'd jinxed the place.

"Put Murdo on duty."

That suggestion teased at Jamieson, pleased her. Murdo on duty. *That'll be a change.* A half-smile formed on her lips. She rolled the idea around in her head, felt the tense expectation. This was surely community policing. Exactly what she'd been looking for. Becoming a part of the village. A part, but still apart, she warned herself not to be getting sentimental. She still had a job to do.

Jamie jumped down from the stage. He grabbed Jamieson's sleeve, looked up at her with pleading in his eyes.

"Oh, please, please." He tugged at her arm. "Please be my prince."

More than any of the other arguments, this moved her beyond measure. The child's shining eyes of expectation. She had the power to make this child happy at Christmas. She'd been a child at Christmas. That tragic Christmas. An innocent child...no, not innocent, but still a child, robbed of happiness. No one after that had ever wanted her to do something at Christmas. They had tiptoed around her. She'd pretended she didn't care.

"Ple...e...e...ease..." Jamie tugged at her sleeve again. Suddenly there was a rush of caring she couldn't hold back, as if her skin had opened and let it out.

"Okay." She smiled. Jamieson actually smiled.

Jamie clapped his hands.

"You can wear your boots."

The moment had passed for Jamieson. She wondered now if it had been wise to agree. But if she did this, played the prince, even if she weren't on duty, she'd still be on a kind of duty. That pleased her.

"No. Absolutely not in uniform. Plain clothes."

Jamie's hand slipped from tugging Jamieson's sleeve into her hand. Another surprise that sent strange, unfamiliar sensations through Jamieson.

"Could I be a Mountie when I grow up? Like you?"

"If you qualified. Of course, but not exactly like me. More like Murdo."

Jamie scrunched up his face. "Murdo doesn't work very hard." Jamieson stifled a smile. Murdo didn't, but he could be depended on when things got bad.

"No, but Murdo's a man. That's what you'll be."

"Oh, yes," said Jamie. "But not on Christmas Eve!"

Hy was thinking: A boy playing a girl. A girl playing a boy. A Shakespearean Christmas pantomime. How much more traditional could you get? Farce was a tradition, too, though, and she was trying to imagine the most outrageous princely outfit she could concoct for Jamieson to wear.

Not in uniform? Done.

Chapter Eighteen

The rehearsal had just begun when Oliver slid into the Hall, exhausted by the double exertion of walking up to Wild Rose Cottage and back down again.

"The world doesn't know the true story of Cinderella. For one thing, it happened in The Shores." Hy was narrator, weaving the scenes together and telling the story, so that the cast didn't have to worry about too many lines.

"And the girl's name was not Cinderella. Her name was simply Ella. But there was an Ella Cousins at Port Corner. Ella Campbell on the Butter Road. Ella Gallant in Mermaid. So people called our Ella…Shores Ella."

Oliver realized that, in spite of his excitement, he was going to have to wait it out. He slumped down on a wooden chair with metal legs, and it cracked under him. He stood up again, and chose the sturdier-looking bench that ran down one wall of the Hall. It creaked, but didn't crack.

Jamie opened and closed the skit on the piano. Hearing him play, Oliver was even more convinced he was on the right track. Jamie's nimble fingers would unlock the secret.

When the rehearsal ended, Oliver approached Jamie.

"A talented actor, yes," he said, "but a much more talented pianist. Will you play for me?"

Jamie looked over at Hy.

"Yes, we're finished."

The women chattered their way out of the Hall, fussing over their coats and boots, returning for something forgotten, in and out, until finally they were all gone.

Oliver had no idea what he was looking for, what clue would be found in the keys of the piano, so he simply asked Jamie to play. Anything.

The notes trickled out of the boy's hands, his movements smooth as velvet, sure and strong, soft and yielding, everything they needed to be to coax…no, not coax…draw the instrument's music out of it, so that even this old piano could make beautiful sound.

Oliver was rapt at first, and then joined in. He was not a musician, but he loved music and understood it, and soon was standing by Jamie, calling out the moods, rhythms and pace.

"…a poco…a poco…subito!"

It wasn't as if Jamie understood any of the words, but he had the feeling for the music.

The feeling in his fingers…dare say…in his soul.

Oliver was beaming and undulating his rotund physique in a marvelously harmonious rhythm with the music. Chopin. One of the nocturnes.

"De capo. Pianissimo."

And on they went, the cultured man and the talented boy, with their separate languages. Oliver, with his profound understanding of the music and the beauty of the Italian language that described it, but no ability, no ability whatsoever to play. Jamie, with no understanding of Oliver's language, of the language used to describe the sounds he made, yet making those sounds, as if he had been born to it.

He was, thought Oliver, *born to it.*

And somewhere in those sounds was the Sullivan legacy. Could it be found through this boy?

The sounds faded out, and Jamie grinned up at Oliver, turning from child genius into just another kid with a big toothless grin.

Toothless, like his father. But it didn't deliver the same message.

Oliver clapped Jamie on the back.

"Well done, son. Now let's try some Beethoven."

Oliver always said he couldn't play an instrument, but that wasn't exactly true. He played the original instrument with perfect pitch. His voice.

And so he sang Beethoven's Ninth, The Ode to Joy, to Jamie, and Jamie listened attentively, all his concentration focused on the sounds coming out of that barrel chest – deep and deadly accurate. Tentatively, note by note, he picked it up, and his fingers began to fly over the keys, with a sureness of where the next note would be, until man and boy were in harmony – the big deep voice, and the out-of-tune piano.

There had never been quite such a performance there before.

When they had finished, forgetting his previous exertions, Oliver walked Jamie home, the two of them humming the Ode. He had been so elated by the experience that he had forgotten that he had left the diary with Rose. Now he remembered. He quickened his pace. Jamie was surprised that Oliver could move so quickly and had to run to keep up.

At the driveway, there was black smoke rising from a fire pit by the shed. Oliver abandoned Jamie, and almost ran. He had only one – sure – thought.

The diary.

It was an illogical thought, but a correct one.

Fitz had grabbed it from Rose when he saw her reading it and made off with it. He'd gone to the shed to have a look at the contents. He had hardly read a thing. Some woman sniveling on. This wasn't the book. This was worthless. He had just tossed it on the bonfire.

Oliver moved faster than he ever had before, scooped it up, cradling it to him, the soot singeing his immaculate suede gloves black.

"You bastard," he shrieked, his face turning a deep red. Oliver rarely used such language. It showed how upset he was.

"Jeez," Fitz was chewing on a toothpick. "It's only a fuckin' book."

The phrase stunned Oliver. Stunned him into silence.

Fitz took a step forward, his look and his stance threatening.

"That wouldn't be *the* fuckin' book, now would it?"

Still, Oliver was silent.

"My guess is yes." Fitz sneered. "And my guess is, you owe me for that."

"But I found it – not you."

Fitz stepped forward suddenly, and whisked the book out of Oliver's hands.

He held it over the fire.

Oliver paled.

"Now, how much is it worth?" He waved the book over the flames.

"Whatever you want." Oliver tried to prevent himself from moving forward and grabbing the diary. He knew Fitz would think nothing of dropping it in the flames again.

"Five hundred bucks?"

"Yes, of course." Too eager. He was too eager. Fitz could see that, and he played it.

"Let's say double that."

"Fine. Fine." Oliver's eyes were riveted on the diary. His muscles were taut, ready to pounce, but he didn't want to make a false move. Better to pay this thug whatever he wanted.

"Good, then let's say triple."

The money didn't matter to Oliver. He'd pay four – five times, to get the book back in his hands. How careless he'd been.

"Yes. Done." Oliver reached for the book. Fitz pulled back, wondering just how far he could push it.

Finally, wanting to end it, to be in possession once again of the diary, Oliver turned around. "That's all it's worth to me," he said. It was a gamble that made him nauseated, but he had to stop the dance.

Fitz looked down at the book. *It was only a fuckin' book. It could only be worth so much.*

"Okay," he said, and Oliver tried to mask his huge relief as he turned around.

"Then give it to me, please."

A sly smile spread over Fitz's face.

"I'd like to see your money first."

"I can give you a deposit."

"So – give me a deposit. An' I'll give you the book when I get the rest of the money." He tucked the diary inside his shirt.

Oliver shuddered to think of the precious leather cover close to Fitz's sweaty skin. The fine thoughts and sentiments attached to that foul and stinking body.

But what could he do?

In that moment, the idea of killing Fitz flashed through his mind.

Oliver reached inside his coat for his wallet. Fifteen hundred dollars. He had a thousand-dollar bill, even though the mint had stopped printing them. He peeled off the rest and held the money out.

"So ya did have it. You was lyin'."

"I didn't have it to spend on you."

"Well, now you have." Fitz grabbed at the bills, but hesitated before producing the diary. Maybe...maybe...he could get more out of him.

Oliver stepped forward, and grabbed Fitz by the collar.

"I've killed a man before," he said. "Don't think I wouldn't now."

Like most bullies, Fitz was a coward.

"Okay. Okay."

Oliver released him. Fitz pulled the diary out and handed it over.

Jamie was numb with a hard realization. First the scene with his mother, then with Freddy, and now this. Something took hold of him, a sensation he didn't like, a feeling of disgust for his father, his father whom he'd always loved. As disillusionment seeped in, love seeped out. Jamie tried to catch hold of it, to blank out the ugly scenes he'd seen, but he couldn't. He looked at his father, and his small child lip curled in repulsion.

"I hate you," he yelled at his father across the flickering fire. The flames cast dark shadows on Fitz's face and made him look evil.

"I hate you." Repeated in a tone and with such force that Oliver turned around sharply to look at the child. The flames were flickering across the boy's face, too, and making him look evil.

Like father like son? What might he do? Was that why the cards had brought him here?

"I wish you were dead." Jamie's words leapt across the flames, on sparks of anger.

He didn't wait to see if the words had hurt his father. Afraid they hadn't, he turned and ran into the house.

Buddy watched. Buddy had seen it all. But Buddy didn't know what to do.

He watched Oliver make his way down the road, clutching the diary to his heart, and he watched as Fitz jumped into his truck. Then he went to the door, trembling. His heart beat harder as he approached the door. With fear and love. He looked through the window, with longing, at the mother and the golden child made magical in the glow of the candlelight. It looked like heaven, not a hovel, to him. He lifted a hand to knock. The child laughed and his mother kissed him on the head. Buddy ached to be that boy, but he knew he didn't belong there. He lost his courage, and turned away.

Fitz went straight to Jared's. Jared had scored hash and cocaine. "Enough to get us through the winter." He had his own stash, his "homegrown," but he knew that with Fitz around it wouldn't last long.

Jared was a very minor dealer. He had almost no customers at The Shores. There were a couple of badass fishermen, and he sold the occasional small bag of marijuana to Billy Pride, but now he had a real customer. Based on that he had extended his credit with Winterside's biggest dealer, and now had a stash in his house that could land him in real trouble, were the police to find out about it.

But there was only that chick. How good could she be? People died all the time when she was around.

Fitz whistled his admiration when he saw the stash of hash and the brick of cocaine. He laid the thousand-dollar bill on the table.

"What'll that buy me?"

It was Jared's turn to whistle.

The lot. It would buy him the lot. But Jared needed some for himself. He scooped the money up.

"It'll buy you half. Half of everything. Including what you owe me from the last time."

It wasn't enough, and Fitz knew it, but he didn't care. He was pissed already and now he wanted to get stoned. So he didn't have to think…think about…anything.

Blasted. He wanted to get blasted.

But still –

"That and what else?" he asked.

Jared produced a mickey of rum and shoved it across the table.

Fitz grabbed it.

"Deal." He unscrewed the cap and knocked back half the contents.

Jared whistled again.

The man was a pig. A complete pig. Jared smiled. He liked Fitz.

He liked Fitz less when, after they smoked and snorted and drank, he passed out. When he came to, all the drugs were gone. Again.

There was no thousand-dollar bill either.

Chapter Nineteen

Rose was cleaning up the dishes and Jamie was reading by candlelight inside the tent when Fitz came home.

He walked in the door, the rifle in his hand. On the way back from Jared's he had worked up an anger. He always did when he got drunk. This time it was Jamie and what he'd said. And it was Rose, too, and the bastard she was carrying.

She turned, and registered only calm as he advanced toward her. He had the gun held at his hip, slanting down toward the floor, but as he got closer, he raised it to waist level, aimed straight at her stomach. He poked her with it and she drew back.

"I'm going to blast that bastard out." He lifted the gun, her belly in his sights. She didn't budge. She knew better.

"And the other bastard." He looked around. "Where is he?" He used the rifle to push open the tent flap, where Jamie was sitting, frozen upright, more scared than he'd ever been of his father before, the fright bringing tears to his eyes.

"Little bastards, both of them." Fitz slurred as he spoke.

Rose pulled herself together. She was used to his drunken

scenes. This was nothing compared to some of them, though it was disturbing. Gently, she touched his shoulder, then turned him away from Jamie and led him toward the door. She used a technique that always worked.

"Jenny needs feeding," she said. She knew Fitz cared more about the donkey than about them.

"I've got a nice stew I'll heat up for you when you come back in."

Fitz stumbled out, and Rose turned back into the house.

Better not to raise the temperature by meeting anger with anger until it boiled over. Keep it at a simmer, and let it cool off.

Like the stew she was spooning onto a plate when Fitz returned.

Fox stew. Stringy and tough. All lean muscle. She'd had to cook it all day. Fox. A bullet through its head. The gun was useful. But sometimes she thought that if she knew how to use it, she'd put a bullet through Fitz's head. She picked at her food. Jamie picked at his. Fitz wolfed his down, and, without a word, left the house, hauling the mickey out of his pocket as soon as he was outside. He looked blankly at the driveway. Shit. No truck. He'd walked home. Why, he didn't know. He couldn't even remember.

Must be at Jared's. He stumbled down the road as the snow began to fall.

Behind him, Jamie followed. He'd slipped out of the house unseen. Why, he couldn't say.

Ian looked out his window. The snow had begun suddenly and was falling rapidly. In ten minutes, there was already more than the slight dusting that had been promised. Carpenter Harold MacLean was The Shores' self-appointed weather forecaster. He was usually wrong – except when the weather was bad. His forecasts were always gloomy. He had prognosticated a big one, and it looked as if he were right.

There, making footprints along the road was Fitz Fitzpatrick, weaving and swaying, mickey in hand, singing, not Christmas carols, but ribald take-offs of seasonal songs learned from Jared, who'd picked them up in jail. He stumbled and fell, right in the roadway, and didn't get up.

"Dead drunk," said Annabelle, blowing through the door with the North wind at her back.

"Dead for all I'd care," said Ian. "Better off dead for those two up there."

"That's as may be," said Annabelle, "but we better get down there and pull him off the road."

Neither of them noticed that Jamie had slipped in behind Annabelle, and heard what Ian said. He went white, and whipped out the door ahead of them. When he got down the hill, there was his father passed out on the road.

Dead? Hope and fear together leapt inside him. Guilt, panic, confusion, desire all intermingled into an emotion he could not have named. He ran to his father. He tried to roll him over. Fitz grunted. Relief and disappointment blended in Jamie's eyes. His father was alive.

Then he heard the swishing of wheels on the new, wet snow. He jumped up and stood in front of Fitz and began waving his arms. A truck was headed straight for them. Jamie kept waving. The truck kept spinning forward.

Ian and Annabelle reached him just in time and yanked him off the road, he screaming for his father as the vehicle advanced, braked, skidded, and swerved, just avoiding Fitz, and landing nose down in the ditch.

"Nathan!"

It was Annabelle's son and his girlfriend Lili. She emerged from the vehicle.

Too calm to be injured, thought Annabelle.

She tried to control herself as she hugged Lili. She reminded herself that it wasn't the first time Nathan had skidded off the road into a ditch. He was a daring driver – excellent – but wild. He always emerged unscathed.

When Nathan tried to get out of the truck, which was nose

deep in the muddy ditch, a shot of pain stabbed through him from his ankle, cut through his body, and came out from his eyes. He threw up, and fell forward, unconscious, leaning on the horn. The airbags had not deployed because Nathan had disabled them. He'd done it because Lili was so tiny they could have killed her.

The blaring horn awakened all of Annabelle's maternal instincts. She slid down into the ditch and wrenched the car door open. Lili was right beside her, and both began to drag Nathan out of the cab.

Ian hopped down beside them.

"Are you sure you should be doing that? Moving him?"

Annabelle looked around wildly.

"What choice do we have? It will take them forever to come from Winterside."

Nathan was the volunteer paramedic at The Shores and had a van rigged up to act as an ambulance. They called it Florence.

"Leave him in there, then." said Lili. "I'm going to go get Flo."

"Take my car. The keys are in it." Everyone left their keys in their cars in The Shores. Except Jamieson.

Annabelle stood in the muck seeping over the top of her short boots, cradling Nathan's head, unaware of the vomit that was smeared all over her.

Jamie and Ian dragged Fitz off the road.

"Wait here with him," Ian said to the boy. "I'll go get my truck." Ian was glad, not for the first time, that he'd replaced his hybrid Insight with a truck. The previous vehicle had been an environmental statement, but at The Shores a truck was more practical.

When Ian returned, Annabelle was still holding on to Nathan, stroking his head, thinking about the other son she'd lost and how she couldn't bear to lose this one. And at this time of year. Fitz was still groaning by the side of the road, alternating snippets of the drunken songs he'd been singing while panic erupted around him.

"Bastard." It slipped out before Ian could check himself.

"What's a bastard?" Jamie asked, hearing the word again. His father had used it about him and now Ian was calling his father one. The word had been bothering him all evening. His smooth young forehead crumpled in concern.

Annabelle quickly shook her head, signaling Ian not to get into it. Ian went ahead anyway.

"A blessing. Some of my best friends are bastards."

Jamie's expression cleared.

"So it's good?"

"Well, it can be."

"Are you a bastard?"

"I've been called that, but no, I'm not."

Jamie turned to Annabelle.

"Are you a bastard?"

"No, dear, I'm not."

"But I am?"

"No," she said. "Who called you that?"

"My father."

"Why?"

Ian wondered, too.

Why?

Lili arrived in Flo, and they got Nathan into the back, strapped into one of the two cots. He was still unconscious.

"I'm going, too," said Annabelle.

"No," said Lili firmly.

"Why not? I'm his mother."

"I can't drive you. In this weather. I'll risk my life for Nathan, but not yours as well."

"Then let me drive."

"No," Lili insisted. "I know this vehicle. Nathan has taught me all about it. I just can't take the two of you."

Lili was not usually stubborn. She was generally a very accommodating person. Ben, thought Annabelle, as soon as Ben got back, she'd have him take her to town.

She looked up at the sky, worried. If and when Ben got back. He'd left in the tiny Matrix, no four-wheel drive, no snow tires. And the snow was no longer a dusting. It was thick, heavy, and worsening.

Would Lili even make it across the causeway?

The windshield wipers couldn't keep up with the snow. It didn't matter. The view through them was a wall of white. Lili was depending on the odometer to tell her where they were, by distance. Near the causeway now. The causeway – a thin kilometre of land that joined The Shores, uncertainly, to Red Island.

A storm surge had scoured across it a few years back, and ripped it apart at its most fragile spot. It had been shored up, tons of rock brought in, but a subsequent storm surge had shifted the massive rocks that had seemed so solidly planted.

This fall, the province had put sandbags all along the ocean side, in fear of another storm surge during record rainfalls. Not likely to be very effective. Still, the sandbags would be something soft to bump into if she went off the road. She tried to banish that thought.

Lili's hands were gripped so tightly on the steering wheel that they were turning white. She worked on bringing back the calm that was her usual state. It was hard to feel calm with Nathan in the back. Conscious or unconscious?

Nathan was having a dream. Two dreams, really. In one, he was tearing down a gully through the snow, after little Jamie. But he got there too late. In the other, it was her he was following. Her? Rose? And then there were Oliver and Jamie, both in the woods in the snow.

And then the snow took over his brain, a cloud of snow blanketing his thoughts and dreams.

Nothingness.

I hate him. I hate him. I hate him.

Jamie had slipped away, leaving his father with Ian and Annabelle. He was fearful of what might have happened to his hero Nathan. Nathan – unconscious in a ditch, Jamie's father to blame, lying drunk on the road.

Jamie ran all the way up Shipwreck Hill and down the other side. He turned into the driveway, but he didn't go into the house. He just kept going. He wandered, desperately, on the snowmobile trails through the woods. Soon he was on no trail at all, but battling his way through, the spruce scratching at him. He didn't care. He didn't know where he was going.

He didn't know what he was going to do when he got there.

Chapter Twenty

Ian pulled out of the driveway at Wild Rose Cottage. He didn't wait to see Fitz into the house. He couldn't bear to look at him – stumbling along in the snow, still singing those disgusting songs. There was puke in the cab of the truck. Vomit, the smell overtaking the brand-new scent.

As he drove back home, there was a streak of lightning, so unexpected he almost swerved off the road. He braked slowly, stopped, and looked at the sky in wonder. He listened carefully and heard the low, muffled rumble of thunder.

He smiled. Thundersnow.

He'd heard about it, but he'd never experienced it. It delighted his scientific mind. Then he frowned. It was rare, thundersnow, and when it occurred, it usually meant a big storm. He thought about Lili and Nathan. They should be over the causeway by now, that is, if – Ian tried not to think about it. When he got home, where Annabelle had stoked the woodstove and made fresh coffee, he had to suppress his excitement about the thundersnow experience. On a normal day Annabelle wouldn't care much about his weather discovery, but tonight everything about the weather would concern her. She would pepper him with questions about what it meant. He didn't want to tell her what it meant.

A severe storm, a blizzard, up to three inches of snow every hour, that's what it meant. Annabelle didn't need to hear that. He breathed in the smell of the coffee. It almost wiped out the smell of sick in his nostrils.

He searched his mind for something to talk about, to keep Annabelle's mind off Lili and Nathan and the hazardous journey they were on as the wind picked up and the snow drove sideways into the window, blurring the outdoors. Still, the village lights could be seen. *Light. Hope in the darkness,* Annabelle thought, and broached the subject that had brought her to Ian's in the first place.

"You know Germaine has gone to Halifax."

"Yup. Heart surgery."

"Well someone needs to read the Christmas verses. Hy asked me to find someone."

"Uh huh." Ian was only half listening. He was thinking about the thundersnow, wondering, if he went out again, would he hear it? See the lightning? Now that was rare, really rare.

"You must do it. There's no one else."

All thoughts of thundersnow swept from his mind.

"Me? I can't do it."

"Almost anyone could do it better than Germaine Joudry."

Germaine couldn't speak English very well, and certainly couldn't read it. In spite of this impediment, he'd been reading the biblical passage at the Christmas show for twenty years. The ladies liked it because they thought he had a "biblical voice" – baritone-deep and judgmental.

"But it's the principle of the thing. I'm not a believer."

"Oh, c'mon, Ian…"

"What about Ben?"

"I love him dearly, but he can't read two words in a row without stumbling."

Ben, she thought, *still not back*.

"Abel?"

"Do you think he'd show up?"

Ian went through the list of potential males, even including Jared MacPherson, to which Annabelle sputtered. The suggestion helped pull her out of her anxiety over Nathan and Ben.

"Any of the ladies?"

"Too shy, most of them."

"Not Hy."

"But she's got enough on her plate already. Besides, she wouldn't have asked me to find someone if she was prepared to do it."

"Maybe she was being modest."

"Hy? Modest?"

There was a silence, a silence long enough to bring Annabelle back to her fears. She had a sunny personality, but her eyes were clouded, and her fears for her son showed through. She couldn't lose Nathan. She'd already lost one son.

The worst thing that can happen to a mother had happened to Annabelle – she and Ben had lost their first child. A beautiful bouncing baby boy – ten pounds, five ounces at birth. So what could possibly have happened? Sudden Infant Death Syndrome. One moment, alive and chortling, then falling asleep with Annabelle's good milk trickling out of one corner of his always-smiling mouth, and then gone. Gone.

Ian knew the story even though he hadn't lived in the village at the time. It's why he finally agreed to read from the Bible at the Christmas show. To brighten her up. It did, for a moment.

"But don't tell anyone," he added.

"Well, Hy – "

"Especially not Hy."

Annabelle didn't get it, but she agreed to it. How was she going to keep it from Hy? Hy would be badgering her to know if she could think of someone, if she'd found someone.

The Christmas Pageant was the last thing on Hy's mind at the moment. She'd gone up to see that everything was okay at Wild Rose Cottage, to try to convince Rose and Jamie to come to her house "for the duration" was how she put it. Fitz was nowhere around. Rose was glad of it. He'd gone out and hadn't returned. She hadn't seen Jamie in a while either.

Rose wasn't concerned about Jamie. She had no idea he'd gone out. He always told her when he did. She assumed he was knocking around the house somewhere. She could lose track of him for hours in this big place.

Rose refused to go with Hy, but invited her to stay instead, as the snow thickened outside. Hy worried about getting her truck up and down the hill, but she had snow tires and four-wheel drive. It should be okay. The two were sitting around the wood range, sipping tea, when a biting pain sliced through Rose. She jumped up and doubled over.

"What's wrong?"

Rose was in too much pain to answer, but Hy could tell it was serious. She got on her cell phone and rang Nathan, but his cell phone was vibrating in his pocket in the back of his ambulance and he was oblivious to it. So was Lili, streaking through the snow, trying to remember everything Nathan had told her about driving in bad weather. Thank God she'd finally convinced him to put snow tires on the vehicle – just last week he'd given in and done it. Even so, the van had only a tentative connection to the road. That's what it felt like to her. Just as she drove onto the causeway, she shut her eyes and began humming "om." It was not as foolish as it might seem, closing her eyes. She couldn't see anything anyway. She might as well have the spirits guide her. It was not a technique Nathan would have supported, but there was nothing he could say about it now.

Rose bent over suddenly, grimacing in pain.

"What's wrong?"

"Contraction."

Contraction? "You're pregnant?" So there was a baby.

"Not going to be anymore." Rose sat down, slowly, the pain easing.

"How far along are you?"

"About four months. Maybe more, maybe less."

"So, if this is it, there's no hope?"

"No hope," said Rose. "Just as well."

Lili negotiated the causeway, and all the curving roads on the way to Winterside through sheer love of Nathan. She almost went off the road twice, but managed to correct the vehicle the way he had taught her.

Lili pulled the van in front of Emergency and jumped out. A nurse and a doctor came flying. Dr. Diamante and Ed weren't even on emergency room duty, they were on a smoke break outside, but there was something about Lili, something that galvanized them into action.

The doctor immediately took Nathan's pulse, put a stethoscope to his chest, and opened his eyelids, one after another.

"Hay-zoos," he said. "Get him in – quick!"

Lili paled further, if that was possible.

Ben almost went off the road when he saw his son's truck in the ditch. He pulled to a stop in front of Joudrys'. Estelle waved him in from the window. She'd been staring out when the accident happened, and had maintained her post ever since, content to steep herself in others' misery, full of guilt at not being with Germaine in Halifax where he was having the long-awaited heart surgery. But Estelle had never left The Shores, not for any reason, and now she was afraid to. Sixty years, all of them here. Never a trip to Charlottetown or Winterside to shop, see the eye doctor or dentist. Her teeth were bad, but her health was good.

Ben burst through the front door, never used in The Shores, but it was the closest. His snow-wet, clay-red boots stomped all over Estelle's treasured hooked rug, the last one her mother had made, sewing the border on her deathbed. Estelle pursed her lips, looking at the imprint of his boots. Not easily cleaned. Then he made it worse. Noticing the mud, he scuffed at it to remove it, only grinding it deeper in. She'd have to wait until it dried. She'd have to look at that mark all that time. Even if she got it out, she'd never see the rug again, only the stain.

Ben grabbed her and shook her, forgetting himself in his panic. He'd lost one son. He couldn't bear to lose another.

Chapter Twenty-One

"I've done plenty of them." Gus looked around – at the smoking wood range, the windows that let in the draft, the quilt hanging over the door and billowing out as the wind hit it. And at the tent.

"But not here," she said. "I won't be doing it here."

Rose was crouched down on the floor, bending over from the pain of another contraction. Hy looked at her watch. Only one minute apart.

She grabbed Gus by the arm.

"Gus, you've got to. It was all I could do to drive down and bring you here. It's like someone poured grease on the roads. There's no traction."

"Just contraction," Rose huffed through another one.

"Well, all right then." Gus rolled up her sleeves, gave her hands and arms a good wash, and said. "Better get up on the table. If I crouch down, I'll never get up. Happened the other day. Went down on my knees to wax the floor, and it was an hour before I could pull myself up again, with Abel the Lord knows where."

She turned her attention to Rose again.

"Has your water broke?"

"N-nooooo…" the word rose with the contraction.

"No water." Gus looked over at Hy. Hy shrugged.

"No good." Gus shook her head and bent to her task.

Annabelle flung herself at Ben when he came through Ian's door.

"How did you know I was here?"

"Estelle."

"Of course, the truck. How awful for you."

"And Lili's driving? You let her go?"

'No. She wouldn't take me. We have to follow."

Ben shook his head slowly, sadly. "No, Annabelle. The Matrix won't do it. I barely made it here."

"The snow tires are in the shed. If you'd only – " She stopped. It was no time for recriminations. Ben had been busy this fall. There hadn't been time.

"I won't have the whole family out on the road tonight." It was unusual for Ben to take such a firm stand against Annabelle or anyone. "We'll just have to hope Lili and Nathan make it to Winterside. When did they leave?"

It seemed like hours to Annabelle, but it had been only forty-five minutes. Enough time to get there in normal weather, but tonight –

Ben put an arm around her. Chilled by fear, she was still wearing her coat. He coaxed her out of the house, Ian following, not knowing what to say or do.

At the last, Annabelle turned to him.

"Our secret," she said.

Ian nodded and smiled.

"What secret?" Ben looked at them, puzzled, on the way out.

"You'll see," said Annabelle.

It had been a long time since Gus had attended a birth. She'd never been a midwife, but she'd helped lots of times, so often that the time melted away, and she knew exactly what she was doing.

Delivering a dead half-formed baby.

No water. No amniotic fluid. No hope. This would've been a bed-rest case. This baby couldn't flourish in its mother's dry womb.

Hy was amazed at how much Gus knew about babies and birth.

She ordered Hy about, and the mother, Rose, telling her to bear down. But this wasn't a birth, was it? The baby would be dead, pray God the baby would be dead, for it wouldn't live long, not at four or five months. Not having done what she knew it had done. Crushed its own umbilical chord. Unable to float freely in the desert of a womb. No oxygen.

What else could an old lady bring into this world? A dead baby. *Good for nothing,* thought Gus. *I'm good for nothing but dead babies and poorly patched quilts. Eight kids and not one I'll hear from at Christmas. Eight kids and not one grandchild.*

Why women went through it, she didn't know.

Rose bore down again.

The Diary:

Elizabeth had a baby girl today. It was stillborn. I asked what she would name it. She said, "Rose." She wants to contain the name, amongst the non-living. She thinks there's a curse on the house, on the name. She fears that there's a legacy of murder. The Sullivan legacy. Not great wealth. Murder.

The Sullivan legacy – murder? Oliver shook his head. Surely not. He'd been re-reading the diary, looking for any clue, any small clue. He looked out the window. It was a blur of white, blinding, the snow tapping on the glass, the wind gusting, retreating, gusting, and making the metal storm windows rattle.

He was comfortably cradled in the bed, atop the marvelous quilt, pillows supporting his back, one leg crossed over the other at the ankles, his jeweled slippers perched on his feet. Ginger lay on his lap. White, in his preferred place, circled the back of his neck, and Oscar was fast asleep on his chest.

Oliver read on, but in just a few moments, was asleep.

Jamie was rushing through the woods in the dark and wild night. In the woods, the storm was not so bad. He was sheltered from the wind by the trees, which held back the snow, so that it drifted down and landed softly. Here, in the woods, it was a winter wonderland, a deceptive beauty.

A beauty that was marred by Jamie as he went crashing along, stumbling in the snow, colliding with trees, whipped by their branches, falling over stumps. His eyes were closed. But it didn't help. He could still see the image of his father lying on the road, having forced Nathan, his hero, into the ditch. He'd protected his father on the road, with a strength that had come from somewhere, and then he backed away from the stench of liquor on Fitz's breath, and watched the adults take over. Watched as Nathan was pulled out of his truck.

Unconscious? Dead? Did my father kill him? I'll kill my father. He hurts everyone.

Jamie thought about Freddy. *He kicked her. He tried to shoot her.*

Jamie was crying, crying from the gut, heaving sobs as he ran, the salt tears scouring his cheeks. A surprised rabbit, and a fox in pursuit of the rabbit, stopped as he passed, then began the chase again.

"Just one more push. One more." Gus was encouraging as Hy held onto Rose's hand. Rose was gripping hard, her nails digging into Hy's flesh. Hy was trying not to cry out from the pain, so much less than Rose's.

And suddenly, she was there. Gus held her in her hands, bloody and slimy – a tiny, tiny child. A little girl. But her skin was blue, and she wouldn't cry, no matter what tricks Gus used from her vast experience. She had been born dead. If you could call it born. It was a miscarriage.

"Dead. Of course she's dead, isn't she?" Rose's voice was unemotional, resigned to losing a baby she hadn't really wanted in the first place, looking away from it. She had known it – the baby had stopped moving. When Fitz had pointed the gun at her belly, she'd felt the baby go still, and not a movement from it since. She was sad for the unwanted child, but angry too, angry because she thought it was Fitz's fault.

"How did you know?"

Hy felt helpless. She was still standing, still holding onto Rose's hand, staring at the baby, which Gus quickly bundled up and put on Rose's stomach.

"That she was dead?"

"No. That she was a girl."

"Oh, I knew that. I always knew that. I knew that she was gone, too." Rose held the little thing, looking at her perfect nose and lips, and a tear slipped down her cheek. A single tear.

Gus was cleaning up and setting things straight, and feeling herself foolish to think that she, at her age, could deliver a baby. That it was not her fault, she knew, but it didn't alter the feelings of inadequacy. Her role would become a local legend, exaggerated over time into a heroic, desperate battle to save a doomed child.

The child was doomed, born or unborn.

"Thank God." Rose drifted off to sleep on a whisper, the words barely escaping her lips.

Gus and Hy thought they must have misheard. Did she think the child was alive?

No. Rose knew exactly what she was saying.

Hy drove Gus back down to her house, in spite of the bad roads.

"I won't be sleeping in any bed but my own," she had announced when Hy asked what they should do.

"And if I was to be sleepin' somewheres else, it would not be here." Gus looked with disgust at the tent.

A mouse skittered across the floor.

That sealed it.

"I'll put my faith in the Lord," she said, as Hy started up the truck, having promised Rose to return. "That's what I always do when Abel drives."

Hy smiled and shook her head. Abel was nearly ninety and his license had been taken away. With Jamieson now in the neighbourhood, she was bound to catch up with him, if she could find him.

Hy had to weave from one side of the road to the other, zigzagging all the way up the hill, her driving style almost as erratic as Abel's. She had four-wheel drive and snow tires, but the way she was sliding around on the hill made her feel as if her four-wheel drive wasn't working.

It wasn't.

Gus gritted her teeth and grabbed the door handle. The door came open. The snow blew in. Gus slammed it shut, and jammed her hand up against the dashboard for safety. Just at the top of the hill, the truck slid back, and Hy prayed with Gus to make it go forward. It must have worked, because the truck stopped sliding when it hit a drift. The back wheels found traction on a small bare patch created by the drift and Hy managed to crest the hill. They slid all the way down toward the Hall, Hy clutching the manual shift, changing into first gear, her foot slammed helplessly on the brakes, popping the emergency brake, none of it working, reminding herself she'd always meant to take a skid control course. But was this skidding?

Gus was praying the prayer she always prayed when driving with Abel, and remembering the time sixty years before when their own car – the first one at The Shores, the pride of the community – had failed to make it up this hill. They'd had to get out and climb, in a blizzard as bad or worse than this. She had thought at the time that they would never make it. They'd even got lost part way. *Imagine. Lost. In full view of home.* But they hadn't been in view, because they hadn't been able to see a thing.

The truck reached the bottom of the hill, Hy still out of control in the driver's seat. The Hall loomed ahead of them, so close it was now visible through the intense snow. The truck leapt ahead, sliding straight at the Hall and the huge spruce tree, its sparkling lights slicing through the thick snow. Gus started praying again, and so did Hy.

The lumpy grass underneath the snow slowed the truck's momentum. It came to a stop just shy of the tree trunk, swallowed up in the branches, a couple of strings of lights on the hood.

The two women sat a moment without speaking. Gus was first.

"Close call."

"Yup."

"No one should be out on these roads," said Gus.

"Unless they have to be."

They both thought of Lili and Nathan – safely over the causeway? Now Gus prayed, for them.

If she'd been alone, Hy would have left the truck there, and walked home. But Gus had a hard time walking between her home and the Hall in good weather, so Hy got out, unstrung the lights from the truck, and tossed them back on the tree. She managed to manoeuvre the vehicle onto The Way and down the lane to Gus's.

"Abel's got the place lit up like a Christmas tree," said Gus.

It is a Christmas tree. Hy looked at the icicle lights dripping from the eaves all around the house. The six shining penguins along the walkway, Santa and his reindeer on the lawn, cleverly executed in plywood by Abel, and all wearing strings of light. The Jolly Elf was also perched at the chimney beside a sleigh full of presents.

But Gus didn't mean the outside of the house. That was just as it should be. It was the inside. The place was ablaze. Every light inside the house was on.

"He misses me when I'm gone." Gus smiled, indulgent.

Hy said nothing. *Misses Gus?*

"He's scared to be alone."

Scared? Alone is all he ever seemed to want to be.

Gus eased her way out of the truck, puffing with the effort, her old bones cracking.

Hy got out, too, and helped her up the walk and into the house, secretly hoping to get a glimpse of Abel in the kitchen. But no. *No one.* Just Toby the dog, in from the weather, unwilling to walk the few houses down to his own home at Ben and Annabelle's. There were cookies here, real ones. The human kind.

He looked up and smiled when the two women came in. Gus automatically went to the cookie tin and gave him one.

"Cuppa tea?"

"No, I've got to get back to Rose."

Gus opened her mouth to protest. *But someone must be with the woman.* "Happen you should. Be careful driving."

"Not driving. Walking."

"In this? You'll lose your way."

"Nope. Got a hiking stick with a compass."

It was a dark stretch of road up to Wild Rose Cottage.

Armed with a thermos of tea, Hy went into the wild night. The snow stung her face, snow that was half ice. She pulled her turtleneck up over her nose. She was wearing a classic Canadian trapper's hat, its earflaps snugly fastened down. For the first time, she found herself using the forehead flap. She'd always wondered when a person would need that. Now she knew, as the snow scoured every bit of exposed skin. By the time she was up Gus's lane, her toes were frozen, feeling like little ice balls sitting outside, not inside, her boots. Her hands, inside a double layer of wool mittens, were balled up into fists, to keep the tips of her fingers from freezing.

Soon, the effort of walking up Shipwreck Hill began to warm her, just like it did when she was cross-country skiing. She wished she were now. *Funny that, how a hill was easier to climb on skis than on feet.*

The north wind was at her back and helped propel her forward. And she had traction, special ice soles she'd pulled onto her boots as a precaution. She was glad she had. The hill was slippery and it took two steps to move ahead one. It was no better on the other side, going down. She had to prevent herself from sliding all the way, the snow was so greasy.

She never for a moment lost her way. She was even exhilarated at times, safe and secure in the knowledge of where she was, where help was – the light on at Ian's, the lights at the police house. On both, no Christmas lights. Ian and Jamieson shared that.

And anything else? Did they share anything else?

She was tempted to stop in at Ian's, but she was compelled into the dirty night. She couldn't leave Rose alone.

But when she got to the house, Rose wasn't there.

Chapter Twenty-Two

When Gus and Hy left, Rose stood over the sink, washing the child. Gus had offered to do it. So had Hy. But Rose had declined. She could still feel Fitz's rifle pressing into her stomach. The moment she had stopped feeling the movement of the child. She touched her belly with a wet hand. Still distended, though she had lost its contents, the tiny human she cupped in one hand. She patted the child dry with the cleanest tea towel she could find. She wrapped her up, her little Angel, in her mohair scarf. Itchy, but the child wouldn't feel it. She placed her gently in the basket she'd been using for bread. The little thing fit perfectly.

She would lie down, stop this dripping from her womb. She opened the flap of the tent and leaned in. Jamie. Where was Jamie? She'd forgotten all about him. Instinct told her she was alone in the house, that he was nowhere inside.

She looked up sharply at the window. Snow falling, the wind blowing, the house shuddering, the door creaking on its hinges, sounding as if it might be blown in at any moment.

She'd lost track of time and of her son. He might have gone

out, but surely he had come in? Had he seen – heard – the birth? Had it upset him? Her blood emptied from her veins, left her cold with fear. He must be somewhere in the rambling old house. Certainly not out – in this. White on dark. The white, white snow, caking to the window screen outside.

"Jamie?" She called for him as she moved toward the window and peeked through it. Nothing. She could see nothing. She turned and crossed the room into the front hallway, the wind wailing through the door, sending the horse blanket she'd attached to the frame, flapping up into the hall. At the bottom of the stairs, she called again: "Jamie!"

Could he hear her above the whine of the wind?

Her back ached. So did her belly, her insides, her womb. She was wet with blood in her groin, trickling down her legs. But she took the stairs, pausing every few to call again.

"Jamie." Her voice was lost on the wind, taken up in its whistling. She had no force to call louder. She got to the top of the stairs and called again. She was silent for a long time, listening for him. She heard only the wind. That – and the mice and the rats scurrying inside the walls, disturbed by the wind.

She went downstairs.

Jamie was not in the house. She knew it, the same way she'd known the child in her belly had given up on life. Back in the kitchen, she grabbed her thick shawl from the hook by the door and went out into the weather, the snow, almost ice, whipping at her naked face like sand. Huddled in the shawl, she made her way, step by step, fighting for balance with the wind, past the back shed and into the woods, a trail of blood following her.

The Hanged Man

The card stared up at him. This reading was no longer about the legacy. With Death in the core position, that is most certainly what it was about. There were cards of loss, grief, abandonment throughout the reading, and so many from the Major Arcana, and they were foreboding: The Devil, The Fool and Death. Over and over again, death.

Death was coming. Or had it arrived?

Oliver stared out the window, and then he did the unthinkable. He put on his coat and went out into the night, leaving White and Ginger – even Oscar – behind. The rat was safely nestled into White's fur, disappearing into the cat, so that when Moira went snooping in the room after Oliver left, she didn't see it.

Moira had managed to force Oliver into his big fur coat, but could not get him to stay in.

"On such a night," she said, thinking about what it would cost her to get her walkway shovelled, and wondering if she could get Billy to do it. He'd be home now, and in the morning that witch of a mother of his would have him shovelling *her* walkway.

After Oliver had gone, Moira laid newspaper on her floors again, adding more layers than usual against the weather that would bring dirty boots into the house. She wondered if she could get Billy to turn the front porch into a mudroom.

Oliver had always been surprisingly agile for his size and weight, but he was having a tough time getting up Shipwreck Hill. He was driven there by the cards, one card in particular. The one he clutched in his hand. It impelled him forward.

Oliver walked all the way up the hill, propelled not so much by his legs, but by determination, by a certainty that this was a night out of which no good would come, and that it was up to him to –

To what? He stopped at the crest of the hill to catch his breath and to think for a moment. The cards had held death in them. In the reading, the critical one had been in the reverse. What did that mean? He realized then that there was a card in his hand.

And there, on the top of the hill, where the wind blew most brutally, he stood and stared at it. The card. In reverse. He began the mental journey into it. He searched around it. He saw what he was meant to see, and slowly, very carefully, he came back out of the card, not feeling the biting wind, the snow accumulating on the shoulders of his coat, his bare hand aching with the cold and the razor edge of the card biting into it. He turned into the woods, and he walked to his certain destination. He knew exactly where he was going and he knew what he would find there. Or create there. That part he didn't know. Either he – or someone close – Rose, the child? – was about to do something they might regret.

Sometimes the cards told Oliver things he'd rather not know. This was one of those times.

Then he saw the boy.

First the boy.

Then the woman.

Whether they saw each other, he couldn't tell.

But it was playing out just as the cards had said it would.

He crushed the card in his hand. Dropped it.

The Hanged Man lay bright and dreadful on the snow.

Jamie still didn't know where he was going, what he was doing in the woods. He wasn't lost, not physically lost. But his love for his father was lost. Gone. That's what he was running away from, but he couldn't get away, stop the thoughts about his father. His wretched father. Layer by layer, Jamie's love for Fitz had been peeled away, until there was nothing left, until his soul was raw with disappointment, with his father's failures, one after another, that had turned love to hate. Eye-shining admiration to disgust. The last layer had come off tonight, on a raw and unhealed spirit, reeling from the sight of his father lying in the road, of Nathan unconscious in his truck.

All it had taken was a few decent men—Ian, Nathan, Oliver—to show a genuine interest in him, for him to realize what a poor father Fitz was. Jamie didn't have the experience to know what Fitz had done to his mother, but he could imagine. And what he imagined was a dark place he didn't want to visit. A dark place his mind was entering now, as he thought of turning back, finding Fitz, and…and…What could he do?

The tears came in a fresh flow, his discouragement welling up and wetting his face, so that he could not tell what were tears and what was snow, falling wet and heavy.

His billy boots impeded him, making him trip and stumble face-first into the wet snow, which washed him of the salt tears. He kept falling, plunging his freezing hands into the snow. They were red and raw and hurt around the wrists, where the moisture had gathered under the cuffs, rubbing at him. The same thing was happening to his ankles. His boots were wet through inside and were causing blisters on the bottom of his feet. The third time he fell down, he didn't get up right away. Instead, he pulled off the boots. His feet were bare underneath. He had not, as his mother always told him, put on heavy socks to keep his feet warm and make the boots fit. He wished he had them now. His feet were red and, curiously, warm. He could feel heat, not cold, in them, so he put the boots back on, got up, and continued on his way. Where?

It was then that he saw his mother.

He followed her. And soon, she was following him, though neither knew it.

On the way into the woods from Moira's house, Oliver passed a dumping ground from before the politically correct days of waste management. There were oil tanks, bits of old farm machinery, all rusting or rusted out; but the pride of the Wild Rose Cottage dumping area was a 1950 Chevy, its original soft turquoise colour still visible in patches, the rest stripped clean, its perfectly round headlight openings gaping emptiness. Every usable piece had been taken and used for something – including engine parts, car seats, and windshield wipers. The doors and trunk had been pulled off, the window glass smashed, and there was moss growing on the dashboard.

Fresh urine was dripping down the hood of the car.

Oliver's sensitive nose picked it up. He followed the trail with a surprising nimbleness, down the long hill to the gully. He was following a trail of blood.

When he saw Fitz, anger boiled up in him and turned him red with rage.

Ben and Annabelle had arrived home to a phone message from Lili, letting them know that she and Nathan had arrived at the hospital, but that Nathan was still unconscious. They called the hospital several times through the night, but there was no change.

Dr. Diamante talked to them personally.

"I cannot say when – if – he will wake."

"If?" Annabelle's voice rose in terror on the short word. She was on the kitchen phone, Ben on the mobile extension, both clinging to the receivers and to each other.

"We cannot say, with injuries to the head...the brain...what may happen."

"But he's young..." Annabelle.

"...strong..." Ben.

"It doesn't matter that he is all these things. We don't know what the extent of the injury was to the brain. It floats around in the head, you know. It depends how hard the impact was when it hit. Until...when...if he wakes, we won't know the extent of the damage."

"Can't you do an MRI?"

"If we but could, we would."

The Winterside hospital was equipped with nothing so advanced. That would mean a trip to Halifax.

As if reading Annabelle's mind down the phone line, the doctor said, "We cannot risk moving him now."

Nathan had been hit – hard. Ben had examined his truck, shaking with anger that Nathan had disabled his airbags. They'd had an argument about it, a rare blowout. Both were by nature too easy-going to get worked up. Ben saw, though, that airbags might not have helped. Nathan had been struck in the back of the head by a toolbox that flew up from behind him. There was dried blood on the box and a new dent in it. Ben smiled grimly. Hardheaded kid.

"There is the vomi….vomi…" Dr. Diamante had lost the word, and turned to the easier one. "Pook. He pooked. This is not good."

"Pook?" Ben didn't get it. *Puke.* Annabelle mouthed the word.

"I am sorry I cannot tell you more. Perhaps the family should come in when you can."

Annabelle paled at the doctor's words. He was famous for them. "It's time to call the family" meant he thought someone was dying.

But that's not quite what he'd said, Annabelle reassured herself as she put down the phone.

Rose scrambled along the side of the creek, looking for her son. She was following his prints. She didn't know they were old prints, left from his running around in circles in the woods, distraught and disoriented by his new-found hate for his father. They were also becoming quickly obliterated by the heavy snow and the wind creating drifts along his pathway. She wondered why he'd come out. She wondered why she had, too, and pulled her shawl around her. She'd only meant to step outside the door, to call Jamie in. Then she'd panicked when he didn't come, and came out herself. The wind was whipping the snow up and at her. Her feet, wearing indoor slippers, were freezing and wet, her face red with the snow hitting it like sand. There was a bright red trail on the snow behind her.

The evergreens were thick and beautiful on either side of the trail down to the ravine. The branches hung heavy with snow, some clumps knocked off by passing humans. There were fresh footsteps in the snow. The trail sloped gradually for a while, and then became steep. The foot treads slipped down the hill to the gully below, the creek running high, the trail just barely cresting it above the culvert.

A couple of coyotes were huddled in the trees. They'd watched the young, tender boy, deciding if they were going to make a move. Now they watched Rose, and smelled her blood on the air.

The battery level on Hy's flashlight was low. It produced a weak wash of pale light that illuminated very little. She was searching through the house, looking for Rose, calling out to her in a loud whisper.

Stupid, she thought, *why can't I make more noise?*

The house was so big in its silence, it unnerved her to crack it. The place was creepy, but even creepier when she made noise.

She could hear and sometimes see mice and rats skimming across the floor. The sound of shredding coming from the library grated on her ears. It was a big sound, not like a mouse or a rat, not like a squirrel – she'd had encounters with those in her own attic. She was compelled to look in. The bright eyes of a raccoon stared back at her when she shone the flashlight on it. It was ripping apart Volume III of *The Encyclopedia Britannica* 1942 Edition and eating its pages. She saw the word *crustacean* hanging out of the creature's mouth. She felt queasy.

The raccoon froze when she saw Hy, stayed statue-still. So did Hy, paralyzed for a moment. She backed out of the room, slipping the door closed behind her. Raccoons could be vicious.

She hoped that it had another way out.

Her skin was shot with sensitivity, goose bumps all over it, hair rising. Inside her skin, her blood was fueled with adrenalin.

Why am I doing this? Rose can't be up here. Unless –

Unless something has happened to her.

And then it occurred to her. *Jamie. Where was Jamie? He hadn't been here all night. Had something happened to him?*

Rose clambered up the hill out of the gully, away from the horrible scene, from the man who had destroyed her life. Away and home. The home of her ancestors. She had some feeling for it, in that way. Otherwise it was just another crazy scheme that Fitz had cooked up. How they'd go to her family home, get all kinds of help from the neighbours because she was a local, and soon be sitting pretty. They could even start an inn or a bed and breakfast if she wanted.

If she wanted. There wasn't anything she wanted except for her and Jamie to be safe. Safe. When had she ever been safe with him?

But now she knew she was safe. *Safe from him. Jamie and she both.*

She was breathing with difficulty. She'd been on all fours all the way up the hill. She stood up and dusted off her hands, red with the cold. When she did, she looked down and saw the blood. She looked behind her and there was a trail of it. She kept going, her gut aching, cramps nearly doubling her over, blood marking her way in the tread of her slippers. Deep dark blood, from the very depths of her, spilling out onto the snow, the flakes falling on it, and making it run, turning it pink.

The snow would soon cover it.

She struggled across the field, against the wind, her damp shawl snapping at her shins.

Jamie. Perhaps now –

She shook the thought from her head. Home. Get home. He must be there by now. He'd be wondering where she was.

Unless he'd seen her.

Had he seen her?

The snow was blinding her, disorienting her. She needed to know that Jamie was safe.

Well he was, wasn't he? He was safe now. They both were.

Chapter Twenty-Three

The snow bank on the side of the creek had given way under Jamie. He lay in the water, just out of Buddy's reach. Buddy was terrified of water. Even of this water, this creek, only waist-deep. He didn't know why. He'd erased the memory of his father trying to drown him like a kitten, at birth. It was his first and only real memory, a sensation that stayed with him. The sensation of being dropped into the cold dark water. Not warm, like the water of the womb. Dropped in and held down. He could remember his own infant cries, reverberating in his ears. He remembered struggling. He remembered a creeping feeling of euphoria, on the tipping point of drowning, when he was suddenly yanked out of the water, back into the world. That's all he knew. That's almost *all* he knew. He didn't know that if his father had not tried to drown him, he would have been normal. Ugly, but normal. A hare lip and bulging eyes. A big mouth over which he seemed to have no control. He drooled when he was born, and he would drool constantly until the moment he died.

His father had tried to kill him because he was ugly. But this child was beautiful.

Buddy stared at Jamie. At the water. He put a foot forward, tentatively, touched the water and yanked it back.

Jamie moaned. The beautiful child with the golden hair, now wet and pasted to his skull, making him look very young, very vulnerable.

Buddy must. Buddy must do this. Buddy forced himself to step into the water, his own infant cries shrieking in his ears, the world around him losing focus as he reached toward the child he could no longer see. His hand hit the water and he reeled back for a moment, pulled himself together, and tried one more time. His hand landed on Jamie's face. He felt the soft cheek.

Tenderness welled up in him. He picked him up gently. Forgetting his fear of water, he took a couple of lumbering steps to the edge of the creek, and, with a strength he didn't know he had, stepped up onto the bank and out of the water.

Jamie was semi-conscious, a wet weight in Buddy's arms. Burdened by his own laboured walking, he had the extra weight of the child to carry up the hill and out of the gully. But he did it – through sheer determination. Up and out of the shelter of the woods into the furious night, with nothing to guide his way other than his sure knowledge of the terrain, and the tiny flicker of candlelight in the house off in the distance. Buddy headed straight for it. When he got there, he slowed his pace, came within a few feet of the door, stopped, and looked in.

Hy had just come back into the kitchen. Buddy smiled. His friend.

Hy saw the shadow flitting at the window. *Rose?*

The door burst open, and she jumped. There stood Buddy, with Jamie in his arms.

"What!" Hy rushed over, about to grab Jamie from him, when he put a hand up to his lips.

"Sleep."

"But what?...where…?" Stupid to ask questions. He couldn't

answer them.

"Little one safe. Buddy keep safe."

"Here, give him to me."

Buddy looked puzzled, resisted. "Safe," he said. "Safe with me."

"And me." She gestured impatiently. "Please, we have to get those wet clothes off him."

Roughly, she took Jamie from his arms, and, oddly, the child did not wake. A spike of fear pierced through her. Not dead? She laid him down and touched his cheek, felt the warmth of breath coming from his slightly open mouth.

"Where have you been? Where did you find him?"

Buddy stood, holding his arms as if he were still holding the child. Open and empty. A tear slid down his face, and met up with the drool sliding down his chin from the right side of his mouth.

"Buddy woods," he said.

"I could figure that out," she said. Why was she being nasty to Buddy? Buddy knew friendly from unfriendly tones. He'd protected the child, and now Hy had taken him away, making Buddy feel bad.

Buddy turned and slipped out of the house before Hy could offer him tea. She shook her head in annoyance with herself for being short of patience with him, frustrated that he couldn't tell her what had happened.

Buddy left, confused. He should be going home, but his mind was back at the creek. With that man who was there, but gone.

Gone. Will Buddy go away someday, too?

Jared turned and ran from the culvert. *Should he help Fitz?*

Jared didn't know and he didn't care. They weren't going to pin this one on him. He went out the way he had come in – through a trail in the woods that joined with his own woodlot, and out onto the lane that took him home. He didn't think about the footprints he left behind him. He'd worry about that if he were questioned.

Questioned. His blood buzzed with fear. He'd be questioned, he was sure. Somehow the cops always got around to it, whenever anything happened near him. What would he say if he were questioned? It had been just a simple dope deal? Had they argued? Should he admit that much? Just a bit of a disagreement over price earlier in the day. He wouldn't say that Fitz had walked off with all his drugs. What if he were charged with murder? It could happen. Just because that old lady had died when his truck hit her, they'd think he'd done this, too.

He stopped in his tracks, and in his thinking, turned and approached Fitz, slow step after slow step. He jumped back when the feet jerked and the body moved. Not dead, then. But soon. Jared reached and grabbed the twisted plastic bag of drugs hanging out of Fitz's pocket. And the money.

All there. He grinned, and lit off once again into the night. He'd need a joint when he got home.

Hy was trying to get Jamie's wet clothes off when he woke and wriggled away from her.

"You're soaking wet."

"I can do that," he said, squirming away from her. Hy realized he was just old enough to be embarrassed about someone other than his mother undressing him. Old enough that maybe he wouldn't let his mother do it anymore. She threw a blanket around him and he slipped into the tent.

When he emerged, in dry clothes, Hy gave him a mug of hot tea. He lifted his head to drink. He saw the basket. He saw the baby. The dead baby.

"What's that?"

"Oh, Lord." It shouldn't be she who told him. The burden of the responsibility overwhelmed her.

The door opened. Rose, her hair sticking to her head, her neck, her chest, was blown in on the wind. She struggled to close the door, and then leaned up against it to hold it fast. She was trembling.

"Thank God you're here." Hy felt instantly unburdened.

"I got lost. I thought I'd never make it back."

Jamie leapt up and hugged his mother.

She winced. He pulled her into the room. They both stood shivering by the wood range. The house was freezing, so cold it was cracking in places. But that wasn't it. Not all of it. It was the baby. His sister. He looked at the basket, then up at his mother. Gently, very gently, she explained to him. He listened, face falling.

"You lost my sister?"

"Yes, dear."

"Does she hurt?"

"Not anymore."

Something else to lay at his father's door. But not anymore. Not anymore. Another reason he was shivering.

He couldn't rid himself of the image of his father. He couldn't rid himself of the sense of relief. Nor that of guilt. Shame. Fear. But relief was the strongest emotion. Relief that now his mother would be free. Free to be with someone else who would be good to her, who wouldn't make her lose babies. Oliver?

As if Jamie had called him up, Oliver walked in the door.

"Here you are, my lad." He swept in, red in the cheek, his jeweled slippers soaked, his feet frozen.

Then he did what always amazed people. He folded down into a Lotus position at the front of the tent, uncurled, and stuck his feet out toward the fire.

No one spoke for a moment.

"Been out in the weather, son?" Oliver asked Jamie.

"Been out," Jamie mumbled back.

"Well," said Oliver, coming to the point immediately. "What shall we three do? What shall we say?"

They stared at one another. They cast glances at Hy. They were silent.

For the first time, Hy felt unwelcome in this house. She was curious, but knew she had no right to be here, that something was going on between the three of them that she had no right to know.

She excused herself, not looking forward to the walk home in a blizzard. Perhaps she'd stay at Ian's.

No one tried to stop her from leaving, which meant her instinct was correct.

After she left, the three sat up most of the night, saying little, and that all lies. The only eavesdropper was the dead child, wrapped in the mohair scarf in a basket on top of the table, away from the rats and the mice.

The snow stopped just as dawn was breaking. Ben fired up Nathan's snowplow, a blade attached to Ben's farm tractor, and went into the village to plow out his neighbours. The villagers had bought the blade and paid the gas, so it was an obligation to clear them out first, no matter his personal problems. The villagers paid what they could for Nathan's labour. After he'd plowed everyone out, Ben edged down The Way, making a lane across the causeway.

When Ben got back home, he went to the shed, rolled out the snow tires, and put them on the Matrix. Annabelle had her coat on already, and had packed food for Lili. Nuts and seeds. Some dried fruit. Not enough to feed a bird. But it's what Lili had requested. She wanted to keep her body and mind clean through this difficult time with Nathan – as if by starving herself he would recover. It wasn't starving she sought, but purity, an open route for the life energy to flow from her to him.

If Ben and Annabelle hadn't been so troubled, they might have appreciated the beautiful winter world, the sun gleaming on white drifts, multicoloured diamonds sparkling on the snow. The wind had whipped it up like meringue or April Dewey's thick white icing, carving sculptures, creating a world of dark and light, blue shadow on snow tinged with pink – the red clay that the wind scraped up and mixed with it. It was a different world, The Shores in winter.

Ben and Annabelle drove across the causeway. After that it was slow going, because no one had come to plow the provincial highway, not at this end. They never hurried. It could be two or three days, even a week.

Who would be going to The Shores?

Chapter Twenty-Four

As soon as Ben had plowed her out, Jamieson went down to Ian's. She knocked on the door, and was surprised when Hy answered. The kitchen smelled of fresh-brewed coffee.

"Jane. Jane. Insane. Pain." Ian's bird went into a squawking gale of laughter, amused by herself, or pretending to be. Jasmine wasn't parroting anyone now. Jasmine had started spouting poetry and rhyming when Ian had left the TV on one afternoon, and she'd watched non-stop children's shows.

Jane? Jamieson looked at Hy. Hy avoided her glance and poured two coffees.

Jane? Where had Jasmine heard that? It rankled Hy. *Pain. Insane.* She smirked.

Insane? Jamieson declined the cup Hy offered her.

"Ian's still asleep, if you're looking for him."

Jamieson lifted an inquiring eyebrow.

"I was at Sullivan's last night," said Hy. There she was, talking just like the locals, calling a house by the name of the previous occupants instead of the present ones. Still, there was a Sullivan there – Rose.

"She had a baby."

"Mrs. Fitzpatrick?"

"Yup. Rose. A little girl. A miscarriage really. Four or five months."

Was there a softening in Jamieson's face? If there was, it didn't last long.

"Why wasn't I called?" *They always come in storms, these difficult babies.*

Hy took a sip of her coffee.

"No phone."

For once Jamieson didn't know what to do. *Was it a police matter?*

Hy knew Jamieson well enough to guess what she was thinking.

"I really don't think you should worry about it. I was there. Gus was there. There was no foul play. Simply a baby born dead, poor little thing. You'll have to shortcut procedure, whatever it is."

Jamieson stiffened. She didn't like to be told that she had to do anything.

"I've just called Dunn." It was the funeral home in Winterside. Jamieson looked dubious. Hy pressed her lips together. Disappointed. Jamieson was always disappointing her. With the disappointment came stubbornness.

"To get a death certificate. The baby can't be kept in a house full of rats until the coroner manages to make it out from Charlottetown."

Jamieson nodded slowly, thinking it through.

"The son, Duncan, has a snowmobile. He'll come out and pick her up."

Jamieson looked shocked. Somehow it didn't seem quite right – carrying a dead baby on a snowmobile.

"He'll carry her in his arms." Hy sensed Jamieson's objection. "Besides, what else can we do?"

"Can they afford it?" Surprising compassion from Jamieson, who, until now, had written the Fitzpatrick family off as a bunch of lowlifes.

"I don't know. But I'll pay if they can't. I'll call Dunn now."

"Dunn? Didn't you say you'd phoned already?"

"I phoned Dunn, the undertaker, but not Dunn, the doctor. Same family. Doesn't exactly inspire confidence in the doctor."

"They got you comin' and goin'," Gus always said. *"When one Dunn's done with you, the other will be as well."*

But Jamieson had already forgotten about the Dunns. The thought of the snowmobile had grabbed her attention. A snowmobile would be perfect. She'd buy one herself. She could have justified it as a police vehicle, but Jamieson didn't want to have to account for every time she used it. Sometimes, when she wasn't on duty – which was rarely – she'd like to use it to explore the capes, the fields, and the woods. The Shores was growing on her.

"Will the doctor come then? For the death certificate?"

"Dr. Dunn's too old to get on a snowmobile. Nearly ninety. He'll be going for the family discount soon. But they'll take the baby right to him, and he'll do what's necessary."

"What about her?"

"Rose?"

A curt nod.

"She says she's fine. If she is, there's no need, in these conditions, to move her. If she's not fine, the trip would do her no good."

Jamieson nodded, some kind of agreement.

Moira didn't know what sleeping in was. She had no experience of it. But this was surely what her guest was doing now, unless he was… She paled. Dead, not dead. Bitten by that rat and eaten by those cats. He'd come in so late – or early? – he may have been asleep only a couple of hours. Still –

She tapped at the door, so silently it wouldn't have scared a mouse.

She opened the door a crack, and could see, by the light coming in the window, that great lump of a man, sunk into the too-soft mattress, head propped up on pillows, cats asleep on his stomach. No sign of the rat.

She edged in, and came up close, to make sure he was alive. A book lay open on his chest. *Murder*, she read.

And then she saw the rat, curled up with the cats, and did something she'd never done before. She screeched.

It woke Oliver, of course. His eyes opened and he was instantly alert.

"Good morning," he said. "Can I help you?"

After Hy had made her phone call to Dr. Dunn, and Jamieson her call to the snowmobile dealership, Jamieson had returned to the purpose of her visit.

"Is Ian here?"

Ian, she'd called him Ian. Rose was Mrs. Fitzpatrick. Hy herself was McAllister. Jamieson had never called her Hy. Hy didn't know the reason: Jamieson thought it a ridiculous name. More like a greeting.

"Ian?" *She'd called him Ian. And Ian had called her Jane. He must have, for Jasmine to pick it up.*

"He may be asleep still. I'll go check. Have that cup of coffee. Make yourself comfortable."

Jamieson didn't respond to either suggestion. Was she capable of making herself comfortable? Hy shrugged and went upstairs, calling: "Ian! Someone here to see you."

He still had sleep in his eyes when he finally appeared, and his hair – what there was of it – was sticking up. He was smoothing it down as he came into the kitchen. He was wearing a T-shirt and sweatpants. He'd put on a few pounds since the previous year, when everyone in The Shores had been on a fitness craze, but he was still a pleasant-looking man.

"I'd like your version of events last night." Jamieson's pen was poised over her notepad.

Hy looked at him sharply. What events? He'd been awake when she arrived last night, but she had been so full of news of the baby, he hadn't had a chance to say anything.

"Ohmigod," she said when she heard, hands flying to her mouth. "Annabelle. I better go see Annabelle."

"Just wait a minute," said Jamieson. "You were at Fitzpatrick's last night, when Ian dropped him off."

"Yes, but – "

"But what?"

"He never came in the house, not while I was there."

Jamieson had a feeling. She didn't trust them, but she couldn't stop the feelings. Something didn't feel right.

Nathan was still unconscious, the usual high colour in his cheeks a disturbing white. He showed no sign of coming to, even though Lili was gripping his hand so hard the pain alone might have brought him up from under.

"In his own good time," said Dr. Diamante, lifting the line of his single black eyebrow. It was thick, but not bushy, neatly trimmed, and seductive above his big dark eyes.

When the doctor lifted Nathan's lids to look at his eyes, they were glazed. They were without life, energy, vibrancy to warm them. Lili shivered from the awful sense that Nathan wasn't there.

"In his own good time," Dr. Diamante repeated. Small, dark, foreign, he clung to those five words as his prescription for his patients' friends and families. Five of the words he knew best in English, and he liked the sound of them.

They gave Lili little comfort. Nathan's own good time was as soon as possible. Nathan was always in a hurry. If Nathan were there, inside that immobile body, he'd be itching to get up and out of here.

Lili wasn't herself either. If she had been, she'd have been floating on a sea of calm, aided by her chanting of "om." But it had given her up. Her charm hadn't been working for her. She hadn't been able to utter the sound "om" and make it swell into that beautiful vibration that felt and sounded as if it were circling the world. When she'd tried, it came out as a grating, halting sound that refused to go anywhere – not even around the room, much less the world.

For once, "om" had abandoned her.

Or she it?

And Nathan? Had he abandoned her, too?

There were six other words Dr. Diamante knew well in English: "It's time to call the family." He hadn't voiced that death sentence yet, but he was thinking about it, rehearsing the words in case he needed them.

One more word he was learning. It was coming from that room – suddenly, finally, after a night of guttural attempts. A deep soothing sound, out of that tiny girl. Lili had finally found herself.

"*Ommmmmmmmmmmmmm.*"

What did it mean? How did she hold her breath so long? He played with the sound, softly, tentatively, as it swelled, surrounded him.

"*Ommmmmmmmmmmmmmmm.*"

He felt strange, dizzy. He hummed a little louder, joining with her. The sound began to vibrate. The specimen containers on Ed the nurse's tray rattled as he came down the hallway. He stopped, staring at the tiny Italian doctor making the weird noise.

Was this foreign medicine, this incantation? The deep hum throbbed and absorbed Ed into it. From the tiny girl in the room down the hall, the threads of it had reached out and entangled the doctor. Ed felt its tentacles reach out beyond the hospital walls, clutching at and finding other such sounds spinning in an orbit of sound, circling the Earth, swirling into the whirr of the galaxy, blending with the song of the universe.

Ed had been smoking dope last night. A lot. He caught up the sound and joined in with Dr. Diamante and Lili.

"*Ommmmmmmm.*"

"*Mmmmmmmmmmm.*"

Two snowmobiles buzzed back and forth across the causeway in tandem that day. One driven by Duncan Dunn on his sad mission. The other, by an employee of the Winterside snowmobile dealership. He'd come to deliver the vehicle, bought sight unseen, to Jamieson. Such is the collegiality of the island that the undertaker had agreed to give the salesman a lift back to town.

Rose was shuffling around the kitchen, after a visit from Gus to see that she was all right – not bleeding excessively. Gus was very matter-of-fact about it. They'd never had doctors to attend to these things at The Shores and women like Gus had become skilled in watching for warning signs.

It was perfect snowman snow, sticking itself together when rolled, but Jamie had made only one halfhearted attempt at one ball of snow. Rose could see him through the window, kicking at the snow, turning around in slow circles.

The baby, she thought. He's upset about the baby. In the morning, he had touched it on the cheek, looked up.

"My little sister."

Rose had nodded mutely. She now looked over at the basket on the kitchen table. Little Angel, she'd named the baby, because how could she not? Her little Angel, too good for life. This life wasn't good enough for any baby who came into it. So why was she in it? Why Jamie?

Rose was sad, but not overwrought. She hadn't wanted the baby from the start. Especially not after the way it had been conceived. Fitz – roaring drunk, slobbering all over her, pushing her down – if it wasn't rape, it was close to it. The next day, she knew she was pregnant. Her breasts had swelled and so had she – with rage. She could have killed him.

No, she hadn't wanted the baby, but that didn't mean she'd wanted her to die. She felt she should look at her, little Angel in the basket, to do her some honour, to recognize her existence before she was gone. But she couldn't. The tiny perfect eyelids, the nearly non-existent nose, the pink lips, so sweetly closed. She didn't have to look. That face was burned into her brain, a memory that would always be there when her mind sorted through its miseries.

Numbly, she handed over the child, still wrapped in her mohair scarf, to the undertaker when he came. If only he had not looked quite so much like a corpse himself. Skeletal thin, cadaverous, long hollow lines down his face where there should have been flesh, was only skin. Chunks of brittle hair on his head, as if it had rotted off in the grave. Long boney hands as he took the tiny bundle. And then his face transformed. It was a professional trick, but it appeared heartfelt. Perhaps it was. A slow, gentle, comforting smile on that corpse-like face, before he turned, got on his snowmobile, and roared away.

Rose would never forget that face, that smile, the sight of the child, so briefly hers, taken away on the snow. A snow angel.

She might have wished she could forget both those faces, but she knew she never would, not even when she stopped torturing herself with them. For the rest of the morning, they were all she could see.

Chapter Twenty-Five

Jamieson was in love. With her brand-new snowmobile. She'd asked for black, but they had only red. She resigned herself to it, but the more she looked at it, the more she liked it. It made her feel…happy. Yes, happy. A strange sensation, one she wasn't used to.

She'd waited with impatience as the salesman explained all the features of the vehicle. She was already on it before he pulled out of her driveway on the back of Duncan Dunn's black vehicle. Jamieson had tried not to, but had seen the tiny child, snuggled into the man's sheepskin jacket. Tiny, too tiny for life, looking merely asleep.

Now she was buzzing across the winter landscape, the vehicle vibrating under her, the sound isolating her, so that she was in the machine, a part of it, humming across the snow.

"I see a man."

That's what he always said when a woman asked him for a reading. And since that first one, Moira was constantly asking.

Her lips parted in a half smile.

It always worked.

Oliver believed in the cards, but he could be cynical about them, too. Otherwise, he never would have given a reading, short one card.

That he would be called to account for that soon, he knew. For now, he was content to lay out the cards for Moira and watch the warm glow spread across her usually dull grey complexion, bringing a small joy into a thin life.

There *would* be a man. The cards told him that, and though he'd been prepared to cheat, was pleasantly surprised to find out that he didn't have to.

There would be a man. Not right away, but soon. Not the man she thought of all the time.

Poor man, thought Oliver, looking into Moira's hungry eyes. Not the kind of hunger that pleases a man. The kind that consumes him. And as he laid out the cards, Oliver felt as if he were condemning the man. There would be muffins and smiles for a while, then Moira's offerings would be laced with expectation and bitterness.

"This crosses you." It was a card of desolation, homelessness, the man and woman huddled against the cold, outside a warm and inviting home where they could no longer go.

Not that Moira would ever be homeless, Oliver knew, but her home would always be cold and unwelcoming, man or no man.

And then came the surprises. There were the cards that showed the man and the union, but another card now, The Lover. So the other would not be out of the picture. The other would remain foremost in her mind. And the young one would escape. The little bird would fly the nest, and leave Moira and her man here in their tight distrust and disappointment.

The honeymoon would barely begin and it would be over.

He couldn't tell Moira that.

But the reading could have been worse, if, say, the Hanged

Man had appeared in it. But he didn't. The Hanged Man was not in the deck.

Fitz did not show up the next day. Nobody noticed. Everyone was thinking of Nathan, still in a coma. Nathan, the bright young lad who'd done so much for so many of them, the volunteer paramedic who'd saved lives, the lad who took seniors without transport into town once a week in his taxi – a large SUV that seated eight. He donated the day, charging only a nominal amount so the elderly could afford it, but wouldn't feel as if they were receiving charity.

Now he lay where he'd taken so many of them – in hospital.

Annabelle and Ben stayed in town with Annabelle's sister, Ruth, but spent as much time as they were allowed at Nathan's bedside. Their daughter Rowan, the Celtic singer, had come over from Halifax to be with her parents. Together with Lili, they formed a tight circle of love and desperate wishes around Nathan, who did not stir.

What running was to Hy in the spring, summer, and fall, skiing was to her in the winter – a reason to go outdoors, healthy physical exercise, and a way to clear her head and release stress. It was not something she shared with Annabelle. Annabelle fished with her husband Ben from May to September – and that was enough physical activity for her.

"Running? I run this big house and that damn lobster business," she'd said, when Hy had asked Annabelle to join her. "That's enough running for me." Flopping back into her oversized armchair, she stuck a well-manicured foot on the footstool.

It would be good for her, Hy thought, take her mind off what was happening with Nathan. Hy had gone out early, striking off straight into the sun rising over the cape. She propelled across the long field next to her house.

Hy was headed for the high ground above the shore. Chunks of white ice floated on the navy blue water.

The icebergs looked like a flotilla of ships.

Jagged icicles sliced down the sides of the sea rock. The rock was a distinctive part of the shorescape, a chunk of land that had been carved away by the action of the wind and the waves.

The waves were splashing up against it and against the cape, forming a frosty icing all down its red banks, right to the shore.

Winter sand. Pale pink with the snow mixed in, looking like a marble cake.

Between Hy and that sand was a long hill, perfect to ski down with the fresh snow slowing what otherwise would be a reckless stunt.

She shoved off from the top to gain speed, and took the hill, exhilarated by the cool air on her cheeks, the speed, the sense of control she felt going down a hill of just the right pitch, in just the right conditions.

She came up from the beach, half-tempted to take the run again. Instead, she sped along the top of the cape and performed her annual mid-winter check of the cottages on The Shore. It was a new tradition for her, because most of the cottages were new. They'd been popping up in spite of the notoriety the Shores had gained for all the deaths and murders in the past couple of years. Or maybe it was because of the notoriety – and the difficulty of getting into The Shores when the weather closed the causeway.

"Yes, we have to fly in by helicopter," the drawling voices of the well-heeled would one-up their friends' tales of how remote their vacation hideaways were. And the murders? Just the shock to their sensibilities that their jaded emotions required. Or maybe it just made them feel at home. They could leave the streets of New York, but still take murder on holiday. And be closer to it. There had been some disappointment that the summer had passed without incident.

Hy looked down on the village. All the houses had been built facing inward, away from the sea and into the community. The village was situated in a depression in the landscape, a bowl. The houses circled around the bowl, a cluster of a community, tied together physically as well as mentally, and genetically. In the end, everyone was related.

Except, of course, come-from-aways like Hy, Ian, and Jamieson. It tugged at Hy, who felt so at home here. Sometimes she thought resentfully, *we're all come-from-aways. The only difference is how and when we got here.*

Behind her, the cottages of the other people from away, the summer residents, had their backs to the village, looking out to sea.

That said something.

Later in the day, Hy skied over to Wild Rose cottage with some supplies.

Jamie's eyes popped open as she poled down their lane. He came dashing out of the house without a jacket.

"Can I do that?" he yelled.

Hy came to a stop, almost losing her balance when she did, looking like an awkward stork rather than an accomplished skier. She coloured, her cheeks already flushed from the wind and the exercise.

Jamie laughed, and tugged at her sleeve, making her more uncertain on her skis.

"Can I?"

Hy stuck a pole on the boot fastener to release one foot, then another. Jamie was ready to jump into them right away.

"Whoa," she said. "You have to have boots on."

"I do." Jamie looked down at his feet.

"Not billy boots. Boots like mine." Hy had the old-fashioned kind – squared off at the toe. Jamie screwed up his face, then looked disappointed.

"You have big feet."

"Aren't you the gentleman?"

Jamie shrugged. Stuck out a foot.

"My feet are big, too."

Hy smiled. "Yes, just about as big as mine. A six or more, maybe, and she just barely an eight. "I think I have a pair at home that will fit you."

"I can wear big socks."

"We'll see what we can do."

"And the skis?" Jamie looked down at Hy's long, long skis.

"If the boots fit, the skis will, too."

Hy left Jamie playing with the skis, trying to use them in spite of his boots.

Rose was inside. There was no sign of the baby or the basket. Of course there wouldn't be. Hy would have stayed with Rose when Duncan Dunn came, but Rose had said she'd rather be alone.

"It's done" was all she said when Hy came in.

"Yes, I assumed so."

There was a silence. A silence that went on too long. Hy didn't know what to say.

"How are you feeling?"

"Physically? Fine."

"Don't you think you should see a doctor?"

"I'd rather not, just now. I think everything's normal. Bleeding a bit, that's all."

Her tone ended the discussion. She took the kettle off the stove and poured a pot of tea. She handed Hy two mugs and gestured her into the tent, where they sat down.

"And Fitz?"

"Dead for all I care."

"Do you really mean that?"

Rose didn't answer. She didn't need to. It was clear from the hard cast of her eyes, the grim line of her mouth, that she meant it. *Why is she with him?*

"How did you – ?"

"Ever get mixed up with him?" She looked down, unable to look Hy straight in the eye. "He was charming. I knew he was no good, but that's the attraction, isn't it, when you're young?"

Hy thought of her own past. It was true. "Sometimes, yes it is." She grinned at Rose, who gave her a half-smile, and poured them each a mug of steaming hot tea.

"But Fitz was more than just bad, he was wicked. Evil."

"Was?"

"Well, back then – and now." Rose looked away from Hy. Hy did what she'd seen Jamieson do when she wanted to get information from someone. She said nothing.

It didn't take long for Rose to break that silence.

"Our – his – daughters. The twins."

More silence. Rose took a gulp of tea, as if swallowing courage to speak.

To speak the unspeakable? Hot fear, along with a terrible knowledge pierced through Hy.

"You mean…?" She couldn't speak it either.

Rose flushed, fast and deep. She shook her head, horror on her face.

"Oh, no, not that." Shook her head again. Looked down. "Almost as bad."

She murmured the last so low that Hy had to strain to hear it.

"Rose, if not that, how bad could it be?"

Rose lifted her head, her embarrassment shifted to anger. She glared at Hy.

"They were sixteen when I met him. I was already pregnant with Jamie when I found him with them, drunk out of his mind, thirsty for more, selling their…favours…to his friends for booze."

"Favours? Not – ?"

"No, he wasn't pimping, at least not quite. Ten bucks for a feel, more for some parts of the body. He traded on the fact that they were virgins."

"Just as bad," Hy murmured in much the same way Rose had, her voice robbed of its strength.

"I helped them get away from him. I put the fear of God in him. Except he was godless." She shuddered, in spite of the warmth of the tea. She brought it to her lips again, and felt the heat through her body, but it didn't stop her shaking and shivering. It wasn't the cold that was chilling her blood.

He was godless. There was that word "was" again.

"And Jamie?"

"Let's not talk about Jamie."

Well, he's a boy."

"Yes," Rose nodded. "Still, I don't know what to think. Fitz might be capable of anything."

But she knew that Fitz wasn't capable at all anymore.

Chapter Twenty-Six

"No news?" Gus was sitting at the quilt frame in the large room behind the kitchen that was only used for family gatherings and quilting.

"Of Nathan – or Fitz?" Hy guessed that Gus was about two-thirds finished the stitching.

"Nathan, of course. Almost gave this up when I heard about what happened." The news about Fitz and Nathan had spread quickly down the Women's Institute phone chain – aided by the fact that a few were still on a party line in The Shores. Many of those who now had private lines were resentful. Some, including Estelle Joudry, had bought police scanners, and found they picked up cell phone transmissions. Just like the old days, they could listen in.

"Yes, I almost stopped." Gus continued pushing the tiny needle through the fabric, picking up four or five tiny stitches at a time. "Then I thought about her, poor soul. She needs every kindness she can get."

"No, I don't know anything." Hy pulled up a chair, threaded a needle, and began to stitch along with Gus, not as expertly, not as tidily or with stitches anywhere near as tiny, but she was no longer shy to join Gus. It was expected.

"I haven't heard from Annabelle since yesterday. If there were good – or bad – news, I'd have heard something by now."

"And Fitzpatrick? Is he back home?"

Hy shrugged. "Don't think so. Went over to see Rose this morning. He still hadn't showed up."

"He'll be on a binge, a bender with that Jared MacPherson." Gus snipped off the thread with her teeth. "Up to no good, that's what they'll be. Has she checked MacPherson's?" It was the first place Gus thought of when anything bad happened in the village. "His truck's down there, you know. In the driveway."

"It is?" Trust Gus to know without going out. Probably got it from Ben. He'd plowed Jared out, too, though everyone wondered why.

"Spect he's lyin' passed out in it, freezin' to death."

"I don't know if Rose cares," said Hy, remembering the matter-of-fact way Rose had greeted her that morning. But then she remembered the trembling hands, the concern with which she seemed to be watching Jamie, wanting to know every minute where he was going, what he was doing.

Jamieson felt a rush of guilt when she spied it. Here she was, escaping onto the capes and the thrill of the snowmobile, and there it was – Fitzpatrick's truck, beside MacPherson's own, in his driveway, an accusation of her delay in taking up the investigation of Nathan's accident. She sped down, came to an abrupt stop, jumped off her vehicle and knocked on the door, but there was no answer. Could the two of them be dead drunk inside? Though she knew the door would be unlocked, she didn't try it. She couldn't just walk into a home uninvited, and she didn't have a search warrant. She had no reason to believe a search warrant was necessary.

Neither was a knock on the door. It burst open and almost swung into her. She leapt back, just missing Jared MacPherson's vomit. It splayed out across the white snow, smelling of sick and of rum, all brown liquid, not a bit of undigested food in it. Drink was food to people like MacPherson, Jamieson thought.

Jared was bent over, clasping his stomach, waiting to see if more would come. It did, but only a few spurts. Then it was over. He'd felt like dying. Now he felt just fine. Until he saw Jamieson. A scowl darkened his face. He swept a filthy sleeve across his mouth, sopping up the moisture.

"Whaddaya want?" His voice trembled a bit. He knew what she wanted. He wished he didn't know. He wished he didn't feel like shit right now, but was on his game, because he was sure she was here to play.

Cat and mouse. The thought flitted through her mind, as if Jared had placed it there. In a way, he had. It was always cat and mouse with people like Jared. Even if they hadn't done anything. And there was nothing to say he had.

Except for that truck in his driveway.

"Looking for Fitz Fitzpatrick." She stared at the truck, more to avert her eyes from the disgusting sight of Jared than for any other reason. "He here?"

Jared looked at the truck, too. *Jeez, why'd he have to go and leave it here?*

"Nope."

"But that's his truck."

"Yup."

"Why's it here?"

"Left it here. Too drunk to drive when he went."

"I'm surprised that would stop him."

"Too drunk not to know better." Jared grinned.

"Do you mind if I look inside?"

Jared shrugged.

"What do I care?"

He was right. In the end, it wasn't he who cared. It was Jamieson, as she walked into the filthiest house she'd ever been in – and there had been a few of them.

Her feet crushed pizza boxes strewn across the floor. Milk cartons. Rum bottles. Years back, most of it would have been cleaned off by Jared's dog Newt, but Newt had deserted his owner to become a village dog – welcome and fed in every other house. Even a dog couldn't stand the mess.

Neither could Jamieson. In the end, she took only a cursory look around. Every surface was covered in garbage. Cupboard doors were hanging on one hinge.

She couldn't help curling her lips in disgust. Jared couldn't help noticing.

"Needs a bit of work."

You're a piece of work.

"Let me know if Fitzpatrick shows up." She let herself out.

Hy had rooted out an old pair of skis and boots from the shed. Before she'd found them, she had fished almost everything else out – tires, gasoline tanks, whipper snipper, lawn mower, lawn chairs, nothing in order by season, all entangled in one another.

She skied back to Wild Rose Cottage. It was awkward with the spare set of skis, poles, and boots constantly slipping off her shoulder.

Jamie was thrilled. The boots fit him, with the help of the thick wool socks Gus had knitted him. Hy wondered when she'd found the time to do it. *Must knit in her sleep.*

Jamie was soon sliding over the snow, making rapid turns, falling into deep drifts, and laughing at himself.

Rose, watching from the door, smiled, then realized she hadn't seen him laugh or smile since Fitz had disappeared. Jamie, whose features formed a natural smile, her happy child. Her own smile turned to a frown.

"Now you've got your legs, let's go for a proper ski," Hy said.

Rose's frown tightened. Tightened in something like fear, it seemed to Hy. She and Jamie began to ski away from the house, Freddy charging after them. With Lili and Nathan in town, Jamie had brought her back to the house.

"Don't be going down that gully," Rose called.

"No," they both yelled back.

Hy was lying. She very much wanted to go down the gully. With this fresh snow, it would be a gentle downhill run, thrilling and beautiful with the spruce on either side clotted with fresh white snow, like a Christmas card. A Christmas card that had been a long time in coming to The Shores this year.

When they reached the trail through the woods, Hy turned onto it.

"No!" Jamie yelled. He sounded panicky. "Mum said not to."

Hy grinned at him.

"Don't tell me you do everything your mother says?" She shouldn't be leading him astray, but she was dying to take the run.

"*Ommmmmmmmmmmm.*"

Lili had been drifting in and out of consciousness with the mesmerizing sound. Floating in another world, then back to this world, the pings and taps and beeps of the hospital equipment performing the background soundscape, in which the doctor and the nurse, too, had become captive.

Then she would sink deep into that other place, where the roar of the ocean, the cascading of rivers and streams, the sound of the wind circling the earth took her away with them.

Suddenly, she came alert.

There was a new sound in the hum that could change the world. There was hers. There was Dr. Diamante's. There was Ed's. And there was…

Nathan!

Lili's eyes shot open.

Nathan lay on the bed, his lips pursed and the sound of a very faint "om" coming out of them. Holding onto the sound, she crept forward, afraid that the moment might be illusory. Behind her, the doctor and Ed crept forward, too. The director of the hospital was walking down the hall and the sound attracted him to the room. He was so puzzled by the sight that confronted him that he couldn't be outraged.

His best nurse, Ed, and his best doctor, although foreign, engaging in some heathen practice with an intensive care patient not expected to live.

But the patient was involved in the ritual, too. Like the others, he was humming that strange…strange what?…incantation, and his right arm was rising slowly, hypnotically. The arm with the feeding tube in it. It popped out. No one budged.

Nathan pulled off the respirator.

He sat up.

He stopped chanting and the others did, too.

He beamed at Lili, and she rushed into his arms.

"Not so fast," said Dr. Diamante. "We must examine him. This is a miracle."

"A bloody miracle," whispered Ed.

The director of the hospital slipped away from the door, and tread softly for a few steps before moving rapidly down the hall. He didn't want anyone to know that he'd seen. Because what he'd seen was certainly not medical procedure. But it appeared to have worked. He'd have to keep informed on the patient. And an eye on Dr. Diamante and Ed in the future.

Later, he found out that Nathan had checked himself out. In his own good time, thought Lili, as they headed back home, Nathan as fit as if nothing had happened.

Jamie had first called after Hy, then followed her. The skis slid underneath him, smoother than walking, the cold air whipped past him, stinging his cheeks, biting his ears. Jamie moved as if born to it, digging in his poles to pick up speed down the puffy white trail. Ahead of him, Hy was manoeuvring the curve before the gully and the bridge, and had calculated that she would be able to go right across the bridge and part way up the hill on the opposite side on the strength of the propulsion she was building up. She poled hard, increasing her speed in a delighted, reckless way, ignoring Jamie's cries behind her to stop.

Stop? Why would she stop?

Then she saw why. Over the bridge.

She raced right to it. She stuck her poles in the ground to stop, and sent herself flying up and into a solid wall of flesh. A body. She fell down into the water.

Fitz Fitzpatrick fell on top of her.

Jamieson had headed up to Wild Rose Cottage to see if Fitzpatrick was back home. Rose, her nose and hands red, had just finished washing the dishes, and was now stoking the range. Jamieson looked up the length of the battered chimney pipe. Another firetrap. She shuddered. She told herself it wasn't the old fear, just the cold in this house. She looked at Rose again. Wearing boots. In the house.

No, Jamieson thought, taking a look at the tent. Not a house. Her eyes swept the room. How could people live like this?

"Any sign of your husband?" Was this investigation of an accident turning into a search for a missing man? Maybe. She wasn't waiting for Rose to file a missing persons claim. She might never do it, with a husband like that.

"No, no." Rose sounded distracted. And looked it. She kept glancing at the window.

"Are you expecting him?"

Rose realized what she'd been doing and transferred her anxiety to drying her hands on a tea cloth and wringing it.

"No."

"Then – "

"Jamie. He's gone out skiing with Hy. I'm just concerned – "

"About what? He'll be safe with McAllister."

"Yes, but – "

"But what?"

"I'm just not sure where they've gone."

"Do you want me to go looking for them?"

"Oh, no, nothing like that. Please, sit down. Tell me why you've come."

Jamieson kept standing. "I think your husband's been gone too long without a word." Now Jamieson looked out the window. "And with nowhere to go."

"Have you checked Jared's?"

"MacPherson's been seen and questioned. Says he doesn't know where your husband is. That he didn't see him after he left. Said he was on his way home."

Jamieson was standing in front of the stove. It took all her control not to shiver, but this house was cold, even close to the heat. Front, warm; back, freezing. Her toes were going numb in her warm police boots. She was fighting a desire to get out of the house, struggling with a rigid discipline that forced her to get the job done, to hang on like a terrier. Gnaw like a rat.

"Besides MacPherson – any other friends?" It seemed an unusual word to use for a man like Fitzpatrick.

Rose shook her head.

"Acquaintances?"

"We knew nobody."

"I'm not asking 'we.' I'm asking 'he.' Was there anybody he knew around here?"

"If he did, I didn't know them."

"Has he disappeared like this before?"

"The odd time, but his truck's at Jared's."

"I know." It nagged at her, that. But MacPherson's story had seemed plausible – of Fitzpatrick, stone drunk, weaving down the road, mickey in hand, going to find Rose and "have a bit of fun."

"We'll have to start a search." Jamieson felt a slight thrill at the thought of using her snowmobile for real police business, not just transportation or sightseeing. That had been a lapse this morning, riding along the capes for the sheer fun of it, when a man was missing in a place too small to lose a quilting needle.

"A search?"

"Of the village, of the property."

Rose opened her eyes wide. Fear? Jamieson wondered what the woman knew that she wasn't saying.

"I think you can help me find your husband."

Rose had wrung the tea cloth into a tight little ball. It was she who sat down.

"Oh, I can't do that."

"Can't – or won't?"

Chapter Twenty-Seven

Hy shoved Fitz away and pushed her head above water.

"Here, grab on to this." Jamie stuck one of his poles at her.

Where had Fitz come from?

Hy looked up and saw the broken tree branch that had been the hangman's scaffold. It thrust out from the tree like a knife stabbing at the sky. It was thick at the base, held firmly to the trunk, and tapered to a spike that had snatched Fitz's chain and the life out of him. Now the body was jammed up against the side of the creek, where Hy had shoved him, head back, mouth agape. A red ring around his neck where the ridiculous bicycle chain he wore had choked him to death. He must have panicked, flailed about and twisted it, securing it around his neck. His eyes were bulging out, and glazed over.

Jamie was staring at his father, too.

Jamie, she thought. How horrible for him. But he turned his attention from the corpse and poked the pole again at Hy.

"C'mon. Grab this. You gotta get out of there."

Was he deliberately not looking at his dead father? Why? Couldn't he bear it – or didn't he care?

"I've got to take my skis off first."

The water wasn't deep, but her skis were sinking into the mud.

She plunged under the water and unlatched one, but struggled with the other.

"It's caught on something."

"Forget it. Get out!" Jamie yelled.

She yanked off the boot and freed herself. She grabbed the pole and he tugged. She fell back into the water twice, but finally made it up onto the bank, dripping wet and the coldest she'd ever been. Well, almost. There had been that other time. But she couldn't remember that, not really.

They climbed the hill, an agonizing climb, Jamie on his skis, Hy without them, but using her poles to move her along, her limbs stiffening with her frozen clothes, the toes on her bootless foot so numb they were like balls of ice. She couldn't imagine afterwards how she'd done it, those last few steps slow and clumsy as the cold began to take her over. Hypothermia. It wasn't long off.

At the top of the trail, Hy put a hand on Jamie's shoulder to steady herself.

"Ski home now," she said.

"No, I'm going to stay with you."

"You'll do more for me by getting home as fast as you can, bringing some dry clothes and help. Phone Ian. Phone Jamieson. Hell, phone Jared if you can't find anyone else." She was forgetting they had no phone. "Now go." She pushed at him and he took off, already able to work the skis as if they were part of him, moving fast. Hy followed, dragging herself forward with the poles. She had to keep moving. She couldn't risk hypothermia. She'd almost died of it as an infant. She knew the signs – not because she remembered them, but because she had studied them.

She was beginning to feel warm and drowsy.

Jamie was clinging to Jamieson on the back of her snowmobile, a sled hitched to it. In spite of their mission, there was glee on his face, as they tore out of the police house driveway and bumped onto the back field. He felt important. He was there to show them the way. Murdo was right behind on Ron Dewey's machine. Ron had left it behind when he ran out on April, and they were Murdo's now. The snowmobile – and April.

"There she is." Jamieson pointed at a figure struggling through the snow on all fours. They sped up, and just as they got there, Hy slumped down.

Jamieson rolled her over and took her pulse.

"Thank God," she said. In her haze, Hy half-heard. Was it real or imagined? Had Jamieson said that? That way? It sounded as if she cared.

Jamieson wrapped Hy in blankets and they strapped her onto the sled. She was impatient to go down into the gully. The child had said his father was there. Dead. She didn't want to lose a corpse like before, but she felt oddly protective of Hy. She sent Murdo on ahead.

"I'll be there as soon as I can. Don't disturb the scene."

"As if – " Murdo mumbled, the comment drowned in the roar of the motor.

The closest place was Wild Rose Cottage, short on water and on warmth. No, best to go to Ian Simmons'. Jamieson called ahead, dropped Jamie off at the police house where his skis were, and went on to Ian's. He was waiting at the door when Jamieson arrived. Together, they carried Hy in.

"Is she – ?" His face was etched with worry.

"She'll be okay, I think. You'll have to warm her slowly. Slowly." Her tone underlined the word. "Cool water on her hands and feet. Then lukewarm, and so on."

"That's okay. I've read up on it."

Of course he had. McAllister's story.

Jamieson had read up on it, too.

She'd also lost a corpse before. Last year. That wasn't going to happen this time. And now that Hy was safe, her mind was flying back to the gully – the gully where Jamie had told her his father was.

"I'm afraid I'll have to leave her with you. Fitzpatrick's been found."

"By Hy?"

"Yes. Dead." *Another one? Was death stalking her, reminding her of her loss and her guilt?*

"How dead?"

Jamieson almost smiled. You could take that two ways.

"Don't know yet."

"Not another murder?"

"Better not be."

Ian could imagine people would be lining up to kill Fitz. The list of suspects would be long.

"But who – ?"

"Everyone's a suspect."

"But not me," Ian grinned a silly grin.

Jamieson did not smile back.

"You as well. If it's murder."

He should have known better than to joke – or flirt – with her.

Hy was flying down the trail toward the culvert – only this time she had no sense of control at all. And no control over the nightmare. The lifeless body of Fitz Fitzpatrick suddenly swung before her, suspended from – nothing. Flying through the air, and she was flying toward him. She couldn't stop herself.

The impact was horrifying. His body came to pieces, but his head was now suspended by the bicycle chain, and his mouth was in a grimace. His hands reappeared, the body reassembled itself, and he reached for her.

She woke on a scream, and Ian was right there beside her, holding a cool cloth to her head. She began to shake from both the cold of the cloth and the heat generated by her dream, her body thermostat all out of whack.

"It's okay, Hy. I'm here. You've been having a bad dream."

She smiled weakly.

"I thought so, too," she said. "But it was pretty real when it was happening." She told him about it.

He laughed.

"Pretty real."

She smiled, a weak smile.

"I didn't know if I should wake you," he said.

"I probably would have killed you, thinking you were Fitz of the flying face."

Jamieson was staring at the body in the stream, his face contorted, gaping up into the sky and the tree that had killed him. She was examining the broken branch closely. Forensics' decision. That lazy Ralph Wilson had no intention of sending any of his men, or himself, out in the aftermath of the storm a hundred kilometres to the godforsaken Shores. That's why they'd put Jamieson out there. To deal with things like this. Obvious suicide. Murderers don't hang people.

She argued that it was only hearsay, that she herself hadn't yet seen the corpse.

"Then you better get over there," said Wilson, tweaking his mistress's breast and hanging up the phone. Hy had said the last thing she saw before she landed in the creek had been Fitz's legs dangling, that she hit them as she went by, then was thrown into the water as he came tumbling down on her.

Jamieson had no reason to disbelieve Hy, so she could assume that Fitz had died from a broken neck or suffocation. There had been a struggle. The branch was raw in several places, the smell of fresh spruce invaded the air.

The water was high, rushing over the rocks fuelled by the melting of the wet new snowfall, some of it splashing over the bridge, icing over what was left of the footprints there. Spread out and enlarged by the melting. Too many of them. She tried to piece together what had happened. Was it an accident – or foul play of some kind?

The body smelled. Urine. Tobacco. Marijuana. Rum. The scents were accented in this otherwise pristine place. Jamieson pressed a handkerchief over her nose, and leaned in to examine the wound. Terrible bruising around the larynx, the neck raw from grating against the bicycle chain that now lay limp around his neck. What had happened? Not suicide. An accident? Misadventure? Manslaughter?

Jamieson could only imagine the sequence of events that must have taken place on the culvert. She couldn't know, because she hadn't been there. Plenty of other people had. *It looks like the whole village has been here.* As the top layer of snow melted off, there were footprints iced in all over the place. Footprints – so difficult to gauge because they were enlarged in the snow. There were her own. Those she could account for because of the distinctive pattern on the sole of the RCMP boot. Then there had been Hy, on her skis, those tracks cutting through some of the prints. Jamie. Same thing. Then what appeared to be cowboy boots. MacPherson? Billy boots – big enough to be adult? Child? Hard to say. Adult woman perhaps. One large, one small set of what looked like slippers. Slippers in the snow? And blood. Spots of blood. A trail of blood, which led out the other way from the culvert, but Jamieson knew the trail circled back to Wild Rose Cottage. She strung yellow police tape on two spruce trees across the trail, and went to ferret out how the blood got there. It didn't come from Fitz.

His was a bloodless death.

Jamieson examined Fitz's footprints closely. Her interpretation would be crucial.

They were spaced far apart, a leap not a walk, the footprints landing heavily, evenly. In between them, the handprints, smudges in the snow, harder to discern unless you knew what they were. She knew. The handprints, deep into the snow, carrying weight. Rose had told her about the family's acrobatic past, and close examination of the series of prints…hands, feet…hands, feet… told Jamieson that Fitzpatrick had been doing flips. In spite of his reported state of intoxication, the acrobatics appeared to have been executed under control. So how had he gone flipping off the bridge and onto that tree – unless he was helped?

She examined the prints again. Was there a slight turning of the feet on the last landing? Was it enough to have unbalanced him and sent him flying in the wrong direction? It was just possible. She took measurements of the trajectory. It would only be rough, but forensics would have the mathematics to work with.

She couldn't make a casting of footprints in ice, so for now she took photos of Fitz's acrobatics. Hands. Feet. Hands. Feet. He flipped his way down the slope and across the culvert to his death. Such a cluster of footprints around Fitzpatrick's final flip. They could have been put there at any time. They could have been witnesses to the event – or its aftermath. They could have been there even before he did his acrobatics, which some appeared to be, his footfall heavy on top of theirs.

He could have been pushed. He very well could have been pushed. It could have been murder. At the very least, manslaughter.

She imagined Fitz, down here on his own. This was something Jamieson was good at, though she tried to repress it. Imagining what might have happened often led her to the truth.

The snow was falling, at first lightly, then thickening, the wind picked up and began to wail, even in the shelter of the woods. The sound of it circled around, until it became the only sound that he could hear.

He might have been singing and weaving across the culvert, taking a swig from his mickey.

The warmth of the liquor burned down his chest, mingling with the sweet taste of marijuana on his tongue. He was suddenly caught up in a feeling of expansiveness. Joy. A sense of his own strength and abilities. Immortal. And he began to flip. Back flips. One after another after another.

And then he misjudged, and in a freak occurrence had hooked himself onto the branch. Or was it something more? He would not have heard footfalls behind him, cushioned by the snow, not – at first – have felt hands on his back, had there been any, at the height of the final in a series of flips, hands that might have been both soft and insistent.

With the keen sense of the acrobat, in an instant he knew it was wrong, all wrong, and he went tumbling to his fate. A broken tree branch, jagged and menacing, thrusting up to the sky, caught the chain around his neck. He had struggled, and only wound it tighter. His hands grasped to tear himself free, but that just made it worse. His legs began to shake, independently of his desire. It seemed that every movement that he made only tightened the band around his neck that was robbing him of life.

His eyes glazed over. Bulged. His feet stopped kicking. His hands dropped to his sides, limp, giving up their doomed struggle to save his life.

There was one final sharp pain. And then cold. Only cold.

As life left Fitz Fitzpatrick, he smelled of rum and marijuana.

She stood on the bridge, staring at the tree, looking down at the footprints for some time. The acrobatics were obvious, and there seemed to be a clear trajectory to that ugly stub of a branch. A one in a million unlucky twist of fate. She'd seen accidents almost as strange. That's what accidents were, mostly. Unusual, and unanticipated, until they happened. But was it just an accident? Had someone helped Fitzpatrick to his fate? A push at the right moment, if not to kill, to harm? She ought to report her suspicions to detachment. It was becoming quite a habit not to. She wanted to report the murder, if it was a murder, when it was solved. Or clearly establish it as an accident, if that's what it was, before she made an official report.

In the absence of forensics, it was Murdo who dragged Fitz out of the creek. Jamieson watched, but didn't offer to help as Murdo rolled Fitz onto a trailer hooked up to a snowmobile. They took him to Big Bay Harbour, where there was an old ice house still in use. Forensics would send someone to pick him up – eventually.

When Jamieson returned, the whole village *had* been there. The scene of a death – escalating to a possible murder as the story went the rounds of the community – was much more exciting than a new cottage going up.

Jamieson had put her yellow police tape on only one side of the culvert – and there were at least a half-dozen ways through the woods that she didn't know about, snowmobile trails that approached it from the other side.

Everyone wanted to see where the man had hung. Hung himself? It gave the woods a new fascination. The villagers came, one after the other, on snowmobiles or foot, and stood there, right on the culvert, right on the evidence, staring at the tree, its jagged branch slicing upward. They speculated about how it had happened, and agreed that the tree looked malevolent. Lester Joudry had phoned Hy to ask her to pose beneath the tree for him.

Lester's call was the last straw for Hy. She'd been keeping at a distance from the case, because she didn't want Jamieson accusing her of interfering again, like she had the last time. It had ended with them on good terms, and Hy didn't want to break that fragile link. Part of her liked Jamieson, admired her even. Now that she knew something about her past, it helped explain that cold exterior, those glimmerings of a warmer heart inside.

But Hyacinth McAllister was like a cat – curious and unable

to stop sticking her nose where it didn't belong. Besides, she told herself, she didn't see Jamieson getting close to finding out what had happened.

Hy thought she might have a better chance through her friendship with Rose and Jamie. She'd see what she could dig up from Jamie at the rehearsal this afternoon, visit Rose in the evening, and collar Jamieson first thing tomorrow morning, to squeeze out of her whatever it was possible to squeeze out of her about clues at the scene. That there were footprints, and plenty of them, she had observed. If she were smart, she might manage to turn Jamieson's interrogation of her – it was bound to come – into an interrogation of Jamieson.

Chapter Twenty-Eight

"You were the last one to see him alive."

Ian knew that the last one to see a person alive was often a murder suspect. But was this even murder? And surely Jamieson didn't suspect him.

"The last one you know of."

"All right," Jamieson conceded. "The last one we know of to have seen him alive."

"Well, you surely don't think – "

"I have to think of every possibility. Please, give me all the details."

"Well, after he threw up in my vehicle – I could've killed him for that – " Ian smiled. Jamieson frowned.

" – after he threw up on my dashboard, Annabelle, bless her, cleaned him up, and I drove him home."

"And that's it?"

"That's it."

"Not quite. Can you describe how he got out of the car, when you pulled out, your last sight of him – "

"Stumbling through the snow. He fell a couple of times."

"Where was he headed?"

"For the door, as far as I could tell."

"And Annabelle?"

"Annabelle?"

"Where was she?"

"She was at my house that night. She witnessed the accident. You know all about that night. She was here all night."

"All night?"

The bachelor and the married woman. Jamieson raised her eyebrows and asked again.

"All night?"

Ian flushed. "No, of course not. Until Ben came."

"Nothing more?"

Jesus, she was persistent.

"She had something to ask me."

"What?"

"I'd rather not go into that right now, unless I have to."

"Not right now, but you may have to. I'll be speaking with Annabelle, of course."

"Of course."

"I'd rather not say, if I don't have to. It's between Ian and me. We don't want the whole community to know."

Good Lord, thought Jamieson. What had she stumbled on? Nothing that was any of her business, though she had thought…it seemed that once or twice…Ian had been looking at her a certain way. He'd called her Jane, and she hadn't objected. She'd felt warm when he did, but there was Hy. Was she just a friend – or more? And now this Annabelle? She hadn't pictured Ian as the village Lothario.

Jamieson shook her head clear of the unprofessional thoughts and returned to her line of questioning.

"Who was there on the road that night?"

"Myself, Ian, Lili, Nathan, and, of course, Fitzpatrick, and, for a while, Jamie."

"For a while?"

"Well, he disappeared."

There was a silence. One of Jamieson's famous silences that sometimes more than a question got a witness talking.

Annabelle leaned forward, shock on her face.

"You don't think – "

"I didn't say anything."

"But when I said Jamie disappeared – "

"I was silent."

Annabelle nodded. Jamieson looked out the window onto the Shore Lane, and was reminded of last Labour Day weekend. That disastrous weekend, when four people had died on Jamieson's watch, three of them murdered.

She looked back at Annabelle.

"I was silent because I was thinking – as you guessed – that Jamie was a possible suspect. Frankly, I wanted to see if it occurred to you, and it did. I've learned not to rule anyone out."

"But Jamie – "

"Jamie what?"

Hy barged through the door and hugged Annabelle.

"Annabelle. How is Nathan?"

Annabelle smiled.

"Lili's bringing him home."

Hy hugged her harder. "Oh, I'm so glad…"

Jamieson waited a few respectful moments, but her impatience was visible in the tapping of her pen on her notepad.

"I'm sorry, but I must continue my questioning."

Annabelle nodded and pulled herself together, sitting upright, Hy's arm around her shoulder.

"Any idea where the boy might have gone?"

"Jamie – you surely don't suspect Jamie," Hy blurted out.

Jamieson held up a hand.

"We've been there already. You must realize I have to know

everything that happened that night."

"Yeah, okay."

Annabelle answered, with reluctance. She didn't want to implicate the boy.

"No. I never saw him leave. I assumed he'd gone home to tell his mother."

"Logical," said Jamieson. But did he?

Unrelenting, Jamieson circled back to the scene of the road accident.

"Who else might have seen it?"

"Estelle Joudry, she sees everything from that front window of hers," said Hy.

"And Moira. Moira Toombs. She might have," said Annabelle. "She's always spying."

Jamieson looked up at the choice of word.

"Spying?"

"On Ian and Hy."

Jamieson looked at Hy. She flushed.

So there was something between them.

"It'll be Jared. We already know he's a murderer." Gus had the tone of conviction that she always used when she made statements that were short on fact. In her world, they were fact. And the fact was, she'd been telling Jamieson that Jared was a murderer.

"A murderer?"

Jamieson had just stopped in on her way up from Annabelle's, not expecting that Gus would have anything to tell her helpful to the case. Half a dozen quilt squares lay on the floor. She was unpicking an error in one of them. She tossed it down.

"What else would you call it? He'd been drinking and smoking drugs before he got in his truck and hit that old lady just crossin' the road to get her mail."

"When was this?"

Jamieson didn't wait for an answer. She hurried out and jumped on her snowmobile and headed for Jared's, wondering *Murdo... where was Murdo?*

Murdo was as comfortable as a cat, sitting in front of April Dewey's cookstove, breathing in the scent of her double-double chocolate chip cookies. He was preening himself like a cat, too, internally. Everything that Ron Dewey had despised about his home and family – the uber domesticity – was an elixir to Murdo, perhaps because he'd never had it as a child. He'd been raised by just his mother – no father, no brothers and sisters. He had two dreams, growing up. His mother had encouraged him in his first dream to become a police officer. His other dream had been a solid family life. It had evaded him until now.

He frowned. It was still evading him.

April was married. And she had six kids. That was part of her appeal.

Married, but less married than a week ago, he thought, sipping on the hot tea that was a constant in April's kitchen.

He'd left. Ron had left her on Friday. He'd told her he wasn't coming back. She could have the house and the kids, he said. He'd sped out of The Shores to the home of his mistress in Winterside, and hadn't come back. Murdo had spent every off-duty hour – and some on-duty ones – here at April's house, happily taking care of her and the kids. That mostly consisted of sitting in the big chair by the stove, sampling April's cooking and indicating his pleasure.

But these were early, tentative days, and Murdo knew he'd have to be as careful as a cat on the prowl if he wanted to catch this mouse.

He'd started by shoveling her driveway and her walkway and presenting himself at her kitchen door, *fait accompli*.

She was delightfully dishevelled when she opened the door;

the smudge of flour that usually appeared somewhere on her face was on her chin today.

"Oh, thank you," she hugged him spontaneously, something she'd never done before. For the first time he felt the pleasure of her plumpness in his arms. As delicious as her baking.

She invited him in and plied him with squares, which he did not refuse. That hadn't changed.

He forgot all about Jamieson.

That hadn't changed either.

A cat jumped on his lap, kneaded his thighs, dumped patches of white hair on his uniform, curled into sleep position, and began to purr.

If Murdo could have, he would have purred, too.

"I go down there, regular-like."

"In a snowstorm?" Jamieson shook off the wet beads of melting snow clinging to her hair. There was a light snow falling, making The Shores look deceptively like a fairyland. Jamieson was back at Jared's, sure MacPherson knew more than he had told her. She wasn't discriminating against him because he was a scumbag. She suspected everyone knew more than they were telling her. She was generally right about that.

Jared was feeling better today, recovered from the drink. His eyes could focus on the cop and he liked what he saw.

She's a nice piece, Jared thought, *even if she is a cop.* He wondered what it would be like to do it to a cop.

"Well – "

"Why did you go down there? You said he left here, drunk, to go home. You didn't say you saw him again. Met him?"

"Well – " How could she know? As if in answer, she looked down at his feet. Cowboy boots. The only one in the village who wore them.

"Your boots. The tracks were there in the snow. I took pictures.

Forensics will be able to confirm."

Jared squirmed. It was exactly the reaction she'd hoped for. A gesture that was an admission of guilt. Guilt about something. Murder? Probably not.

"Did you arrange to meet Fitzpatrick?"

"No – "

"If you leave me to imagine what was going on, you might regret it. A murder charge is a lot worse than a drug charge."

"You're not sayin' I kilt him?"

"I'm not saying anything. Did you?"

"Jeez, no."

"Then what were you doing there? You said he'd left here. Drunk. You said you didn't see him after that."

There was a long silence. A silence that produced nothing.

"A drug deal?"

Jared dropped his head.

"So it was."

"Not eggsackly."

"Not exactly. It is or it isn't." Black and white were Jamieson's shades of grey.

"He had sump'n of mine."

"What? Drugs? Cocaine?"

"Just some grass." A lie, she thought. It's never just some grass. "I wanted it back."

"Bad enough to go out in that night?"

"I was pissed. That's why I went out."

"Bad enough to kill him?"

"C'mon. Just a bit of grass…"

"Did you get it back?"

*Yes…no…yes…no…*the words flitted through Jared's brain. What was safest to say? He'd got the grass all right. And the coke. Would she know? Would she search? *Yes…no…yes…no.* She wouldn't find it on the body…he could've lost it…

Yes…no…yes…no…

"No."

Jamieson was disappointed.

No. What was no? How could it help the investigation? Probably a lie.

"How did you know where to find him?"

"I went up to his house. I followed his trail from there."

"To the gully?"

"Yup."

"Was Fitzpatrick dead or alive when you got there?"

Jared smiled.

"We smoked a joint together, so I guess he was alive."

"And he was still drunk?"

"Yeah, he was tanked. Like I told you before. Pissed."

"And you left?"

Jared nodded. "I don't like it down there. We was standing on the high ground over the culvert. It made me feel woozy."

"And did you give any thought to how your 'tanked' friend was feeling? I could have you on criminal negligence as well as dealing. I'll have to think about it. In the meantime, watch your ass."

But it was her ass he was watching as she left the house.

Chapter Twenty-Nine

"The show must go on." Hy got a kick out of saying the words, but she wasn't happy about the position she was in. Jamieson had made it clear that, with a death under investigation, she couldn't possibly take part in a Christmas skit. Moira was still staying away and keeping Madeline with her. And how could she expect Jamie to take part when his father had just died in such awful circumstances?

"The show must go on," she repeated to the buzzing press of villagers who'd come with their children to the Hall, expecting, surely, that this rehearsal would be called off, if not the show. A man was dead, his son playing a key role in the Christmas skit.

Unnatural, thought Gladys Fraser.

"I'll not be part of this." She tugged on her dusty rose parka. It was quilted, and, when buttoned up, made her look like a small, square, padded armchair.

"Not this day," she mumbled as she bent over to yank on her naugahyde boots, stained by salt. Salt wasn't used at The Shores, but she made Wally put it on their front walk and driveway. She'd have liked to spread it all over the lawn to be rid of it.

"The show will go on," repeated Hy. Amidst grumbles, the

group dispersed and found seats around the Hall, continuing to mutter their disapproval of the whole thing.

Most of them hadn't known Fitz Fitzpatrick. Those who had, hadn't even liked him. But he was dead now. That made a difference. Certain respect was owed the dead. A respect they might not have had in life. Some dignity graced all who'd passed on, even the ones from away. Even Fitz Fitzpatrick.

"Of course the show will go on," piped up Rose Rose, with her high reedy voice. The minister's wife's word put an end to the complaining. Although why they were whining, Hy couldn't understand. In a couple of nights they'd be laughing until they ached, as they did at the show every year.

It was the last rehearsal before the dress rehearsal and half the cast was missing, including Jamie. He came crashing through the door, just as they were preparing to start without him. He jumped up on the stage with an agility he must have inherited from his father, thought Hy.

He turned round to face the audience with a big grin.

That started up the murmurs and mumbles again.

"Hardly seemly," Glady Fraser said from onstage. It wasn't a stage whisper. She could be heard at the back of the hall.

He's coping, thought Hy. *More than coping.* It disturbed her.

The first scenes went well, with Gladys and Annabelle doing a grand job as the ugly sisters.

Hy stood in for the prince, and in the scene where Shores Ella tries on the fisherman's boot, Jamie thrust a bare foot forward, holding it up high so Hy could see the sole.

It was red and blistered.

He thrust a second foot forward. The same.

Hy was shaking as she slipped the second boot on. Frostbitten. She hadn't seen it. Hadn't suspected it. Jamie had skied and seemed in no pain. Jamie was young. He either didn't feel it or didn't show it. Rose hadn't mentioned it. Did she know? Frostbitten feet. Had Jamie been there, that night? In the culvert?

Did he see his father die?

Had he killed him?

The fish had been swimming around on the screen saver in Gus's kitchen for days. She'd become used to them, and was having a nice doze when Hy came up from the Hall with Jamie after the rehearsal. Gus had plastered ointment on his feet, and he'd gone skipping out as if there were nothing wrong with them.

Now Hy was on her second mission – to put Gus in contact with her family.

"You can forget about the boys," she said. "Not one of them has one of them things – " she pointed at the screen full of fish.

"But Dot does. Dot will."

"Where she is? I doubt it."

After seven boys, late in life came the girl. Gus had been forty-five. Her namesake, Aunt Augusta, had looked down on the babe and in the accumulated wisdom of her years said, "But Gus, she's so young."

She was. Very young. Abel spoiled her silly, from the get-go, said Gus.

Dotty, Gus thought of her, a pet name. After all those boys, she'd finally had a girl, but not a real girl, one who cooked and sewed and wanted to be a nurse. No. A boy-girl. A tomboy with a desire to see the world, save the world, and photograph it while she did so. Dot was a doctor. She'd gone and got a medical degree, Gus would say in a disapproving voice. Doctor was better than nurse. But for a girl? Gus had set her sights on a nurse, but had to settle for a doctor.

Then Dot "upped and chucked it all away." She'd joined UNICEF as a doctor and photographer, her newest passion growing out of a desire to photograph the misery and terrible beauty of the Third World.

Gus never knew where Dot was. It's not that she purposely didn't keep in touch. A lot of the time, she couldn't. The last six months she'd been in Africa. Somewhere. Every now and then, a parcel would arrive, containing a bundle of magazines in which Dot's photographs appeared. There was even a *National Geographic*. Gus was impressed by that. At least she'd heard of it. But she couldn't show it to anyone in the village. She flushed red when she opened the magazine to the photographs of near-naked men and women. Dot had taken these photos.

Gus did show the villagers the parcel's outer packaging. She'd twisted it up and waved it in the air.

"Fifty dollars. Imagine. Fifty dollars to send me this…this…" Photographs in magazines she'd never show to Abel. Or any other man. Or woman.

Hy wanted to put Gus in touch with her daughter by Skype, if possible. But she was having a tough time finding out where Dot was. Gus had forgotten.

More likely it had never registered with her.

"Try to remember, Gus. Where is she?"

"Some forrin soundin' place."

"Well, ya, we can assume that. But where? Africa? Indonesia?"

"Sounds like you're sneezing."

Desperate, Hy began reeling off country names as they came into her head.

"Botswana?"

"No."

"Somalia?"

Gus perked up. So did Hy. *Of course.* All the agencies were in Somalia. Dot would be bound to be there. Alleviating, photographing the misery. Then Gus shook her head.

"No," she said.

"But you recognized it."

"I did. Been in the news and such. Thought she might go there. She's allus helpin' others."

"Like her mother."

Gus shook her head again, deliberately misunderstanding. She chuckled.

"Oh, no, there's no help for me anymore."

Hy kept going. When she got to Eritrea, which she wasn't sure still existed, she gave up, having exhausted the number of countries that she could think of. There was a long silence while she tried to produce the name of a country she hadn't already mentioned.

"I've found Dr. Dot!" Ian came tramping through the door, snow all over his boots, giving not a thought to the shining linoleum of Gus's floor. Authentic linoleum that had survived the monthly polishing Gus still managed to give it.

"You've what?" Gus didn't know that Hy and Ian always called her daughter Dr. Dot.

"Found Dot. You can Skype her. Now."

Ian grinned a grin big enough to split his face. This was a coup. Genuine coup. And so exciting. Soon they would be connected to Dot in Antarctica. He'd made the arrangement with her moments ago, then sped down here to connect. He fumbled as he worked the keys of the computer.

The floating fish screen saver disappeared. Gus had become quite used to the fish. She found them soothing and much easier to care for than live pets.

But a few keystrokes later, there she was. Dot, looking like, well, Dot. Wavy hair, a rich brown and slightly disheveled. High colour in her cheeks. A broad grin and a sparkle in her eye. That sparkle came from her mother.

"It's great here," she said. "The quality of light, the barren landscape."

Gus's chest rose and fell. Offended.

"We have all that. Of course, if you want real barren, there's the Magdalene Islands, though why anyone would go there either, I don't know."

"It's not the same, Ma."

And then the question she always asked. Dot might not be able to hear her biological clock ticking, but Gus certainly could. In fact, for her, the alarm had gone off, and there was only one way to stop it ringing. The only thing that Antarctica had to recommend it, in her figuring, was that there were bound to be many more men than women.

"Is there someone?" she asked tentatively, a question she'd learned was the polite way to ask from listening in to Hy and Annabelle's conversations. It beat, "Have you got a man yet?" or the not-so-subtle: "Are you gettin' married anytime soon?"

Dot's grin broadened.

"You mean someone special?"

Gus grunted.

"Well, yes."

"Who?" *Mebbe a doctor. A scientist.*

"The cook."

"The cook? A man?" *Please God, Dot didn't like women.* Gus had first heard about "that sort of thing," as she put it, well into her thirties, and she was still trying to figure it out. One thing she knew – it didn't produce babies. Grandchildren.

"Yes, Ma. A man."

Gus was suddenly glad the cook was a man, although she believed in the division of labour. When she was young, she'd had to cook twenty pounds of potatoes a day and bake a dozen loaves of bread to feed the farmhands. She didn't mind that. She was glad she didn't have to muck out the barn. There were jobs for men and jobs for women. Period.

"Yup. A genius with food."

Dot would think that. She couldn't cook a hot dog. Well, she wouldn't. Dot was a vegetarian. That was another problem for Gus.

And then, the other inevitable question:

"When are you coming home?"

"I don't know, Ma. It depends."

"On what?"

"Well, I signed up for a year."

"A year!"

"Yes. And…I have to tell you – " The image cut out. Her daughter disappeared. Ian fiddled with the keys, tried to reconnect. Finally, he shrugged his shoulders at Gus, apology in the set of his mouth.

"That's all right," she said. But it wasn't all right. It was uncomfortable watching the image of her daughter disappear like that. Sliced off the screen. As if she didn't exist anymore. Communication ended, with no power to control it. The end of the conversation perhaps not worth the start of it, it left such an unsettling feeling.

Dot had been about to say something. What?

Murdo knew he should be getting back to the police house, especially as there was an investigation going on. Jamieson was so single-minded, he wasn't sure she even missed him, except when there was dirty work to be done, like fishing Fitzpatrick out of the creek.

He was too comfortable to move, sitting here in April's kitchen, smiling when her horde came tumbling into the room, grabbing at her apron and demanding cookies.

They almost didn't hear the knock at the door.

Murdo heaved himself up and went to open it.

A small man with a black moustache and a ski hat that made him look like a hairy grade-schooler, stood there, mustering up all the dignity he could over the roar of a snowmobile whose young driver was eyeing the rolling hills, barely concealing a desire to go zooming up and over them.

"April Dewey?" The man's thin voice could barely be heard under the roar of the snowmobile.

"No." Murdo was distracted.

"Not here?"

"Oh, yes…yes…do come in."

The man declined with a curt shake of his head. Murdo turned and called to April.

She wiped her hands on her apron as she came to the door. She looked at the man, not speaking.

A Jehovah witness?

He thrust some folded papers at her.

She opened up the papers, and went so pale you couldn't see the flour smudge on her chin.

"You've to sign," he said, thrusting out a clipboard, and handing her a pen. He pointed to the place where he required her signature.

She scribbled, her hand shaking, Murdo, curious, watching.

"Aren't you gonna read it?" asked the man. Murdo was thinking the same thing.

April shook her head dumbly.

The man – the bearer of bad news, or good, depending on how you looked at it – shrugged his shoulders, and walked back down the path to the snowmobile. As he got on, April slammed the door.

April, slamming the door? The news could not be good, thought Murdo.

"Divorce papers," she said, a tear trickling out of the corner of her eye.

The news was good, thought Murdo.

He put an arm around her shoulder to comfort her.

He was surprised at the force with which she reacted. She spun into his arms, and pressed her sweet plump body up against his.

Murdo felt faint with pleasure.

He couldn't leave now.

Chapter Thirty

The next day brought sunny skies, above-freezing temperatures, and melting snow. Some, like Jared, were hoping the two feet of snow would melt away and they wouldn't have to lift a finger.

"It's heart attack snow." Gus was keeping an eye out the window at Jamie shovelling the walk, his cheeks turned a high colour of red. When he shovelled the last bit, Gus hauled herself over to the front door and invited him in.

"Hot chocolate and chocolate chip cookies."

He was soon stuffing cookies in his mouth and slurping back the drink in spite of its heat. He had a chocolate-brown moustache and crumbs all over him. He swept a forearm across his face.

Gus grinned. He might have been her own grandchild – or great grandchild – except she didn't have any. Eight children and not one grandchild. How had that happened?

She blamed her daughter. Not her sons. They were all out in Alberta, those that were still alive. Somehow, none of them had ever married. They were "living in sin," Gus said, and her opinion of that was never tested by the birth of a potential grandchild. None of them had ever come back to Red Island. They had, as men often do, joined the families of their partners. Her only daughter was single, and Gus never saw her either, not with her living all over the world like that. And now in that frozen place.

Dot was her father's daughter. Abel had been around more when she was a child than at any other time in their long marriage. Most of the time it had been work – the farm, fishing, the store – that had kept him away. After? Maybe just habit.

Gus wondered how she'd ever managed to get pregnant eight times, but she had. And what did she have to show for it?

Jamieson was staring at the footprints again. They were teasing her – the woman's slippers, the cowboy boots, Chinese slippers, rubber boots – all growing larger in the melting snow. The footprints told her who'd been there, but didn't tell her whether Fitz's death was an accident or intentional. Her gut told her it was more than an accident. There were simply too many people who would be glad he was dead.

A tiny bright splash of colour caught her peripheral vision. She pried at it, pulled it out of the snow. A card. A Tarot card. The Hanged Man. *Oliver.* She imagined him waddling through the snow. It was hard to imagine, but he had done it, because here were his footprints and here was his card. His calling card, she thought grimly. What had he seen? Done?

The brightly coloured card dropped in the snow, just a few feet away from where Fitz Fitzpatrick was hanging. Had Oliver tipped him off his balance? Deliberately pushed him? A lucky push. The tree snatched the man and his life. Oliver turned away. He dropped the card, and left Fitz gasping for life. Was that how it was?

She climbed back up from the ravine and went straight to

Wild Rose Cottage. She knocked on the door. Rose answered, dressed oddly, Jamieson thought, in a flowing flowered robe, her hair loose and hanging and shining from the effect of being brushed a hundred times. Her face, usually pasty, was glowing, her cheeks flushed.

Oliver Sullivan was sitting in the lotus position at the entrance to the tent in front of the stove.

Cozy, thought Jamieson, as she took it all in.

This case might be going somewhere after all.

Now she had them together, the interviewing might prove more fruitful. She hoped she'd be able to tell if one was protecting the other. She'd be able to read their body language.

For one so in control of her emotions, Jamieson was markedly perceptive about other people's silent messages. What made her seem cold was the same thing that made her so perceptive – she hid what she was feeling, so that she seemed hard, unyielding. It wasn't so. Jamieson was afraid that if she let any of it out, it would all pour from her in one tidal wave of sorrow and drown her. In the effort to contain herself, she had become highly attuned to other people's small giveaways, studying them so that she wouldn't commit the same mistakes herself.

She towered above Oliver, who wasn't prepared to stand up, even though it put him at a huge psychological disadvantage. This actually threw Jamieson off. She wasn't used to people – guilty people – allowing that to happen. *Did that mean he was not guilty? Not feeling the need for psychological advantage?* She always felt the need for it. That's why she always stood. It gave her a big advantage. But now the gap was widened even more, and it put her off-balance. She couldn't look him directly in the eye, not unless she crouched, and her authority would dissolve in that.

Rose was fussing with the teakettle, looking away from Jamieson.

What was she hiding? Her face, for one thing. The place where her emotions rested, revealed themselves.

"No tea for me," said Jamieson, in an effort to get Rose to look at her, to see if there was guilt – *something* – on her face.

But she didn't. *Guilty?*

It put Jamieson even more off-balance, which is why she charged in like a bull. She pointed at Oliver.

"You killed a man once." She had Ian to thank for that piece of information. She didn't like civilians interfering in investigations, but she was grateful this time. He'd told her just this morning, over coffee. She'd dropped in with a few computer questions, and when he'd offered coffee, she had accepted. She had called him Ian again. He had called her Jane again. She'd let her guard down.

Why? Was it the way he looked at her? At her hair?

Rose turned, shock on her face. *Killed a man? Oliver?*

He was looking benignly up at Jamieson.

"Once. But not twice."

"So you say, but you are able – you have done it."

"It was not my intent at the time."

"So the judge ruled, and I accept that ruling. I wouldn't contradict the justice system. You had your reasons, noble, we are supposed to believe."

Rose stood, holding the kettle aloft, her jaw dropped, her mouth partly open, unable to speak.

"The point is, you have blood on your hands. That makes it easier to kill a second time, doesn't it?"

"I couldn't tell you, because there hasn't been a second time."

Silence. Punctuated by the sound of metal on metal as Rose dropped the kettle back on the stove. It began its boiling-over hiss almost immediately.

"Oliver, what happened, what did you…? "

It was Jamieson, not Oliver, who answered.

"Shall I tell her, or will you?"

Again, the benign smile.

"Why don't you? I'd be interested to hear your version."

If he had hoped to pounce on opinion or conjecture, he was disappointed. She listed the bare details, as toneless and lacking in emotion as a voice messaging system.

"Young girl. Back alley. Rape in progress. You come around the corner. See it. Jump on him. Pull him off and slam him to the ground. Hits his head. Dead."

"Correct in every detail, madam, except nothing said about my emotions. You might term them the motive, I prefer emotions. Were they those of a killer? Or were they somewhat nobler?"

"Only you can know that."

"All I can say, and trust you will believe me, is that it was accidental. It did not give me a taste for killing, as you seem to suggest. I may have blood on my hands, but not in my heart."

Rose had turned away again, pouring hot water into the teapot, hiding her face. Relief. That's what Jamieson would have seen, if she had seen it.

But she didn't. She pulled out the card and threw it down in front of Oliver.

It stared up at him, damaged from the snow.

"This is yours, I believe."

He nodded, but didn't speak.

"You know where I found it?"

He inclined his head again.

"How did it get there?"

"I dropped it."

"Before or after you killed him?"

Oliver's face broke into a broad smile, like the Cheshire cat. His eyes narrowed to nothing.

"He was dead before I got there." A dead man. The Hanged Man. Destined to die. It had little to do with Oliver. It would have happened even if he hadn't come here.

She flipped the Tarot card over.

The Hanged Man.

"If he was dead already, how did you know to bring this card?"

"Ah, that is the magic of the Tarot. It is the Tarot that speaks, not I."

"If you didn't kill him, why did you go down the trail, why did you bring this card, why did you leave it there?"

He held up his hands.

"One question at a time, please. You are making me dizzy."

"Dizzy like Fitzpatrick was? Dizzy enough to lose his balance on the fly – if pushed?" Jamieson was angry with herself for drilling him with questions. One at a time. That was the method, unless you were going in for the kill. She wasn't sure that she was. She backed up.

"Why did you go out?"

"I sensed trouble in the air."

"We call it snow."

"That, too." He shivered. "Nasty stuff." He clicked his fingers, and Ginger jumped on his lap. White leapt onto his shoulders and wrapped himself around his neck. Instant warmth.

"And the card? Why did you take it?"

"I was doing a reading. It happened to be in my hand."

"In your hand as you put on your coat and your gloves?"

"Ah, but I didn't."

"In that weather, you went out in your clothes?"

"No. The coat, of course. The gloves…"

He shook his head, his brow furrowed in that peculiar V.

"…apparently not."

He held up a hand as Jamieson began to speak.

"And don't ask why – as you seem so fond of doing. I can't tell you why. I don't know why. I was called to do it."

"Called to kill Fitzpatrick?"

"Of course not."

"Then what?"

He sighed. It seemed they were going around in circles.

Jamieson frowned, pointed to the card, and began all over

again. Something here didn't make sense. He'd either killed Fitzpatrick himself, or knew who had.

Jamieson began a second round of questioning at Jared's. He was nursing a hangover, looking very rough with bloated face and bleary eyes. His voice was rasping. Jamieson wanted to avoid looking at him, but she had to, to see those giveaway signs that he was lying, or, less likely, that he was telling the truth.

"Were you there when he began the flips?"

Jared grunted.

"Is that a *yes?* Were you there when he started?"

Jared grunted again. He'd learned to say as little as possible to police.

She made a note of it.

"No."

Silence. Jamieson's signature technique.

"I'd gone by then," he offered. A small offering, thought Jamieson. She'd get more out of him yet.

"Did you hear anything?"

"No." Jared swiped a sleeve across his nose. Jamieson looked with distaste at the snot he'd left on the arm of his coat. His dirty fingernails.

"Mind if I smoke?" he asked.

"I do," said Jamieson.

Jared didn't usually let that response stop him. Especially in his own house. But there was something about this Jamieson even he didn't want to cross.

"You heard nothing?"

"Not a thing." Jared stood up and went to the fridge.

"Mind if I have a beer?"

She did, but she just shrugged. Maybe it would get him talking. He opened the fridge, stuck his head in. "Would you like one?"

"No, thank you. Not on duty."

"I was gonna mention that," he said. "So when you're not, how 'bout you 'n me, we do the dirty?" Moist lips curled in a yellow smile.

Jamieson's lip curled in distaste. Jared slumped back in the chair.

"You were saying you heard nothing."

"That's right." He took a swig and burped.

"Not a shout?"

"No."

"A cry for help?"

"No."

The sound of branches bending, breaking?"

"No."

"The sound of a man squirming in a tree, trying to get free?"

"No."

"A struggle? Guttural, choking noises?"

"No."

"What *did* you hear?"

"I told you, nothin'. I was wearing my iPod."

What a waste of time he was. Jamieson had been hoping to wear him down into some kind of admission. Murder? An accident? He might have caused it or been a witness to it and might be scared to say.

"Do you think Fitz was murdered?"

Jared was silent. He took another swig of beer.

Why should he help out the cops?

"Nah," he said. "I think it was an accident."

"Why? What makes you think that?"

"Cause I didn't do it."

"You killed someone once."

"That *was* an accident."

"That's what the judge ruled." Jamieson's tone told him she was unconvinced.

"That's always comin' back to bite me."

"Didn't you think it would?"

"They don't pay me to think. That's your job."

Jamieson left. Of all the people who might have killed Fitz, he was the one it would give her the greatest pleasure to arrest.

Any of the others – no pleasure at all. That thought had been with her for a while. It had finally surfaced, and had begun to work at her. *No pleasure. No pleasure at all.*

Rose was slicing a turnip when Hy came in. *As if she were killing it... Or killing Fitz all over again?*

That was the thing that troubled Hy – and she bet it troubled Jamieson as well. When a woman killed, it was often in rage. Stabbing repeatedly. Shooting a load of bullets into the victim. Working out years of anger and frustration in a volley of hatred.

Not tipping someone off balance. That was for someone more subtle. Oliver. That would be his style. Just a bit of a push and... *voilà.*

"He wasn't always bad, you know."

Rose finished slicing the turnip. *Dead.* She scooped the pieces into her apron and slid them into the pot of boiling water on the wood range. She wiped her hands on the apron and sat down on the stool by the stove. Hy sat in the recently reclaimed rocking chair opposite.

"He had a hard life."

Hy's mouth was set in a grim line. She wasn't inclined to soften on Fitz. She'd seen too much she didn't like.

"The real story is – "

Hy leaned forward, eager. New information. Information Jamieson wouldn't have.

"The real story is – he lost a child."

That was careless of him. The uncharitable thought whipped through Hy's mind, fast enough that she didn't utter it.

"He killed his child."

Hy's mouth dropped open. She couldn't speak.

"His son."

"When...where...how?"

"His only son."

What about Jamie?

"Your child?"

"No. Not my child. That other marriage. There were the two girls and then the boy. Just three years old. Sticking his head out the window of a trailer as Fitz backed up. The boy fell out and under the wheels. Fitz never saw him, couldn't have seen him. Everyone, even the coroner, agreed. He backed over the boy, then dragged him before he found out."

"How horrible."

"That's what started him drinking. Seriously drinking."

"Was he drunk when it happened?"

"Well, yes, but – no one blamed him for it, not even the mother."

I do, thought Hy. *I do.*

"How could you have got hooked up with him – with that history, his alcoholism...?"

"I told you. It's the old story. I was young and foolish. I thought I could save him."

"Yeah, well I've done that, but I didn't have babies."

"Jamie is not his son." Rose stood up, and began stirring the turnip in the pot.

Not his son. She'd said that before – to Fitz.

"Not his? Then whose?"

Rose didn't turn. With her back to Hy, she just said, "Mine. Jamie is mine."

End of conversation. But not the end of Hy's curiosity, or the conclusions she was coming to. Rose was lovely, but she was weak. That's why she'd allowed Fitz to happen to her. And now she and Jamie were paying for it. No matter whose son he was.

Oliver's? No, that was just crazy. But Oliver did sometimes call him son.

Chapter Thirty-One

The Hall was ablaze. From the outside it looked as if it were going up in flames. There were Christmas lights everywhere – strung along the wainscoting, the ceiling, the stage, the window and door frames, even the kitchen cupboards and fridge. The portraits of Queen Elizabeth and Prince Philip were draped with spruce boughs and shiny ornaments. There had been hot debate over festooning the royals. Gladys Fraser and Olive MacLean were on the "over my dead body" side; the others thought that the fading photos of the royal pair could use some sprucing up. Literally. Spruce boughs crowned their portraits.

It was the dress rehearsal for the Christmas Pageant. All the performers and a sprinkling of mothers and fathers were there. Little Violet Joudry was murdering a fiddle – it sounded as if it were in its death throes. All the while she was step dancing, and doing that not very well either. But her mother Celeste was beaming from stage left, glowing with pride, thankful that, for once, Violet had decided she did feel like doing it after all. Usually she didn't, and her mother was finding it harder and harder to justify the expense of lessons to Violet's father, who sat glowering in a chair at the side of the Hall, from where he could slip out easily and, he thought, unnoticed. The other fathers envied him as they whispered, "There goes Frank." He didn't really care if they noticed. He'd much rather be with his cows.

Violet's screeching and thumping came to an unfortunate crescendo, and then, mercifully, died out. She performed a much-too-precious series of curtsies, and her mother, unable to resist, ran onstage and hugged her, peppering her blond ringlets with kisses. Violet screwed up her face and pushed her mother away.

Moira and Madeline had shown up after all, unwilling to be left out at the last, and Moira with the certainty that she had cowed her younger sister sufficiently to be assured, herself, of the lead role.

She'd certainly done a job on Madeline.

As soon as she walked out on stage, Madeline had a panic attack. She couldn't even spit out one word.

"I can't do it," she whimpered after she finished hyperventilating. "I'd rather just open and close the curtains, please."

Moira smirked and stepped forward. She knew all the lines. She'd been undermining her younger sister for days, nagging away at any small shred of confidence Madeline might have. Moira wanted Ian to see her as the beautiful Shores Ella, not as a mannish prince. She stepped forward, mouth open to volunteer.

"I'll do it." Jamie jumped down from the piano bench. "I'm the understudy. It should be me."

Everyone looked at him. Then they looked at Moira. Her mouth wide open, silence coming from it, her voice strangled by this new possibility.

"I know all the lines." His big eyes open and appealing. "You've seen me do it."

"A boy – playing a girl? I never heard of such a thing." Moira found her voice. Gladys Fraser marched over to Moira in a gesture of support. Gladys took every opportunity to be offended.

"We've been through this. It's quite Shakespearean, actually," said Hy.

"Well, that's different." Gladys folded her arms across her chest.

Her standard approach to life. Especially when she didn't know what was being talked about.

Hy would have liked to tell Moira to leave, that she'd been replaced as prince, except that Jamieson had pulled out because of the investigation. Hy resigned herself to Moira.

"We need you as the prince." The word "need" stuck in Hy's throat, but she could tell it placated Moira, who patted her hair smugly.

"Oh, all right."

Hy nodded at Jamie.

"Okay. You're on. Let's take it from the top."

Madeline tugged the curtains, jerking more or less open as Jamie stood on stage, sweeping and waiting.

And waiting. For the screeching sound of the stepmother to come from offstage.

Estelle was just putting on a last dab of lipstick and missed her cue. When she did scream, it didn't happen offstage. She came sailing out and obliterated Jamie from view, until he peeked out from behind her skirt with a cheeky grin.

The skit bumped along with forgotten lines and cues, but with Jamie giving a stellar performance as Ella. Moira walked through her part with flat expression as the prince, and Annabelle and Gladys made a pair of funny wicked sisters. Gladys wore her usual frown and Annabelle had a wide lipsticked smile and her hair pulled into two bunches on either side of her head. Their feet slipped too easily into the rubber fisherman's boot. Too small. The prince was looking for the girl with the biggest feet.

The rehearsal ground to a conclusion with forgotten lines, inappropriate remarks, and all the makings of a perfect Christmas skit. Hy, as narrator, wrapped it up:

"Every good fairy tale's supposed to end: 'And they all lived happily ever after.' But of course they didn't. The Prince didn't like living

*with his step mother-in-law and went back to his castle. There
was no fairy godmother, no pumpkin coach, ratty footmen or
mousey horses either. Because this was a true story.*

*"And if you believe that, I'll show you a prince who married a
fish girl in rubber boots."*

Madeline jerked the curtains closed. She had to jump up to
put her weight behind the pulley. Why she had ever been chosen
for this particular task was a mystery. But she loved it. And it
had saved her from being Shores Ella. That made her like it even
more.

Buddy hadn't been seen in two days. Jamieson had sent Murdo
looking for him. Murdo might as well be missing, too. Missing in
action, spending his time doing odd jobs for the divorcée. That
was Jamieson's unkind tag for April. She pigeonholed people,
gave them a hook to identify them. It was usually not flattering.
Annabelle was the tart, Jared the scumbag, Gus the old fool. Ian?
Well Ian…had become Ian. On at least two occasions recently
she'd called him by his first name. Hy, as close to a friend as
Jamieson had ever had, was still not quite a friend. Hy was the
woman with the ridiculous name.

Jamieson didn't like the idea of Buddy hiding and lurking
about. Was he in the woods? Had he killed Fitzpatrick? It nagged
at her. He was mentally defective, so he might do anything, she
thought. These villagers might trust him with their children,
but she did not.

As for murder, she was not sure Buddy could have accomplished
it – could have known just when to give that push that would
have sent Fitzpatrick somersaulting off the culvert and into the
tree.

He could have done it accidentally, of course. But there were
at least three other suspects, three people who knew far better
than Buddy when that precise moment would be.

Rose had told her she'd worked with Fitzpatrick in his acrobatic act, that she had spotted him, so she had to know, with precision, all of his moves. Of all of them, she was the most likely to have killed him. She was the only one who could know the intricate details of his movement, know what would throw him off balance, know –

And then she always came to a halt in her line of thinking. Rose had seemed so protective of Jamie. If Jamieson had read the signs correctly – one of her skills – Rose thought her son had killed his father. But if she thought that, she couldn't be guilty herself.

Could Jamie have done it? Jamie of the bright open face, who had studied his father's acrobatics. He performed some of them, in fact, better than his father, because he was so light and flexible, and because Fitzpatrick had been out of the habit of performing and very much in the habit of drinking himself insensible. Not to mention the drugs.

And then there was Oliver. He had trained suspicion on himself by admitting to being down at the culvert. Otherwise, Jamieson could not have imagined him being able to get there, with his squat Humpty Dumpty body and legs you could barely see. He seemed to think Rose or Jamie was guilty.

What did any of the three know about one another? Were they knowingly withholding evidence? Did they have a pact – two protecting one? But which one?

Jamieson kept staring at the photographs, as if they would hold some clue to what had happened on the bridge that night. They should, but they didn't. All the people whose footprints were there had said they were there – without any particular coercion. Their stories sounded reasonable, plausible. So was it an accident? Just an accident? She could just accept it and leave it at that.

But it was gnawing at her – because, in spite of the plausible reasons, there were as many arguing for murder. The murder of a man who didn't deserve to live? Maybe not. But justice could not be swayed by that.

Or could it?

Could it – if it were the boy? The child would live with guilt, she knew that, even if it were an accident.

She was burdened with her own guilt. She couldn't allow herself to experience joy. She didn't deserve to be happy. She had killed her family – her mother, her father, the unborn child, the relationship with her sister that she couldn't sustain, the closeness she couldn't bear, didn't deserve.

The child would suffer whether she made him suffer or no.

But the child must be questioned. It was her duty.

She awoke the next morning, with that duty oppressing her.

The boy. She would have to talk to the boy. She wasn't looking forward to it. She had never interviewed a child before – not as a suspect. It was hard to tell who was more nervous – Jamieson or Jamie – when she sat down to question him in the comfort of the police house. She wasn't going to endure that tent anymore.

She sat down because he was a child.

Of course his mother was with him. Whether that would help or hinder her, she wasn't sure.

"When your father was lying on the road, you were there."

"Yes."

"And you left – before or after the truck went off the road?" It was still there, in the ditch. Ben Mack had said something about hauling it out with his tractor.

"After."

"So you saw the accident?"

Jamie's head dropped.

"Answer, Jamie," Rose said, her voice gentle, reassuring.

"Yes." Jamieson knew that from her unfinished investigation of the accident, but she'd never asked Jamie outright – just taken Ian and Annabelle at their word.

"And?"

"And I ran off."

"Why?"

"Because I hated it."

"Hated it – or hated him?"

Rose's sharp intake of breath alerted Jamieson that she had gone too far. She knew it herself. She'd never done this before, but that was no excuse.

"Jamie loved his father." Rose had taken hold of one of Jamie's hands, and was exploring his face for signs of distress.

The mother was becoming intrusive.

"Please – " It was a word Jamieson rarely used in questioning. "Let the child answer for himself."

"I'm not a child." Jamie aimed a stubborn look at Jamieson, then at his mother. "And I can answer for myself. I did love my father."

Jamieson caught hold of the word "did."

"Did? Do you still?"

Rose was about to object again.

"He's dead," said Jamie, his tone flat, emotionless. It tugged at Jamieson. She remembered saying the same thing, in the same way. *But not the same circumstances.*

"Yes," said Jamieson, "and that's why I'm speaking to you, trying to find out what happened that night."

Footsteps. She'd seen the footsteps. Bare feet. A child's or an adult's. She looked down at Jamie's feet. He'd taken his boots off. They weren't child-size. They were the feet of small adult.

"Did you see your father again that night?"

There was a long silence.

"Answer Jamie." Rose prodded. "Did you?"

Jamieson shot her a look.

"I'll do the questioning."

"Of course. Excuse me."

A decent woman, thought Jamieson. A decent child, too. But decency didn't mean a thing when it came to murder. She must not be swayed. She must go on what the evidence told her – though there was precious little of it, and even that was confusing.

"Did you see your father again that night?" She repeated the question to bring them back on track.

After a moment: "Yes. Yes, I saw him."

"Where?"

"In the culvert…" He was about to say more, but Jamieson – uncharacteristically – jumped in on him.

"Why were you there?"

"No reason. Just wandering in the woods."

"And then you saw him?"

"Yes."

"Performing acrobatics?"

"No."

"Are you sure?"

"Yes."

"What was he doing when you got there?" No answer. "What was he doing?" she prompted.

"Twirling around."

"That's acrobatics, isn't it?"

"No."

"What is it then?"

"That's dead. He was dead. Hanging from the tree. Twirling around. Dead."

"Are you sure?"

"That he was dead?"

"No, that it was then that you saw him. Not before."

A slight pause. "Yes. After. Not before."

"Why didn't you tell anyone?"

"I was afraid."

"Afraid of what."

"That someone might think I'd done it. Like you." Jamie jutted his chin stubbornly at her.

"No one's accusing anyone of anything here. I have to get all the facts. Did you notice anything, anyone there? Anything unusual?"

"Well, it was unusual to have my dad hanging dead from a tree."

Jamieson flushed, her pale skin turning pink. She remembered. She remembered what it was like to have a father – and a mother – die. Different circumstances, but both terrifying to a child.

But Jamie was still composed enough to withhold vital information.

He had seen someone else.

His mother.

He looked at her now.

And he thought she'd seen him, too.

Their eyes agreed to keep that knowledge from Jamieson.

When the pair left, Jamieson sighed. This was a tough case. Those three – Rose, Jamie, and Oliver – were so busy protecting themselves and each other that it was hard to tell who did it.

If any of them did.

She slumped down in the armchair by the window that looked out on the road.

She stared out at some children building a snowman in front of the Hall – a Santa Claus. One of them was fashioning a fabulous ice sculpture of a whale. Wasn't that one of the Dewey boys? And helping him – a Fraser? She craned forward to get a better look. Weren't all the Frasers off on some family reunion in Winterside? It couldn't be a Fraser. It must be –

Community policing was having its effect. On Jamieson, not on the village.

She was becoming a bit like them.

Chapter Thirty-Two

Jamieson interviewed everyone – even Lili – who had not been in the village at the time.

The moment Lili answered the door to her sharp knocking, Jamieson knew the girl knew something. There was a certain wariness about her as if she were guarding some nugget of knowledge. She was – and it would not take much for Jamieson to have it out of her.

"Tea?"

Tea. Always tea. Jamieson wondered why the village didn't float away on a sea of it. She shook her head. She drank coffee. One. In the morning.

"Some water then? I have some lovely – " She reached for an exotic-looking green bottle.

Worse. What's wrong with what comes out of the tap?

"Please, sit."

Jamieson didn't budge.

Lili stayed standing, too, out of politeness to her guest. Jamieson towered over her. Lili was used to that. She was not just smaller than most people, she was tiny.

"What do you know?"

"Know?"

"About the death of Fitz Fizpatrick."

"Nothing. I know nothing."

"Nothing?"

"No. Nothing." Lili's voice wavered almost imperceptibly. Almost. The kind of thin fissure Jamieson could wedge into. Jamieson, an expert listener, heard the slight inconsistency. Lili knew she'd heard. She resumed control of her voice.

"I wasn't here." She sounded strong, sure.

"I know that," said Jamieson. "But I think you know something. I think it would be wise to tell."

"Well, I – " The crack reappeared and opened up.

"Yes?"

"It's nothing really."

"Everything matters when somebody dies and we're trying to find out why. Besides, it must be something, or you wouldn't be trying to hide it from me."

"I wasn't hiding it."

Jamieson pursed her lips in disbelief.

Lili gripped the back of the chair. "Well, I suppose I was, but I don't know that it means anything."

"Let me decide that." Jamieson softened her tone slightly to soften Lili, to make her speak.

It worked.

"It's Oliver..."

Jamieson remained silent. *Give her room and it will all come out.*

"I think he may dabble in the black arts."

Spare me.

"I think he may be evil."

"Do you have evidence – or are you just speculating?"

"I'm not sure." Lili pulled out the chair and sat in it. Suddenly Jamieson's height seemed a disadvantage. She towered so high above Lili that she felt a bit dizzy, as if she might fall over. She, too, sat down.

"He had this…book."

"What book?"

Lili couldn't name it. She felt if she did it might materialize, here at this table, desecrating this house and this village. The book Oliver had sold to the church to feather his nest forever. It would be a miracle if he hadn't been tainted by his possession of that book. He must have been. It must have come to him because he was evil, and gone from him for the same reason. *And wasn't he here searching for another book? Was it like the other one? Could there be two such books in the world?*

"I can't explain about the book. It's known – and his possession of it is known – by certain people in the spiritual community. Word gets around."

"Can possession of a book make a man evil?"

"Oh I think so – or, at least, the evil in the book can rub off on him, and then on others."

"You really believe this?"

"Yes. Look what happened to Nathan, who was in contact with him every day. Look what happened to the Fitzpatricks – he was in and out of their house all the time. I think he got rid of that book, but he brought its evil with him."

"Are you suggesting Oliver killed Fitz Fitzpatrick?"

"Killed?"

"Murdered."

Lili's hands flew up to cover her mouth.

"Oh no," she said, after a moment. "I just think evil follows him."

"Or comes with him."

"Right."

Some nugget of knowledge, thought Jamieson. *Useless. What I need is a confession.*

Jamieson ought to have been careful what she wished for.

Although it was Hy, not she, to whom the trio confessed, one after another.

"I did it."

Jamie came up behind Hy when she arrived at the house. Her back was to him. That's why he was able to say it. She whipped around.

He looked defiant, not confessional.

"Did you?" She kept her tone even, but the words caught in her throat.

He didn't answer, not at first.

She took a step toward him. He lowered his head.

"But why?"

"My father. Because of my father. Because of the way he was."

Hy was doing her own rounds of the people who might know something about Fitz's death. In her case, it was not to find a guilty party. It was to find reasons to believe that none of the people she'd come to care about had anything to do with it.

She got the opposite, starting with Jamie, who had been outside in the yard when she'd arrived at Wild Rose Cottage. Inside, Rose was sitting, staring blankly at nothing. A soup of root vegetables that Gus had given her was boiling on the stove.

Hy didn't even say hello.

"Jamie told me he did it."

Rose went pale, paler than usual.

"I did it."

She looked defiant, not confessional.

"I thought it was an accident."

"I...I hoped that's what people would think." Her head was dropped down, she was looking at her own hands, clasped too tight in her lap.

"That's what people do think. So why not leave it alone?"

"But if they think Jamie..."

"I don't believe anyone thinks Jamie did it. I think he's protecting you."

Now Rose's hands came up and covered her face.

"Oh, no. I hope it's not that."

"I think it is. Tell me, Rose. You can tell me. Did he do it – or did you?"

Rose uncovered her face and looked up at Hy.

No guilt there. Just anguish. If she was reading it right.

She didn't stop there very long. She marched down to Moira's, banged on the door, and shoved past a startled Moira. She tangled up the layer of newspapers under her feet and dragged them across the floor. With them, some road sand striped Moira's sparkling clean hardwood.

Hy walked straight into the dining room, where she knew she'd find Oliver. She'd seen him from outside through the window.

She didn't say hello, but dove right in.

"Both Jamie and Rose say they did it. I think they're protecting each other. I don't believe either of them did it."

"No, because I did it."

"You did it? Are you sure?

"Absolutely. It wasn't either of them."

The look on his face like Rose and Jamie – defiant, not confessional.

"Maybe not. Maybe not you, either. It could have been an accident, easily an accident."

"No, it was I." You couldn't fault his grammar, but was the statement true – or false? She asked the question she hadn't asked the others, because she didn't believe they did it. Was she beginning to think he had?

"Why haven't you told Jamieson?"

"The time has not yet arrived. We three must agree."

"Three? Rose and Jamie?"

He inclined his head.

"Agree on what? Who did it?"

"I told you I did it."

"Then tell me how you did it. What did you do?"

"It's in the cards," he said, and began to lay them out. They were all, as he knew they would be, cards of the Major Arcana, starting with the Hanged Man. The Hanged Man, streaked and buckled up by the snow. It was Jamieson's evidence, but somehow the card had slipped away from her, back into Oliver's possession. She couldn't have said how it had happened. She didn't know it was gone.

"This is the nature of the question," he said as he laid it down.

"This covers him." It was one of his own cards. The Magician. "This crosses it." Obstacles in the way. The card of Justice. And on through the reading.

"I don't see that this proves anything."

"Perhaps not." Oliver gathered up the cards. "But to me they do. You'll have to trust me. I did it."

"I trust you, but I don't believe you did it. I believe you're protecting Rose and Jamie, just like they're protecting each other."

Oliver inclined his head. He had said what he wanted to say, showed her what he wanted to show her. He could do no more.

Hy left, more puzzled than ever. If Rose didn't do it, Jamie didn't do it, and Oliver didn't do it, then who had? Buddy? Buddy who'd disappeared, casting suspicion his way?

Possible, but likely?

Wasn't it more likely that it was an accident?

She had a gut feeling just like Jamieson that it was not. Even so, she wanted Jamieson to think so, and to let this whole thing drop. How was she going to do that?

Hy was pacing the floor in front of Ian's woodstove.

"Rose said she did it."

Ian handed her a glass of Pinot Noir, and sat down on the couch. It creaked.

"Jamie said he did it. And Oliver. He said he did it."

Ian leaned back on the couch and stuck his feet out, just grazing Hy. He hoped she wouldn't pull away as she usually did.

"Jane said that Jared was there."

Hy pulled away.

"When?"

"Well – uh – " He sat up.

"When she questioned you?"

"No – "

"Well when?"

"She borrowed – "

"A cup of sugar." Hy's lips settled somewhere between a smirk and a sneer.

"No, a thumb drive. She needed one for backup."

"And so how'd it go? Thanks, Ian, for the thumb drive – and by the way Jared was down in the gully. When did she become Jane?"

Ian's face had gone bright red. He liked Jamieson, but not as he liked Hy. Hy seemed to be jealous. Did that mean she felt something more for him than friendship? He'd never dared to find out.

"We had a talk. I don't know. It was a slip." It was – if it made Hy back off, just when he thought she was warming up.

"On her part, or yours?" *Jamieson doesn't make slips.*

"What? Her mentioning Jared? Or me calling her Jane?" He was hot. Sweating. Why?

"Oh, well, it doesn't matter." She shrugged and took a sip of wine. But it did matter.

"I don't think it's Jared, anyway. I think it's one of those three. I think murder has come to Wild Rose Cottage again."

"Are you saying murder is the Sullivan legacy?"

"No. Still, these patterns sometimes play out in families."

"But this is nothing like those others. It could easily have been an accident."

"One that leaves a widowed Rose again in possession of the house. For the third time in as many centuries."

"Ian, you're sounding like some kind of psychic." Hy laughed. It was so unlike him.

"No, I'm a realist. I think Fitz was murdered. By Oliver, Rose. Or – " A long pause. "Jamie."

"Oh, God, you don't think – "

"I do. I don't think Fitz mistimed in that gully. I think he was pushed at the critical moment. By someone who knew when that was."

"But he was legless – and neither Rose nor Jamie has the strength."

"It wouldn't take much. If he were drunk enough. Besides, they would both know the timing."

"You haven't told Jamieson what you think, have you?"

"No. I don't expect I'd have to. She should have figured it out herself."

Sudden, inexplicable panic gripped Hy.

"You haven't shown her the family history?"

"No. I don't expect Jane would consider it material or evidence of any kind."

"Jaaaane." Jasmine had picked up the name again.

So had Hy.

It was the word Jane, not the word murder, that Hy had on her mind as she left Ian's.

Chapter Thirty-Three

Rose Fitzpatrick had asked everyone to call her Rose Sullivan now that Fitz was dead. She looked happier, more alive. She didn't have to have killed him to feel that way, look that way, but still –

Jamieson was back for another round with Rose, like a dog chewing a bone. She felt ridiculous inside the tent, but the whole room was now leaking with the melting snow. At six feet, she had to bend over. It was uncomfortable, and put her at a disadvantage.

"And so you went out. Why?" They'd covered this territory before, but a second interview, Jamieson found, could be more revealing than the first. It was a test to see if the stories matched – version one and version two. Jamieson had the notes, detailed notes, and she'd be comparing everyone's first and second interviews tonight.

"I was looking – " she hesitated.

"You were looking for…your husband?"

A pause.

"Yes." Almost eagerly. "Yes." As if she'd found a solution.

Lying. She was lying. Why?

"And you found him?"

"Yes."

"Dead or alive?"

"Alive," she said quickly.

Lying. She was lying again.

The way she said it told Jamieson that she was lying. Jamieson was keenly attuned to tone of voice and the meaning hidden behind the words.

"So you found him alive?" There was a shade of disbelief in the question.

Rose picked up on it. She nodded, and looked down at her hands, clasped in her lap. They both looked at them. Rose's hands were trembling.

Jamieson was also attuned to body language. She'd attended several workshops in it. All the trembling hands could tell her, though, was that Rose was upset, not guilty. As imperfect as a lie detector. Agitation, fear was easy to see, but not necessarily interpret. Upset didn't equal guilt.

"You found him alive. Was this before or after he met with Jared?"

"I can't say. I don't know if he'd been there or not. All I know is, I found Fitz."

"Where was he standing when you found him?"

A moment's hesitation. Jamieson marked that, too, in her book.

"On this side of the culvert."

"This side?"

"Yes."

"Not the far side?"

"No."

The content of the questions and the answers were barely important. What Jamieson was doing now was wearing down the...witness? Suspect?

"Was he performing acrobatics?"

"No, of course not."

"There's no 'of course not' about it. We know he performed some stunts – and that, in part if not wholly, caused his death."

"I suppose."

Jamieson jumped into the tiny opening, the crack in confidence.

"Might he have been – before you came?"

"Might he have been what?"

"Performing acrobatics?"

"I suppose so." Rose let out a sigh. She was weary of this questioning. *When would it end?*

"What time was this?"

"I can't say."

"You can't say – or you don't know?"

Jamieson's tactic was working. She was wearing Rose down. A tear appeared in the corner of her eye. Not for Fitz.

There was nothing of the grieving widow about this woman, thought Jamieson. She noted that down, too, and then circled back to where they had started.

"So you went looking for your…husband…and you found him. Why were you looking for him?"

"I wanted him home."

"Really?" The tone made it clear Jamieson didn't believe her.

"The weather was bad. He wasn't in good shape."

"Was he stoned?"

"He was drunk and stoned, both."

"And you left him there? In that condition?"

"What could I do? I didn't have the strength to force him to come home."

"But might you have had the strength to unbalance him in the middle of a flip? You, of all people, would know the perfect timing for that."

Would this woman never stop? Perhaps this would satisfy her.

"That's true," said Rose. "I would."

Jamieson almost smiled with triumph. Was this a breakthrough in the case? Was Rose coming close to admitting she'd done it?

It was one of them. One of the three. Which one?

The woman, the man, the boy?

They were her suspects, in that order. How was she going to prove it? What were their motives? Were their motives... mundane? Or were they...peculiar? She was betting on peculiar. It always went that way in The Shores.

And that thought triggered another in her mind.

Peculiar. Buddy is peculiar.

She didn't even say goodbye. She burst out of the house, jumped on her snowmobile, and made off to the shack in the field. No one was there. There was no smoke coming from the chimney.

She charged up the steps, shoved open the door, half-expecting to find another dead man inside. But there was nothing. No one. She put her hand to the woodstove. Still a bit of warmth in it. She opened it. This time she didn't notice the ember fall out.

Buddy was missing. And she bet she knew why.

Buddy had killed Fitz Fitzpatrick.

She walked around the shack to make sure he wasn't lying in the snow somewhere. The tracks around the shack were at least a day old.

She headed for Hy's, and walked up to the door with new determination.

"Do you know where he is?" Jamieson did not even bother with a hello as she charged through Hy's door. By now, she was thoroughly accustomed to the fact that Islanders expected you to come right in. Jamieson also expected Hy to know what she was talking about.

Hy turned, interrupted from writing a piece about Old Christmas Traditions for her regular website client, the Super Saver grocery store. There were a couple of spruce needles in Jamieson's hair. Hy smiled. She wasn't going to tell her.

"Where who is?"

"Buddy. Second time I've been up there. No sign of him. He's not in his shack."

"Oh, he'll be somewhere around." Hy looked out the window. Night was falling fast. It did that at this time of year. It seemed that the afternoon had only begun, and here it was ending.

"I checked outside. No recent activity."

Hy screwed up her face. It wasn't like Buddy.

"You don't think…?" Surely not someone else disappeared and dead?

"I don't know what to think." Jamieson's tone was impatient. She'd expected an immediate solution from McAllister. "I don't know the man."

Dark. It was dark now as Hy stared out the window, wondering where Buddy might be.

Suddenly, through the window, she saw flames rising in the night.

"It's on fire," she yelled, jumping up and knocking over her coffee so that it shot across the room, the liquid spilling all over the floor and splashing up onto the curtains. The new ones. She'd put them up yesterday as a Christmas present to herself. Creamy raw cotton, now etched with black coffee.

No time for that. She grabbed a jacket, and tugged at Jamieson's sleeve.

"What's on fire?"

"The shack. Buddy's shack."

They ran out the door, leaving it banging open, and jumped on the snowmobile. Jamieson accelerated so quickly it bumped down the lane and onto the road.

Flames were licking the sky, so high up they were leaping beyond the tops of mature spruce trees.

Like a tinderbox.

They couldn't get there fast enough. If Buddy were in the building he'd be dead by now. The entire shack was engulfed in flames.

Outside, the well had an old-fashioned hand pump. Hy jumped off the snowmobile, grabbed the bucket hanging on a hook above the pump, and began pumping water into it. She whirled around and threw it at the inferno. The flames leapt out at her, as if fueled, not banked, by the water.

Another bucket. The flames came shooting out at her again.

Another. No change in the roaring power of the fire.

And another. Until, exhausted, she gave up. Jamieson had not made a move to help her. She was frozen on her snowmobile. She knew the battle was hopeless, but it was more than that.

Jamieson was reliving that other fire – more than thirty years ago. She was paralyzed, unable to respond, and buzzing with fear, an electric jolt through her like those flames shooting into the sky, a reaction that made her unfit for service. Her secret terror, the terror she never talked about, the terror she did not want to confront. And here it was, raging before her, and if she had needed to go into the building and save someone, she would not have been able to.

Two snowmobiles pulled up. Murdo. Ben Mack. Behind them, a half-dozen cars, their occupants running awkwardly through the snow, some with buckets in hand. But when they got close to the building, they could see it was hopeless. The shack and everything in it would soon be gone.

Jamieson managed to pull out of her paralyzed state. There were tracks and ice everywhere, illuminated by the fire. Buddy might have been back, fired up the stove – there were a number of ways a fire could have started. Ember on the floor. Spark from holes in the pipe. A tinderbox, as Jamieson had thought from the first. She had no idea she'd started it.

Jamieson drove Hy back home when it was clear there was nothing to be done until the rubble cooled down, and they could search it to see if Buddy had been inside.

Jamieson took a sip of tea. Hy was surprised when Jamieson accepted. She never had before. *Was she melting? Becoming human?*

In a way, perhaps she was, but not in the way Hy thought. She was undone by the fire, by her memories, unsettled by her weakness, so off-balance that she had accepted Hy's offer of tea.

She didn't usually drink on duty. Anything.

But she had also begun to think that maybe this, too, was part of community policing. "When it cools down, we'll search for human remains."

"Human remains?" Hy hated the thought of that phrase being attached to Buddy, to anyone she knew.

"Yes, shards of bone and such. It won't all have been burnt up."

"It?"

"The skeleton. The body – if there is one in there."

"If there is?"

"Well, we'll have to get forensics to confirm that it is human remains and not a dog, or cat, or last night's dinner."

Hy was not liking Jamieson, not liking her at all in this moment. She was so cold, clinical.

What Hy didn't know was that Jamieson was struggling back to normalcy. She was forcing herself to be analytical rather than compassionate, because it was the only way she could hold herself together.

If she let go of the calm professional view, her blood would flood with panic, her mind would run away from her, leaving her here, a puddle of fear on Hy's floor.

She stood up, suddenly, because she had let that thought run away with her. She had to pull herself together. But her movement was so sudden, her composure still in pieces, that she lost her footing as she stood, grabbed onto the chair, knocked it over, and tumbled down with it.

Landing, a puddle of fear, on Hy's floor.

Hy jumped up to help her, but Jamieson lifted a hand to stop her.

"A minute. Just a minute," she gritted her teeth. The pain of the fall had shocked her. She couldn't move – at all – for a moment. Fear and shock running rampant inside her, unbalancing her, leaving her here, undignified, on the floor.

Finally, she let Hy help her up, and eased back onto her feet.

"Would you like another tea?"

Jamieson shook her head.

"No, no, I have to get back."

"Would you like me to drive you?"

"No, I'll be fine," she said.

Hy watched with concern as Jamieson left the house, got on the snowmobile, fired it up, and buzzed off into the dark, the beam of the craft's light searching the road ahead.

Hy was searching her mind for a clue to Jamieson's behaviour. There had been that fire when she was a child. The loss of her parents. But Hy felt as if there were something more.

Hy had never imagined that she would see Jamieson lack courage. Confronted by a fire, she lost it – and it wasn't surprising considering her childhood tragedy. What Hy couldn't know was the real tragedy. The shadow that stalked Jamieson.

There were no bones found in the rubble of Buddy's cabin – human, canine, feline, or supper. The final word would wait on forensics, when they bothered to get here.

Jamieson was getting used to being ignored by the detachment. She didn't mind it. She liked to have her own turf, and The Shores was becoming more and more hers. It would be better, though, if fewer people would spend their time dying.

If the fire had killed Buddy, there was no evidence of it. She couldn't say she was sorry about him, one way or the other. She knew some of the villagers were – they would miss his smile and his fiddle, they said, one after another echoing the same sentiment. And she would commiserate and pretend it meant something to her.

It didn't. Not the man. Not his music. Just his disappearance.

Where had Buddy gone – if not to his death in the flames of that shack? Or somewhere else? Somewhere that had something to do with Fitz Fitzpatrick? Nothing was out of the question.

Strange happenings around a murder must all be considered in the mix.

Jamieson was thinking about that now.

Where had Buddy gone – if he had not perished in the fire?

Where would she find him?

"Why?" Ian had asked the awkward question.

Jamieson hadn't thought of a motive. She knew it. Just knew that Buddy was to blame. There was a certainty in her that defied logic. She hated it. Wished she could prove it with the facts, but she couldn't. It was just…just this feeling. This unwelcome feeling, this sure knowledge that she was right.

"I don't know why. Because he's nuts." If he were nuts, there didn't have to be a motive.

Jamieson had taken to stopping in at Ian's on the way home to the police house. Home. It wasn't a home. With Murdo gone so much, it was lonely. Jamieson had always been alone, kept to herself, enjoyed solitude. She had certainly never felt lonely before, in town with thousands of people whom she didn't know. But here, in this village, surrounded by people who all knew each other, loved or hated each other, had at least feelings for each other, good or bad, Jamieson felt lonely. Lonely for the first time. Ian's computer screen saver throbbing its light onto the white landscape, chased by the flickering of the woodstove was warm and welcoming, and Jamieson responded to it.

"Help me find him," she said.

Help? Ian found it an interesting choice of word. He was sure Jamieson rarely used the word, didn't ever ask for help.

But she had now, and he was more than happy to cooperate, to be in the thick of the investigation. This would put Hy's nose out of joint, he thought. It wasn't ill will, just part of their friendly rivalry.

Hy's nose would have been out of joint at Ian being so close to the investigation. And, maybe more, so close to Jamieson. He slipped onto the back of her snowmobile, arms around her slim waist, willow-thin like Hy's. He could just feel the drop of her breasts on his arms, her back lined down his torso, her buttocks up against –

Better stop thinking about it.

Ian was very close to making his attraction to Jamieson abundantly clear.

He tried to bring the stirrings under control.

The hum of the snowmobile and the vibration of the engine didn't help.

As they sped across the shining snow, Jamieson went over and over it all in her mind. Jamieson suspected none of them – and all of them. Could it have been the woman? No. No. The fat man? The child? Any of them could have done it, she knew – by accident or intent. She had no desire to bring them to justice, not for that man Fitzpatrick. Lord knows what he had done to his wife and child. She'd asked, but they hadn't said. That didn't mean a thing. She thought of her own guilt, how she, at six years old, had gone downstairs on Christmas Eve and had turned on the tree lights to enjoy them secretly on her own, something that was forbidden, something that had killed her family. Her father never left the lights on overnight – a fire hazard, he had said. But she had done it. Left them on. Not even her sister knew. Or did she? Sometimes, Jamieson thought, she suspected. Perhaps it was why they were not close, this sliver of suspicion dividing them.

Should she have confessed at six years old? Should she have been convicted? No, it was an accident. An accident that had haunted her all her life.

The man, the woman, the child, she wanted all of them to go free, murder or accident. It wasn't about justice in court. It was about a larger justice, for having suffered so and, having got rid of that suffering, as Jamieson herself had not.

And what about Buddy? Could it have been Buddy? Oh yes. By accident or intent.

And Jared? The scumbag. Accident or murder, no, she thought not. He'd gotten stoned with Fitz and he'd left – before someone else had come along, and, by accident or design, finished Fitz off.

Jared was a scumbag, but not a murderer.

But she might be wrong. It wasn't hard to imagine them, drunk and stoned, Fitz performing his flips, down the hill and toward the gully; Jared running, half-stumbling beside him.

Hollering into the night. Spilling rum all over himself, laughing so hard he wet his pants. The moisture between his legs shocked him, and he thrust forward as Fitz executed a flip in front of him.

Jared slammed into him, and Fitz went flying, up into the air, caught by his bicycle chain necklace on the branch of a tree, and, bug-eyed, implored Jared for help. He struggled, and, as he did, he twisted the chain tighter around his neck.

Jared left. Jared went stumbling as fast as he could through the deep snow.

Is that how it had happened? Had Jared MacPherson killed Fitz Fitzpatrick?

Chapter Thirty-Four

Jared had asked himself the same question. In his own mind, he managed to convince himself he hadn't been responsible, unless he got really drunk or really stoned, and then he knew. He had killed Fitz Fitzpatrick. Not in the way that Jamieson imagined, but, true to form, he had let Fitz die when he might have saved him. He had not been there, as Jamieson imagined, to watch the acrobatics. He had come after. After Buddy. After Buddy and Jamie had left, to find Fitz twisting by the neck. And he had done nothing. Nothing, except pull the dope out of Fitz's pocket, which sent the dead man – or not quite dead man? – spinning even faster to his death.

It had been as good as murder. And he got off, because other, better people were suspected.

Among them – Buddy.

Buddy is remembering.

Though he lay dying, the thought was exciting to him. *Remembering.* It was his father trying to drown him. That remembering brought on the other. Lifting out of his body, he looked down upon himself, and remembered the man, hanging there.

When he heard them, Buddy stopped in his tracks. He hunched down, and peered through the trees, the smell of spruce invading his nostrils.

A hare froze in his line of sight. He made himself as still as the rabbit.

He could hear their voices, but he couldn't understand their words. He couldn't understand words easily. Just tone. Tone of voice.

The tone of voice he was hearing was ugly.

Every time, it was ugly – at least from The Man. That's how Buddy thought of Fitz. Every time it was ugly. That is, every time someone else came into the gully.

There were a lot of them. The funny fat man. The Woman – that was Rose to Buddy. He was in love with her. He wanted to touch her soft blond hair. He wanted to thank her, in good, well-rounded words, for the kindnesses she had done for him. He never went into the house, but she brought out tea, and sometimes a biscuit. She gave him books for kindling. They never spoke, just the language of the eyes. He could only grunt and smile and drool.

Buddy had stayed there for a long time, hunkered down in the woods, until he heard the shrill cry of the child. He'd jumped up, and he didn't like what he saw. He went lumbering down the hill into the gully.

Fitz held Jamie aloft, as if ready to toss him into the water. When he saw Buddy lumbering toward him, that's exactly what he did. Threw him into the water. Then, scorn etched on his face, he began his acrobatic flips, escaping from Buddy's slow and stupid steps.

But something took hold of Buddy in that moment, and he began to move more fluidly than he ever had in his life. Forward,

forward, reaching out toward Fitz, coming closer with every step that was like magic to him. His body had never responded before to his desire to move like other people.

Fitz arched in the air, just as Buddy reached out and pushed. Shoved. Shoved him off the bridge and into the tree. The chain around Fitz's neck appeared to leap out and fling itself at the branch, and the branch, co-operating, seemed to reach out and snag the chain.

Buddy stared, confused, for a moment, and Fitz stared back, too, for a moment. A fatal moment. It was already too late when he reached up his hands to the chain and tried to yank it off. In fact, that's what sealed his fate. He set off a spiralling motion that sent him spinning to his death. Around and around so that the chain got tighter and tighter and choked him of life.

You might almost say that Fitz killed himself. But Buddy, in his new remembering, knew that he had done it. And Buddy, who carefully minded spiders in their webs around his shack, who shooed away flies and mosquitoes, who would deprive nothing of life, had just killed a man, and was happy that he had.

Buddy didn't wait around to watch the end. He went chasing down to the water to pull the child to safety.

It wasn't easy.

It was his last thought. A well-formed thought, as he slipped out of his life of torment into peace. Everlasting peace. For someone who had never known peace in this life, death was the next best thing.

Buddy would not remember anything anymore.

In the end, Buddy wasn't in the woods. They'd traveled all the trails, searched the clearings, where trees lay, cut to the ground, waiting to be hauled out in long lengths and then cut and split into woodstove-size pieces. Ian's wood came from here. But he used only fallen trees. Ian didn't want to be guilty of killing, especially not a tree.

Jamieson was looking for a different kind of destruction. A hand, a foot, a trail of blood? Nothing.

The snowmobile was growling them out of the woods, breaking the silence that was descending with the too-early Canadian winter night, when Ian saw him.

The branches of the spruce trees were still heavy with snow, even on the edge of the woods behind Wild Rose Cottage. But the snow had fallen off the bottom branches of one tree, and that's where Ian saw him.

A hand. A foot. But no trail of blood.

Buddy was lying under the shelter of a spruce, the tree that had beckoned him to lie down, called him to death, sheltered him as he gave up life.

Jamieson stopped the vehicle. She and Ian both jumped off, and lifted the branches, to find Buddy lying in the snow, curled up in the fetal position, thumb in his mouth, eyes shut as if in sleep, a small smile of contentment on his blue face.

Jamieson dismounted and leaned down close enough to try to feel his breath on her face. Nothing.

He was maybe a hundred feet from Wild Rose Cottage.

So near and yet so far. For the first time, Jamieson understood what that meant.

So near and yet so far. The phrase was repeating itself in Jamieson's mind as she looked down at the body. It was numbing the horror she felt. After all the death she'd seen, Jamieson was not immune to its effect. Not immune to the fact that she'd been unkind, thought unkind things about this man, who looked now like a large baby asleep on a white down comforter.

But he might be a murderer. She hardened herself to that thought, even though he didn't look it. She grasped his wrist in a futile attempt to find a pulse. No rigor mortis. He'd been dead more than twenty-four hours. That meant rigor mortis had set in and then left the body.

Like Buddy. He'd left his body.

Jamieson shook her head. *What was she thinking? Like those nuts – Oliver and Lili.*

Ian dug deep into the emergency kit in his backpack. He held out a space blanket, crinkly, silver, shiny like tin foil, so thin it didn't look like it could warm a finger.

She screwed up her face.

"Too late for that." *Too late to provide the warmth Buddy had needed. Just a hundred feet from the house. Had he known? Been afraid to approach?* The questions would never be answered. Jamieson hated that. The not knowing.

So near and yet so far. That's how she felt about her investigation.

"For decency." Ian unfolded the foil blanket and she took one end. They laid it over Buddy's body.

"And it may keep the coyotes away."

She looked up, startled. She hadn't thought of that.

Better get Murdo. Better get that sled.

She pulled out her cell phone. The on-and-off reception was off again. She was so frustrated that she threw it in the snow. Ian quickly retrieved it and dried it off, as if it were something precious.

It was, to him. Top of the line.

"Well…" Jamieson's hand thrust out to demand her phone. Ian came back to the present. He mounted the snowmobile behind Jamieson, again acutely aware of her body against his, even through their winter clothing. They took off to Ian's to find a phone and Murdo.

Still, Jamieson did not get through to Murdo. Her phone was on. But his was off. And he was on.

On and off April Dewey's plump little body.

Finally.

April in bed was everything April in the kitchen had promised.

It was something men like Murdo knew about her instinctively. That smudge of flour on the cheek, a catechism of children hanging off her apron, her comforting plumpness held promises. Promises she had just fulfilled for Murdo.

It had started when April's sister came and took the kids for the afternoon. For the first time, Murdo and April were alone. She had a strand of hair caught in her mouth. He reached out to free the strand and stroked her cheek.

He had put his arms around her. She hadn't resisted.

He let his hands slip down to paradise, the round cheeks of her buttocks. He began to knead them, and that's when his thoughts turned to culinary terms.

That's when April led him to the bedroom and made him a happy man. A happy man now lying beside the sweetest treat a man could ask for.

There was still flour on her cheek! And he'd thought he'd kissed it all off her. He'd kissed every inch of that delightful body. It had been a feast.

My little crumpet. Sweet. Delicious. Murdo was playing a game, lying awake beside April, who was asleep, short messy curls on the pillow, breasts naked above the sheets.

The most beautiful breasts. Round. Like apples. No, grapefruits. No, not smooth enough. Melons. Warm. Ripe. A mouthful.

Murdo couldn't resist anymore. He took that mouthful, and then another, and another…until April stirred in her sleep.

Stirred.

Another culinary term.

The policewoman. Jamieson. Jamie-son. Interesting, but not relevant, Oliver decided, as he laid out the cards the way he remembered that they had come up.

The police woman. He had read her in the cards. And there it was. He realized, as he lay it down in the last position – the final outcome was Justice.

Justice. He rolled it around in his mind. Justice, yes, he thought, but not the justice of man, of the bureaucracy, of police stations and courtrooms. True justice. Making all right in the world.

Oliver sat back, his hands propped on his belly, as if it were a shelf. He stared at the card and he memorized it, internalized it. Then when he knew it completely, he closed his eyes, and he walked into it. Right into the card, and the world around him disappeared. He was Justice. He could see her, be her. He stayed there some time, just to make sure he was correct, and then he began to walk back out of the card, slowly, carefully, not too hastily. This was a hard discipline because he was excited, excited by what he had found out.

It would be all right, he knew, as he began to bring his spirit out of the card. He was still half in this world and half in the other when a door slammed and yanked him out of the card, out of the world of justice.

Oliver was shaking at the abrupt return to this reality. He had not fully returned when that door banged. He hoped it wouldn't do any damage. The windows shook. The cupboard door creaked.

Settling down. The disturbance was settling down. White and Ginger were walking around in circles and meowing.

And then all was calm. The card of Justice seemed to glow in the dimming light.

It would be all right.

Justice would be done.

"The case is closed." Jamieson had stopped at the Hall when she saw Hy's car in the lot.

"So who – ?"

"It was an accident," said Jamieson. *If the guilty got away, so be it. And if the guilty were truly guilty? Let it lie.*

Hy sat down with a thump. She couldn't believe what Jamieson was saying.

"But…"

"An accident." Jamieson repeated. She had her face turned from Hy so that Hy couldn't see it. "We don't know how it happened. There was no eyewitness." Hy knew it wouldn't be the first time Red Island law enforcement had turned a blind eye to crime. But Jamieson? Jamieson? An accident? Accidental murder, maybe.

"They should go," said Hy, wishing them gone before Jamieson changed her mind.

"Immediately. The three of them. Before I reconsider what happened."

Jamieson left the Hall, and Hy took off for Wild Rose cottage, as Jamieson knew she would do. Let her make the announcement.

Hy could hardly believe what had just happened, but it had. Jamieson. Fully human. Better than fully human. Hy grinned. She didn't care who'd done it either. The man had been an accident waiting to happen. An accident on earth. Quickening her pace, she came to a full stop at what she saw at the front door.

Chapter Thirty-Five

Oliver had seen something in the cards that had made him move with unusual swiftness up to Wild Rose Cottage. *Of course. Of course.* Why had he not seen it? He arrived there and saw immediately that he had read it right.

It was the three of them standing there – mother, magician, and child – that had made Hy stop in her tracks. She inched towards them, dizzy with the sight in front of her that had so satisfied Oliver.

Rose. Oliver. And Jamie.

Jamie in a dress.

Not the Shores Ella dress. A beautiful emerald green Christmas dress, with a lace collar and cuffs.

"He's a girl," Rose blurted out.

Hy inched a few steps closer, her mouth wide open.

"But – "

"I'm a girl," Jamie piped up, smiling.

"A girl?" The words choked out of Hy's mouth.

"A girl," said Rose, Jamie, and Oliver in unison.

Jamie looked up. And she could see it. The rose-pink lips, the long eyelashes. The face like an angel, that at his – *her?* – age could belong to either gender.

Oliver began to laugh, so hard the ripples of his flesh jiggled. Under his chin, his belly, his arms and thighs, all jiggling while tears ran down his eyes.

He chucked Jamie under the chin.

"The Sullivan legacy." More laughter. "Of course. Of course." He chucked Jamie under the chin again.

"And what a little legacy you are."

The Sullivan legacy. It was Jamie. How?

"Come in," said Rose, looking better than Hy had ever seen her. If killing Fitz had done this to her, then it was worth it. She glanced at Jamie. But perhaps it had been her. She didn't know and didn't want to know.

Inside, Rose handed her a book – the diary.

"In a way, this is the Sullivan legacy. Members of the family have withheld it from one another for generations. Fought over it."

"Killed for it," said Oliver, and all eyes were on him.

"Oh, yes, the first two inheritors. Two young men. One sure the other had the diary. He, as eldest, had the house, but he wasn't happy thinking his brother had the diary. He threatened to burn down his house – and he did. Killed him. But the book, all the time, was here. Someone knew – in each generation, but when the family left, the secret was lost, too. I was interested in the diary itself, but I'll admit the thought of a legacy was…uh… inspiring?

"Now I've read it, and realize the Sullivan legacy is Jamie's musical genius. Until now, the Sullivans had thought it was wealth of some kind. I feared it might be murder. But it turns out it's music. Musical talent. It skips a couple of generations and then re-emerges. Well, we're going to do something about that legacy, aren't we, boy?"

Jamie's face brightened. It was his turn to laugh.

"Girl."

Not his son. Now she understood. Jamie was Fitz's daughter. Hy wanted to know more, a lot more, but there was no time. Not right now.

"Jamieson's ruled it an accident."

"I know," said Oliver smugly, slipping an arm around Rose. "Didn't I tell you so, my dear?"

"I'd love to stay and chat," Hy grinned broadly. "We certainly have a lot to talk about, but showtime's in half-an-hour. I need your little legacy."

Oliver smiled Buddha-like.

"We'll get her there."

"And Santa?"

Oliver bowed serenely. "As you insist on calling him, yes, he will be there."

He smiled over at Rose and she smiled back. The moment was almost – but not quite – ruined when a rat appeared, and ran right over Ginger's back. Ginger stretched, turned, and curled into a new position.

Rose and Oliver laughed.

The cards had been right, he realized, when he'd thought they'd gone all wonky on him. There was love, at least companionship, in the cards. There was the legacy, and he knew now what that was. And there was himself as The Magician who would help bring magic into the lives of Rose and Jamie.

But they should think of leaving soon. That police officer seemed oddly disinclined to pursue the case, and the cards had been favourable, but he'd misread them before, so it would be best if they all just left.

After the show, they'd leave. He looked into Rose's eyes. He could see she understood without his saying anything.

His lost soul – was it with her? Could he reclaim it? Not in any sordid physical way. He'd never wanted a woman for that. Man either. He had many desires, but that wasn't one of them.

He turned to Rose and took her hand. They stood silent together for several moments.

Hand in hand.

If there was blood on either of them, neither knew, nor cared.

Alone in the police house, Jamieson thought of the suspects. Buddy, Jamie, Rose, Oliver. They were all innocents, like her. The innocents could not be guilty, no matter what they'd done.

A flush of warmth rushed through her, straight to her head. She put a hand on the doorframe to steady herself.

She was not guilty. It was not her fault. She was innocent.

Jamieson did what she'd never been able to do before. She forgave herself.

In this new and unexpected state of forgiveness, she was prepared to forgive them, too.

The innocents. However, whoever, innocent or guilty, victim or suspect, she didn't care this time.

Fitz Fitzpatrick's killer – if there were one – would go free. Free from the law, anyway. From conscience? Probably not. That would be the worst punishment, as she well knew. She had suffered it herself for thirty years.

Hy was doing a last-minute check to make sure there were enough chairs for the villagers and guests – and space on the sides for wheelchairs and walkers, more of them every year.

The ticket table was set up with the 50-50 jar, and the Institute women were organizing the food in the kitchen, making pitchers of "juice" and setting the sandwiches, squares, and cookies on plates – for a little lunch after the concert.

Rose and Jamie arrived, well ahead of time.

"Jamie insisted on wearing the dress tonight, and I don't blame her. Gus gave it to her. A dress her daughter never wore."

"Gus?" *So Gus knew? And hadn't said?*

Little Jamie grinned. Jamie's grin. From this girl. Hy looked up, eyes questioning, still not able to fully take it in. *Why?*

Rose saw the question in her eyes. "Gus guessed," she said. "I made her promise not to say anything. Even to you." There was a half-apology in Rose's eyes.

"I was fittin' her for the Cinderelly dress," Gus later told Hy. *"I spent enough years waitin' for a girl. I think I know one when I see one."*

Hy suspected that it was what Gus *didn't* see that tipped her off.

"Jamie herself hasn't always known. I told her a few years ago. I didn't want her to be confused."

Hy raised her eyebrows, tilted her head. *How could Jamie not be confused?*

"She was relieved. She knew there was something, but she didn't have any experience of other boys and girls."

"It was our secret," said Jamie. "The name doesn't change, but I did." She whirled around in the velvet dress. There was a bandage on her left knee, a scrape on her right.

"I don't usually like dresses. They're for sissies. But I like this one." She twirled around again.

It began to make sense – why Jamie would want to play the part of a girl at all.

A clattering of dishes came from the kitchen.

"Is Gus here?" asked Jamie. "I have to show her." She dashed off in a very boyish way, taking the steps up to the back kitchen two at a time.

Rose and Hy watched, then Hy turned to Rose. *More,* her expression said. *I want to know more.*

"It was him," said Rose. "I had to protect her from him. He – well – I told you. His two daughters – "

So that was it.

"I told him she was a boy. It was easy to fool him. He never changed a diaper in his life."

"But how did you hide it from him?"

"He wasn't interested in babies."

"Just booze."

"Yes. Or that's what I hoped. Isn't that sick? Hoping. Hoping he wouldn't be selling a young boy's favours."

"He never saw Jamie naked?"

"No. Never."

"And how long did you think you could keep it up?"

"Not much longer."

Was that a motive for murder?

"Why did you stay with him?"

"I didn't know what else to do. I had no friends, no family – "

"There was Oliver."

"I didn't know him. I knew of him, vaguely. But I'd always been brought up to think him odd."

"He is."

The hint of a smile broke on Rose's lips.

"Yes. Good odd, as it turns out."

"And I thought he might be Jamie's father."

Another broad smile. "He might be now."

"Do you think – ?"

"No. Oh, no." Rose's hands flew up to her face as the word burst from her mouth.

Hy didn't know how to interpret the sudden words and movement. True distress?

Or an acknowledgement of her own guilt and the certainty that Oliver had nothing to do with Fitz's death?

"Why didn't you just leave him?"

"I didn't know how. I didn't know what to do. This was all I could do."

"It couldn't have gone on forever."

Rose thrust her chin out.

"No, it couldn't, could it?"

All Hy could think was *motive*. This was a motive. Was she

required to tell Jamieson that Jamie was a girl?

No.

Let her find out for herself.

Jamieson was writing her report on what she referred to as "the incident." She made every effort to downplay it, because, accident or murder, here it was – another death on her beat. Well two, if you counted Elmira. Three, with Buddy.

Accident or murder?

It kept playing in her head.

Accident or murder?

She sighed. A deep sigh. Accident. She had ruled it an accident. There was no forensic expert, superior officer of any kind, there wasn't even Murdo to gainsay her. It had been an accident.

She stopped typing. Leaned back in the chair. Turned her head toward the window and saw the black, black night, thousands of stars shining in it. A city girl, she had never seen anything like it before. She was mesmerized, her mind emptying of thoughts of every kind, seeing only the bright stars in the dark night, hypnotized by their beauty, paralyzed by her own insignificance, lulled by the rhythmical pounding of the ocean on the shore.

It had never happened to her before.

She felt herself being pulled away, taken up, transformed, and when the moment passed, the word was solidly implanted in her brain.

Accident.

And she continued to write, all the while thinking: Murder. A nice clean murder. That's all she wanted.

But murder was messy. Always messy, as she was finding out.

And this had been an accident.

The images of Rose, Jamie, Oliver, and, yes, even Buddy floated in her brain.

These were not murderers.

Whatever they might have done.

Just down the hill, Ian was Skyping his brother Redmond. He'd finally given into Hy's nagging to get in touch or regret it.

Hy had made the connection for him, and had left just as Ian was making arrangements to see his brother in the New Year.

It hadn't been all warm and fuzzy, as Hy had fantasized. They'd been stiff, formal, but still, what could you expect after so many years? Redmond still recognized Ian, and what he saw he didn't like. He couldn't remember why. He couldn't remember the details of their falling out, but he was holding on to resentment.

Driving down the hill to pick up Gus, Hy still felt satisfied with herself.

She'd brought Gus together with Dot. Ian into an uneasy connection with Redmond. Jamieson? No, she hadn't managed anything there. Hadn't tried. Hadn't had the time.

And herself?

The Shores was her family, she realized, even though she was "from away." Gus, Annabelle, Ian, Ben, and Nathan.

She wasn't alone in the world.

She had family.

Gus was beaming at the computer monitor when Hy came through the door to pick her up for the Christmas Pageant. She was already dressed in her winter coat and boots, hat, and gloves. She had been for the past hour. Not for the show, but so she wouldn't freeze whilst speaking to Dot in that cold, frozen place.

Hy soon saw the reason that Gus was beaming. The screen was filled with a protruding belly, topped off by a Christmas bow.

Gus pointed at the screen.

"My granddaughter," she said proudly. The image shifted, as Dot pulled her sweater over her belly, and angled the screen to frame her face, smiling and glowing.

"It's your Christmas gift."

"And about time, too," said Gus, forgetting that what looked to her like a TV screen heard her as well as spoke to her, and transmitted her words halfway across the world.

"No. Just in time, Ma. It's Christmas Eve."

Suddenly Gus opened her eyes and mouth wide. "It won't be born tonight."

Dot laughed. "No. Not tonight. But soon. Another three months."

Gus's tense body relaxed.

"You'll be home by then." The way Gus said "home" meant The Shores, not any other home Dot might have.

"No, Ma. I'll be having the baby here."

"There? You can't have it there."

"Why not?"

"You have to go to the hospital."

"You never did."

"That was different."

"Yes. You weren't a doctor.'

That silenced Gus. Hy smiled. Touched her friend's shoulder. "We have to go."

"Merry Christmas, Ma. I'll speak to you tomorrow." Dot clicked off the screen and disappeared in that disturbing way.

As Hy helped her down the stairs and into the truck, Gus began to soften to the idea.

A grandchild. Born in Antarctica.

A double coup. It would be the talk of the village.

By the time they got to the Hall, Gus had melted.

A grandchild. A granddaughter. A little girl to love.

A new life.

Good tidings of great joy, Gus couldn't help thinking, though she felt blasphemous. One thing was certain.

It was the perfect Christmas gift.

Chapter Thirty-Six

The show went on at the Hall with much the same success as the rehearsals. Violet Joudry had a tantrum – onstage. Some, outside the family, considered it the best performance she'd ever given. Her scream was much more pleasant than her torture of the violin; her kicking at the floor, more fluid than her step-dancing attempts.

The Women's Institute struggled through *Shores Ella* with Moira, the Prince, forgetting one of the three lines she had. The fisherman's boot clearly didn't fit Jamie – it would have been perfect for one of the ugly sisters. One of the clogger's shoes flew off into the audience, narrowly missing 102-year-old Lydia Dodd, who was attending her hundredth Christmas celebration at the Hall.

In the biblical vignette, one of the three wise men, little Tommy Gauthier, his back to the audience, kept scratching his bum. Joseph was chewing gum. The shepherds had towels on their heads and wore bathrobes – one was tartan. Their shepherds' crooks were hoes.

It was a disaster. The crowd was thrilled, laughing until they ached.

It was a triumph – recorded on video by Estelle's son Lester.

There was a bit of confusion about Jamie in a dress, but not all the villagers knew the child, and those who did assumed they had just got it wrong. She was clearly a girl. That was clear to Jamieson as well, who chewed on it all evening. Obviously a girl. Why hadn't anyone told her? What did it mean in the death of Fitzpatrick? Was there a motive for murder behind this new revelation? She could imagine that there was – that more lay behind it that could have driven Jamie – or Rose – to kill. But she had no plan to reopen the case.

Boy or girl, Jamie could surely play the piano.

And Tchai had made it there to hear it. Now more woman than man, she wasn't at all confused by Jamie's sex change.

"Not surprised," she said, then, "Listen." She spread her bat-wing black sweater sleeves. She closed her eyes and swayed with the music coming out of the – a Christmas Eve miracle? – tuned piano. Out of Jamie's agile fingers. The Sullivan legacy.

People stared at the stranger. First, because she was a stranger. Hy remembered the first time she had walked into this Hall and all eyes had been on her.

But they kept staring at Tchai, because he/she was so unusual.

"Is that a man or a woman?" Gladys Fraser whispered to her husband Wally. He was hard put to say. Gladys had seemed like a man to him most of their married life.

"Easier for him…her," Tchai chuckled as she nudged Hy, both staring at Jamie. "He, she – just had to change costumes, the outerwear, to transform. Unlike me – shots, pills, surgery. Hormone therapy. Psychiatric consultations. Perhaps Jamie will understand me better now, when she comes to me in the New Year."

"I don't think that's going to happen."

Tchai's benevolent smile turned to a frown, her smooth white forehead wrinkled.

"I think they're leaving," Hy explained.

"But for where? I have friends everywhere. The child must be trained."

"You'd better speak to Rose."

Hy wondered, briefly, if Tchai would be willing to spend time at the Hall with the untuned piano and the fumbling fingers of the local children, and then decided against it.

Jamie had been exceptional. *Is exceptional.*

And then Hy saw Jamieson staring at the child, from just below the stage. Staring at the child in the dress. She then looked sharply back, her eyes scouring the audience and fixing on Hy at the back of the Hall. The eyes were full of questions.

Oh, God, thought Hy. *I hope she doesn't reopen the whole thing.*

Hy shrugged. Smiled. Jamieson did not smile back. Hy knew she'd be answering some questions later.

At intermission, Santa appeared to hand children their gifts from under the tree. It was Oliver, resplendent in a red velvet cape, its hood trimmed with white fur.

Gladys Fraser gasped. She stopped breathing, emitted some odd sounds. Hy thought she was having a stroke. Gus beamed. The costume reminded her of the pictures of Kris Kringle in the old story books. Very appropriate. Rose Rose, the minister's wife, wasn't so sure, especially when Oliver greeted the audience.

"I am the Magician from the east."

The work of the devil? Rose Rose wondered.

The children didn't care. They gathered round him, clawing at the cape for their presents. Even Violet Joudry could be bought.

The performances stumbled to their conclusion, the curtains closed in spurts as little Madeline cranked at the pulley, and Jamie, in her beautiful velvet dress, began to play a medley of Christmas tunes. The villagers sang along all the way through the finale, *White Christmas.*

Jamie tinkled a waterfall of notes on the piano and Millie Fraser began to murder "Silent Night."

"All is clam," she sang defiantly. "All is bright."

About that, she was right, thought Hy watching Jamie as she slid seamlessly into "O Holy Night."

Millie was doing too many curtsies. The curtains closed and Annabelle yanked the pouting child offstage. She thought she saw something glisten on Madeline's left ring finger. It was a promise ring Billy had given her before the show started. They'd promised each other that they wouldn't let Moira – or his mother – get in the way of a future together. Fuelled by the thought of that promise, little Madeline pulled the curtains open with more than her usual vigour.

There stood Ian, a Bible in his hands. To Jamie's accompaniment and the surprise of almost everyone in the Hall, especially Hy, Ian began to read in a rich melodic voice of which Hy had only ever been half-aware.

Jasmine, on his shoulder, echoed every line, in that same pleasing tenor.

Fear not: for, behold, I bring you good
tidings of great joy, which shall be to
all people.

For unto you is born this day in
The city of David...

A heathen, thought Gus. We all thought he was a heathen. She looked at Hy, her eyes shining, fixed on Ian. And she, a heathen, too. Hy shook her head, but was seduced into the age-old story and the beauty of the words.

...a Saviour, which is Christ the Lord...

Ian continued, the Hall wrapped in silence, unusual silence,

carried away on his words. Hy was proud. Proud of him. Proud
he was her friend. Big enough to do what mattered, in spite of
his personal reservations.

...Glory to God in the highest, and
on earth peace, good will toward men.

Sonorous, serious, unbelievably Ian, the atheist. He and Jasmine
read the biblical passage. The Hall was silent, hypnotized by his
voice and the ancient words. The only applause was the deafening
silence. So silent it was possible to hear the soft sound of snow
beginning to fall. They'd had enough snow for a lifetime of
Christmases, but slowly, respectfully, without the strangled "O
Canada" that usually ended events at the Hall, the villagers filed
outside and stood and stared at the sky and the falling snow.
Fresh white powder, dusting clean the ugly, dirty remnants of
the storm.

They didn't know the sky was staring at them, too. The satellite
was about to take another photograph – and it would show the
same thing – The Shores as a sparkling diamond in a sapphire
blue sea, a tiny jewel on earth.

A star in the East.

There was an extra sparkle that night that may have been
missed by the satellite, but not by the villagers.

"Look." Estelle Joudry pointed up Shipwreck Hill.

There were lights on Ian Simmons' house.

A simple, single strand. But lights.

It was an evening of firsts, thought Hy, as Ian came up and
slipped a friendly arm around her waist. He grinned.

"Forgiven?"

"Oh, yes," she said, leaning into him.

"Hot chocolate? My place?" He took her hand.

"Maybe something stronger?"

"Sure," he said, pulling her into his arms and hugging her. Tight.

In front of everyone. Annabelle nudged Gus. Gus nudged April. April nudged Madeline. Madeline didn't know what to do. She couldn't nudge Moira, who was beside her. Moira didn't need nudging. Her eyes were slits. She did not appear to be looking in the direction of Ian and Hy, but she was. It ruined Christmas for her. She couldn't erase the image from her mind the whole holiday season, and spent a lot of time staring out her upstairs window to see Hy's and Ian's comings and goings over the next several days. What she saw did not relieve her torment.

Everyone was looking at Hy and Ian now. The hug could no longer be mistaken for just a friendly one. Hy didn't care what people thought, didn't worry for once about how intimacy might change her relationship with Ian. She was filled with the Christmas spirit, a spirit more heathen than Christian, but she was feeling immense good will toward Ian. She let him kiss her.

When the kiss ended, she saw Jamie grinning at her, Rose smiling, the two hand in hand, with Oliver behind them, his hand on Rose's shoulder.

Which of them? Any of them?

It didn't matter.

She caught Jamieson's eye.

They were both feeling good will, not just to mankind in general, but to the men and women in this circle around them, a circle that Jamieson, unthinking, had become part of. She had never been a part of anything, had stood aside from her classmates even at the police academy.

Now she was surrounded by April and Murdo, Gladys Fraser, Olive and Harold MacLean, Ben and Annabelle, Nathan and Lilli, and – was that Abel – flitting like a shadow at the edge of the group? They and the other villagers had encircled Jamieson and Oliver, Rose and Jamie. Jamieson and Hy looked at those three now, about to make their way out of the village – a man, a woman, and a child, any one of whom might be guilty of murder. And they didn't care. Hy didn't care. Jamieson didn't care. They ceased to even suspect Buddy. God only knew what had happened in that gully.

They were feeling good will.

They were feeling, in a heathen sort of way, good will toward men – and murder.

Epilogue

The glow in the sky on Christmas Eve was replaced by another glow on Christmas Day. It was coming from Wild Rose Cottage.

The blaze had begun in the back of the house, where the wood range was. The pipe had holes in it. A spark escaped and jumped out onto the floor, where it had smouldered for hours until, suddenly, it ignited the tent. The synthetic fabric billowed with flame in eerie unnatural colours.

Volunteer firefighters from all three districts came – even though it was Christmas Day. Al Dooley from "over the road" – that being the causeway. Spencer Meghan from "in the holler," Carlton and Boyce Gagnon from "up West." The Shores wasn't even their jurisdiction, and it was hard to get to. That didn't stop them from buzzing in on their snowmobiles.

And this time, Jamieson was in the thick of it, as the flames leapt up onto Wild Rose Cottage. There was a bucket brigade of villagers all the way up, over, and down Shipwreck Hill, some of the women still with their aprons on, the men with napkins tucked into their shirts to stay clean while carving the turkey.

They'd been preparing for Christmas dinner when the call came.

"Fire!" burned down the phone lines and party lines.

"Fire!" a call the village had always responded to as one.

There had never been an official municipal or provincial response team here. The villagers had always taken care of it themselves.

It wasn't easy as Wild Rose Cottage had no running water. The village men had to pump it out of the well. "Thank God it's handy the house," they kept repeating as they filled up buckets with water.

They also knew there was no one inside. Rose, Jamie, and Oliver had left that morning. Early, quietly, having said their goodbyes and thanks the night before. They'd taken Fitz's old truck, with Rose at the wheel. Oliver couldn't drive. He sat with White wrapped around his neck, Ginger on his belly, and Oscar peeking out from his sleeve. Jamie sat between the two of them, grinning a big grin, hugging Freddy. They'd given the donkey to Abel. How or when the exchange took place, no one knew.

Jamieson was in full control of the fire brigade, and though the community was used to acting as one in these matters, they accepted that she was in charge.

She felt – no fear. No fear. She was miraculously free, free of the grip of panic that had been poised to ruin her career. Free of the crippling guilt of the child shadowing her adulthood. What more might she be free of here, with these people? She looked down the line at Wally Fraser, Billy Pride, Harold MacLean, Lester Joudry, and, one by one, she named them off, all the way down the line.

Community policing. This was it.

Together, they managed to contain the fire. Nathan showed up with his plow – Lili had forbidden him to do any more than drive – and plowed snow over the debris.

"We'll have to watch it, to see it doesn't start up again," said

Jamieson.

Why? was the question several people didn't ask. The house had been good for nothing for years, and was in worse shape now. The affected part was only a cheap addition that wouldn't be missed, but the fire had opened the rest of the house to the weather and a sure, slow death.

Property. It was property. Jamieson had been trained, brought up, to respect it.

The villagers straggled away from their posts, back to their warm houses and Christmas dinner.

Ian was eating at Hy's. Hy was thinking dinner would be ruined. He was thinking it wouldn't have been that good anyway, but Ian was grateful when anyone provided him with a meal, and he wanted her company. Oddly, especially now, at Christmas, which he didn't believe in.

Jamieson watched wistfully as the pair walked up Shipwreck Hill. Up and over. As they crested the hill, Ian took Hy's hand. *To help her walk on the slippery surface? Or out of affection?*

Jamieson turned back to look at Wild Rose Cottage. *An accident? Arson?*

Don't start, she told herself. Why had they fought the fire?

We should have let it go, she thought.

She was correct, but she couldn't have known that the magnificent house would rise again to its full glory, like a phoenix from the ashes.

Giving her another murder to solve.

She couldn't have known that. But she sensed it.

She shuddered – from the cold or fear?

Jamieson gunned the snowmobile, trying to drown out the thoughts in her head with the noise of the machine. Thoughts of what had happened and how she might have prevented it – through better community policing. Thoughts of Christmas, as she headed back alone to the police house and a can of noodle soup.

Not knowing what waited for her there.

Murdo. April Dewey and all six kids. The kitchen table laid with a paper Christmas tablecloth and a big fat turkey in the middle. An empty chair waiting for Jamieson. There was a tiny crooked Christmas tree in the corner of the room. No lights. Decorated sparsely with ornaments April's children had made out of discarded paper mined from the wastebasket.

Police reports and bills turned into angels and stars.

Christmas.